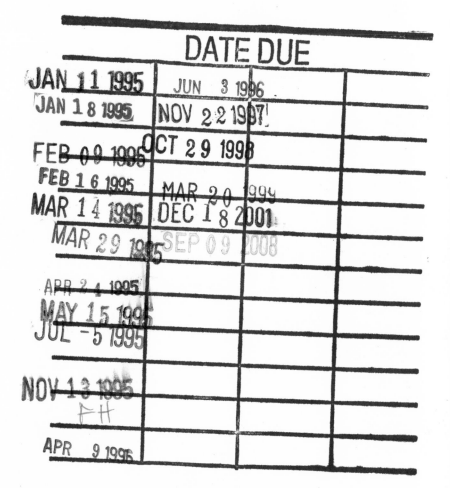

SHADOW PLAY

shadow play

frances fyfield

Pantheon Books   New York

Library of Congress Cataloging-in-Publication Data

Fyfield, Frances
Shadow play / Frances Fyfield.
p. cm.
ISBN: 0-679-42402-4
I. Title.
PR6056.Y47S5   1993
823'.914—dc20
92-50780

Manufactured in the United States of America
First American Edition
9 8 7 6 5 4 3 2 1

For my sister, Susan Styan,
with love.

CHAPTER ONE

It was half-past six in the evening and felt like midnight. Everyone else had abandoned the ten-year-old court building, which was decaying at the edges in the effort to house cars on the roof, prisoners in the cellars and justice in between. Helen West had been discussing handcuff burns all day. Did they constitute assault? Was it only an insult to dignity when the handcuffs bit round your wrists? What was it Logo had said about them being the only legal means for a policeman to make you scream? He had volunteered this remark with his usual, ambiguous smile, harnessing all their sympathies to the scars on his wrists, and that was long before he began to sing. I might be small but I've got big wrists, Logo had said: look, they always put the cuffs on too tight. It was then, with this artless admission so late in the afternoon, that his trial had been aborted. Helen reached her car, quivering with cold. It was wet and dark upstairs, unlike the fuggy yellow warmth below.

The car stood on the only dry piece of concrete roof, next to the ugly spiral roadway which clutched the side of the building like a fat chimney. Children would love this, Helen thought, but children do not know it is here. Drivers began at the top of the spiral and drove down the curving funnel: skateboards would be better. Economy denied the provision of light. There had been no need for her to bring the car today, but since a space on the roof was a hard-won favour she tended not to abuse the privilege. She wanted to get out from under, out of the rain, into the cocoon of the car and not stop until she was home, for an evening with tomorrow's work and, in all probability, a row with Bailey. No, she had to avoid any such thing: he was going away, and although the boat in which they rowed was rocky, she did not want it overturned before he left. The car door clunked shut: she was suddenly in a hurry. It was even colder inside and she fumbled for the ignition. The lack of light was as suffocating as a blanket.

Oh Lord, would she ever be able to pretend she was not afraid of the dark?

There was a man caught in the headlights like a giant moth. A small man, slightly stooped but spry, standing in the rain with his hair plastered against his head and waving her out of the parking space with imperious gestures of exaggerated politeness, as if announcing a royal command performance. Waving her out as if it was necessary in all the empty bleakness of the roof, obstructing her at the same time. Retreating in front of her car, beckoning to it, moving back inch by inch, bending from the waist as if to coax. Nice Mr Logo, with his talent to amuse, the erstwhile defendant of her long afternoon, recently acquitted on a sympathy vote spiced with a pinch of legal technicality, the bastard. Helen felt the desperate urge to accelerate, a mad and joyous anticipation of seeing the smile leave his puckish face as he melted beneath the bonnet, but the sudden rage which had displaced her great leap of fear on sight of him turned back on itself and became fear again. He was a strange spectre, Logo: a trespasser up here, waving his arms in his too short sleeves from which those large wrists grew into enormous hands. Helen wound down the window, kept her foot on the clutch and the car in gear, ready to move, frightened.

'Could you get out of the way, Mr Logo? You've no business up here. What do you think you're doing?' The voice was loud, the authority in it surprised her. Logo moved to the side of the car, stood a respectful distance, sedulous.

'Oh, taking the air, Mrs West, taking the air. I saw a door and walked through it.'

'Get out of the way, Mr Logo,' she repeated.

'I'm not in the way, now am I? It's all your imagination. I wanted to ask you something.' He moved closer. Suddenly his fingers were wrapped round the top of the half-open window, his smiling face close as he flattened his wrists against the glass. In the dark, Logo looked almost respectable, but the clothes were a parody of respectability which made her remember the frayed cuffs of his second-hand suit and the subtle odour of a body in dirty clothes.

'Tell me something, oh so fair Mrs West, just tell me. Can I sue for these burns? Can I, can I, can I?' The voice ascended to a sing song, mocking and pleading, the end of the interrogatory verse and the beginning of the chorus. 'I thought you were so fair, Mrs West. Fair in mind, fair of face . . .' The weals of his old handcuff marks were displayed to good advantage, his fingers relaxed.

'Why can't I sue? Can I? Can't I? None of it's my fault. Why did the police never find my wife? I can't help what I do,' he intoned sweetly.

'Listen you hymn-singing hypocrite, I'll get you next time. Now sod off,' said Helen.

Her car shot forward so fast she was momentarily out of control, dangerously close to the exit wall before she stopped. She reversed, grinding the gears, plunged towards the dark tunnel, sensing him behind her, laughing. Down the spiral she went, too fast for safety, the car careering like a toboggan shying from the walls. At the end, when the portcullis to the outside world opened, she came to an uncertain halt. She stopped to breathe, subject to a terrible desire to scream, and grateful for the light which graced the bottom floor. From a shabby shed of a room where a television cast extra light, the security man blinked at her, rose without ceremony but considerable resentment, and ambled across.

'What's with you then? You come down off there like a boy racer.'

'There's a man on the roof,' Helen said.

'Oh yeah?' The indifference was palpable. It was warm down here. 'Thought they'd all be home, the lunatics. It won't be someone escaped, I know that.' They were all gone by three thirty, all those who were being taken back to prison for the first or fifteenth time. They went in vans with bars on the windows. 'Dare say he'll come down, whoever he is. I'm not bothered. Is he dangerous?'

Helen breathed out shakily.

'I don't know,' she said slowly. 'I just don't know.'

Logo? Dangerous? No. Only a poor lost soul probably, and it was unprofessional of her to swear at him. Solicitors acting for the Crown should not do that.

This time she moved away without speed. Oh Lord, I must pretend not to be afraid of the dark. The indifference of the security man to the presence of the trespasser on the roof of the magistrates' court was somehow soothing, an attitude which neutralized the sinister and made everything banal. Helen stared at the windscreen wipers, smearing across her vision with their worn rubbers, the rain spattering through the still open window on to her shoulder. She made herself slow down, think of something other than being made a fool of for the second time in a day. Geoffrey would not want to hear because his mind would be elsewhere, packing his mental and emotional equipment along with his clothes. Helen remembered where she was going, Geoffrey's place not hers and she felt the old, familiar resentment which was all the worse for being unreasonable.

Rose Darvey had waited a long time in the office to take the phone call from Helen West at the end of the case. She did this frequently. It was Rose's job to note down the result of the day's cases, to keep a running check in her notebooks of where all the papers were. They were City Branch North of the Crown Prosecution Service, big deal. Since she was not trusted or trained to operate the computer, the god of their existence, all she had to do thereafter was transfer the notes to someone else who logged them in and gave them back. Rose despised the computer, purely because she was not supposed to use it, although she could, it was easy, and because she knew it would be so much simpler if she took the phone calls, logged them on to the screen without an intermediary, and saved time all round. That was too simple for the captains of this ship. Rose was also supposed to know, and made it her business to know, where all the professional staff were at the end of the day and to ensure they collected or had delivered to them what they needed for the next. She did this with a surreptitious disdain for the lot of them. Case clerks of her own stable attracted her fierce loyalty; the lawyers were a joke. Dinsdale Cotton was worth a laugh, Redwood was a pillock, but he was the boss, John Riley was quite sweet, Amanda Lipton was a stuck-up prune . . . Helen West talked to her at least, but they were all congenital idiots. Rose had long since surmised they were all failures of a kind. When Helen West told Rose that she was wasting her brain being a case clerk, and why didn't she try to qualify as a lawyer herself, Rose had shaken her head in disbelief. 'Get stuffed,' she'd said. 'What, be like you and work here for ever? You must be joking.' Helen was all right, condescending old trout, and Rose wasn't being truthful. She loved working here in this great big castle of a building, didn't want to do anything else, but she wouldn't have said so at the point of a gun. Not to one of them anyway.

Today, Rose had waited, not just painting her nails and chewing that thin plait of soft, dyed hair which did not rise in spikes above her head like the rest of it, but curled behind her neck where she could always reach and tease it. Simply waiting without fidgeting, tense, looking at her feet slung over the arms of an old and rocky chair, regarding herself with the sort of half-admiring disgust which was second nature. Admiration for her body because of what so many men wanted to do with it, disgust since she couldn't herself understand the appeal. She was worried about the body, but other worries came first. Worry made many a woman move: it rendered Helen West twitchy, rude, uncommunicative, occasionally funny and finally apologetic, but never listless. It made Rose Darvey very still.

'I'm late, Rose,' Helen said on the phone. 'Mr Logo got off. Why didn't you come and watch? It's good for you to see what it's all about.' She sounded hurt, Miss West, in a bad mood. Lot of those recently.

'Oh yeah?' said Rose with studied disrespect. 'Think I've got sod all else to do? I mean, apart from watching you prancing round some sodding court-room making a tit of yourself for the prosecution.'

'Well, I certainly did that.'

'How'd he manage to get off this time?' They all knew about Logo. Helen West's fury at the inglorious acquittals of him and others had rung round the office.

'He said he wasn't trespassing in the school yard. He'd gone in there by mistake. To sweep it, he said. Just to look, he said. Told us how he got so disorientated through being lonely. He's only a poor creature and this was only a misdemeanour, all that. So I had to throw in the towel. Look, forget what I said about being a prosecutor. Forget what I ever said to you about being a lawyer at all. You'd be better cleaning lavatories. See you tomorrow.'

'Right. Take care.'

Rose put down the phone, but it slipped off the cradle because her hand was shaking and she did not bother to put it back immediately. Would they ever get that man locked up? It was the last call for the evening and the worst. Well God bless you, Helen fucking West, letting that bastard get away with it again. But at least working here, I know where he is. Rose straightened the phone, pushed her fingers through her hair and replaced the single six-inch plait down the back of the neck of her red blouse. The collar felt damp and the front was creased. Well, what else would tonight's man expect after a day at work? The phone rang again. Rose was not particularly jubilant as she picked it up, the receiver still clammy from her previous touch.

'I'm down at the front door, Rose. Fancy a drink?'

'Oh yeah? And a hamburger? I'm hungry.'

'Are you now? Fancy that. So am I, as it happens.' There was a suggestive chuckle.

'Be there in a minute.'

She knew exactly how the rest of the evening would go. A couple of drinks, payment in kind for the company and a lift home and she didn't care. The main thing was always to leave the building with a man. Any man.

Passing through the office, hauling on her coat, teasing up her hair, pausing by a desk to straighten her tights, Rose thought again. Why the fuck should I? Why? Her tights were thick, to go with the weather and they had bagged at the knee. Distracted, she pulled up her short skirt and adjusted them thoroughly, beginning at the ankles and finally hauling them into place above her waist. Tucking in the crumpled blouse, she slung her bag over her shoulder, patted herself down and looked up at the door. Dinsdale Cotton, barrister-at-law, stood there, looking and laughing. Rose was furious.

'Seen enough, have you? Want your eyes back, do you?'

'I'm sorry,' he said. 'So dreadfully sorry. Didn't mean to be a voyeur . . . I really am sorry.'

'Thought you'd gone home.'

'I did. I left half my stuff, had to come back. Look, no offence. Can I buy you a drink? No, not for the view, but because I embarrassed you. And to stop me feeling such an idiot. I really didn't expect to find someone dressing, I'm so sorry.'

He stopped where he was, patently sincere, all his amusement dismissed by the look of fury on her face. Poor idiot, she thought, but not bad. No wonder he fancied Helen West and she him. Apart from his silly name and his wonderful floppy gold hair and the fact he was out of place in anything but a stately home, he was nice, inquisitive but nice, and the best looking man in the office, not that that was saying much. Rose relented.

'No problem,' she muttered. 'Don't worry about the drink though. Another time.'

He bowed, he fucking bowed, he really did. Rose would tell that to Paul later, by way of distraction, as if distraction would work. To Rose's own surprise, she found herself bowing back, both of them acting up, being silly. Dinsdale had this effect.

'Mind your tights,' he grinned. She smiled too this time, right from the eyes. If he hadn't smiled and apologized, she'd have bitten his balls.

They'd had a case like that in the office last week, a woman who bit off a bloke's testicle during a row. Rose had been the only one who wasn't surprised.

She stamped down the corridor, shoved two finished files in the old goods lift for carriage to the basement, adjusted her bag again. There were fifteen ways to the front door. Turn right and you came to the end of a wide corridor, so wide it could take a bus. Then you turned left down narrow stairs, but fifty feet away there were broader stairs which threw themselves against a narrow and futile door, blocked in to lead only to the floor beneath instead of towards the continuance of the sweep which had once been grand. The same, wide stairs continued to the front door, two floors down, with similar interruptions. So did the back entrance and the clattering stairs she trod to the floor beneath through swing doors which creaked. Down, down, down, in a clatter of deliberate noise, because she liked making a noise, enjoying the emptiness without ever being afraid, it was so big you could hide yourself. The room numbers made no sense. It had been a hospital once, a Victorian lunatic asylum. Helen West had told Rose that, in the interests of her education: Miss West was stuffed full of useless information. The conversion to an office had been minimal, hence the wide corridors and the super-wide doors, built for trolleys and strait-jackets with escorts. She had listened to Helen's lecture, wide eyed, blinking, waiting her turn, which came finally. 'Naa, I don't believe you. This was never converted . . . It's just what it always was, still a loony-bin otherwise, isn't it?' Rose trod past the video room for obscene publications, past the library, all law reports incomplete, full of last week's newspapers, past the offices for fraud, tripped on the bulging carpet outside the passenger lift marked 'Out of Order'. Helen West had also said they should all travel up and down in the goods lift, it was more reliable, very funny, and could carry at least

13

one pygmy at a time. Rose supposed this building was all they could afford. More fool the lunatics who worked here.

Suddenly she was unsure she could cope with the evening ahead, and then on the second turn of stairs, she knew she would. Reckless Rose: that was her reputation. Nineteen-year-old Rose, never leaving the office without a man.

Detective Sergeant Ryan and Detective Superintendent Bailey sat in the casualty department of Hackney hospital.

'Fucking lunatic asylum, this,' said Ryan. 'Run by a load of lunatic medics, far as I can see.'

'Don't speak ill of the doctors. We need them.'

'I wasn't speaking ill. Only as I find.'

'Will you watch your mouth then? How much longer, do you think?'

'Oh, ten minutes. Then they'll see you right in five and you can go home.'

Bailey looked at his damaged watch and groaned. His left eye was half closed by a huge purple swelling. A haematoma, the report would call it. To Ryan it was just another black eye, an occupational hazard not usually incurred by officers of Bailey's rank. Ryan was alarmed by the groan, the first yet. The rest had been a string of obscenities, not typical of Bailey either. Ryan wondered about sir's love life; he hadn't been too happy lately, but then he should have known better than to shack up with a solicitor.

'What's the matter, sir? Does it hurt?'

'Of course it doesn't bloody hurt,' said Bailey with heavy irony. 'But I've just remembered I was supposed to get some food in. And cook it, round about now. Damn. She'll have to make do with soup.'

Ryan was incredulous. He thought of his own marriage, far from unsatisfactory, despite its vicissitudes, a history of burned meals left in ovens, but at least they'd been put in the oven in the first place.

'Helen? Make do with soup. Why isn't she cooking the food? Doesn't she cook?' He might as well have said, does she wash?

Bailey turned the one good eye on Ryan. It looked a trifle sad, if not a little frightening, staring at him on its own like that.

'We take it in turns. Her place, she cooks, mine, I do. Only we seem to have lost the knack. Not much taking of turns these days.'

It was as a close to a confidence as he would get and Ryan saw the signal to change the conversation. Besides in the aftermath of

Christmas and this raw January day, he did not want gloom on the brink of a holiday. He rubbed his hands together.

'Never mind. Bramshill. Day after next. Get away from all this. Don't we deserve it? Can't be bad.'

They were both going on extended courses at the police training college. Ryan said his was for reading and writing; Bailey's was for senior command. They'd get him talking to hostages next.

'Not bad today, either, was it?' Ryan continued, still rubbing his hands in a way Bailey found irritating. 'Last day's active duty, five arrests. You put a really good sprint on there, sir, you really did. Never knew you could run so fast.' He means pretty good for a man of my age, Bailey thought.

'No, you didn't know I could run, and you didn't know that the man was waiting round the corner, with his fist out either, did you? Why didn't you tell me? I could have just run into a wall and got it over with.'

They both shook with laughter. Ryan eyed the nurse who came towards them. There'd be women at Bramshill, surely. Time to get the old man out of himself.

'Listen,' he said to the nurse. 'When you've done with Mr Bailey here, would you mind putting a patch on that eye to make it look worse? Only he's got a woman waiting at home. He'll need sympathy.'

Waiting. Helen felt the emptiness of Bailey's flat as soon as she put the key in the door. Late again, always late, but she couldn't even criticize him for it because she had been so herself, often enough. For the grosser occasions of his lateness, she usually managed to pay him back by not turning up at all some other time. The games they played, so childish. The light on his answering machine winked at her. It might have contained a message of explanation since he was scrupulous about such courtesies, but, mindful of his privacy so that he would be mindful of hers, she did not stop to listen. They had a rule that although each possessed the key to the other's house, that was not quite the same thing as being entirely at home in it. Helen craved a sensation of righteous indignation and knew she did not deserve it. Geoffrey was a policeman: he did not have a timetable like other men. They had chosen to have a relationship that was both uncommitted and committed at the same time. It had been bound to bristle with difficulties and it was she who insisted on this awkward format. Living together had not worked particularly well either.

Helen never quite knew whether Bailey's professed willingness to try again, or indeed to marry her, worked as a comforter to their impermanent arrangements, or an irritant. Perhaps they were just stale. Like the bread in his bread-bin. He would have forgotten food. There was rice, tinned shrimps, cartons of soup and more than sufficient wine to dull the day. Not a feast, perhaps. She could have gone out again from this warehouse top floor which was so much cooler than her own cluttered basement and found the late-night shop on the corner to improve on their provisions, but she didn't. Instead she waited for a quarter of an hour and then went home.

It was dark down the street where Logo lived and darker still in the alleyway between his house and Granny's. Neither owned their small houses, impossible on their incomes, even in a street like this where no one in their right mind would want to buy a house. That's what Logo thought anyway. The Estate Agents may have disagreed as their signs festooned five dwellings over the road. Attempts had been made to gentrify Legard Street, but those who tried with the bravery and optimism of youth tended to move after a year or so. Artisans' dwellings, mostly privately owned now, a few left like his and Gran's with sitting tenants. The sitting tenants were old, an endangered and truculent species who did not band together, but jeered at the private owners with their new front doors. All were threatened by the proximity of the football ground. Every second week in season and plenty of other times besides, their street was blocked by cars, their gardens trodden by the thousands on foot who came to worship the team. As the team's fortunes prospered, so the fortunes of the street were endangered. Young Mrs Jones in number seventeen had left after her first baby because she could not stand the prospect of keeping a fixture list in the kitchen so she would know on which Saturday she would be able to get out to the hospital and produce the next. In comparison to the hazards of the football stadium, Logo's singing was a minor irritation.

He sang in a light tenor, his voice blending with the persistent rain, increasing the eeriness, but not diminishing the triumph of the sound.

'Come let us join the Church above
The martyr's praise to sing,
The soldier true who gave today
His life blood for his king . . .'

Tan ter ah! he finished, lost for the words of the next verse. A door slammed. There was the sound of scurrying footsteps in the wet, another door slamming, someone putting out rubbish. Logo did not look round. It wasn't a convivial street. He dived into the alley, feeling for his door key. As if there was any need. All anyone in the world had to do was kick it and they could come in if they wanted, but somehow, they didn't.

'Mother!' he yelled as he pushed the door. Beyond the broken fencing which flanked the alley as it grew into a mossy backyard, light poured from the glass door of the next-door kitchen. Logo stepped over and rapped on the glass. She might not have heard with the rain, but now she would and he wanted someone to talk at. Although she would resent it, just as she hated being addressed as his mother or gran when she was nothing of the kind, it usually took her less than three minutes to come across. Old Mrs Mellors was victim to her own desire for company. Logo was her lifeline. She was also the only one in the street who continued to like his singing long after the novelty had worn off.

'I may as well be your bloody mother,' she grumbled, heaving herself through the battered door he had left ajar. 'What do you want now?'

'Nothing,' he said indignantly. 'When did I ever want anything from you? But it's a wet night and I thought you might like a drink.'

She sighed. 'Well, don't you know me well, but you could have saved me getting wet and brought it in to me. You're wet already. I was doing my knitting.'

'Nobody calls me wet.' He adopted a boxer's stance and squared up to her, the aggression diminished by the smile on his face. Margaret sat down heavily.

'I know,' she said. 'Obviously, you got on all right today. No wonder you're celebrating. Oh I do wish they'd stop picking on you like that, all those police. It isn't fair. Not that prison would do you harm. You'd get fed, put on a bit of fat.' She chuckled.

'Is that what you want for me, you ungrateful old cow? Is that what you want?' From one misshapen jacket pocket he took a half-bottle of whisky and from the other, a bottle of dry ginger. Posh. Margaret Mellors found the sight of the whisky brought saliva to her mouth. She looked down at her own legs stretched across the rotten lino floor in front of her with her stick running parallel. Margaret was waiting for a new hip, felt as if she had been waiting for ever. She was pretty mobile with the old one, but by this time of day, she ached.

'No,' she admitted. 'That's not what I want at all and well you know it. I just wish you'd behave. But you're good to me, Logo. I'd rather have you dead than alive.' Are you going to be all night pouring this drink, then?'

He tossed a pack of cigarettes from one of the bottomless pockets in her direction. She caught them nimbly in both palms. Margaret's hands and her mind were unaffected by more than seventy years' hard labour with no great expectations of life even at the beginning. Blessed are they who expect nothing, she was wont to say, for they will not be disappointed. Logo and Logo's family had given her much of the joy she had ever had. He looked at her with that smile which wooed magistrates and said softly, 'Good to you, Mother? Other way round, isn't it? I don't know what I'd have done without you, but it's fat thanks we get, eh?' She shook her head, not anxious to follow this line of conversation, but he was determined.

'What would I have done with a wife like mine, eh? And a daughter to raise with a wife like that? I don't know. You were mother to us all, Mother, you and Jack, God rest him. And what happens after all that loving kindness, eh? Wife runs off with someone else, and the daughter can't give her father the time of day. Never mind you, Granny.'

Margaret shrugged, still hoping the conversation would die away. She had no real doubt she deserved the accolades but it did not follow she wanted to hear them, and the thought of the missing daughter, as well as that pretty wife, still filled her with anguish sharper than any physical pain. She was accustomed to it and told herself that since Logo was talking about his own blood she might not understand his obsession, having no kids of her own to throw into the balance. She had taken Logo's child instead but she knew she had no right to her now.

'You haven't seen them, I suppose?' he asked wistfully. For a moment she thought he might mean the neighbours who hated him most, the landlord of their identical houses and his wife, but that wasn't what he meant at all.

'Seen who? Oh, I know who you mean. No, you daft thing, of course I haven't. Not in four years. Don't be silly. Why do you always ask?'

The whisky, which she drank sparingly but greedily, was already in the system, dulling the pain, though not the regret and the guilt.

'I did what I could was all,' she said. 'I wish you wouldn't keep on asking. I've never seen your daughter or your wife since soon after Jack died, and you'd be the first to know if I had. Will you let up, you mad son of a bitch?'

Logo threw back his head and laughed with a sound as glorious as the best of his singing. The sombre mood, as quick and flimsy as the rest of him was light and spry, seemed to have fled. Oh, you had to love him: he was a character, rising like a cork over all his difficulties, holding down a job no one else wanted: she admired him for that. Who else would be a road sweeper and trundle that big old trolley around all day, picking up rubbish? She felt as loyal to Logo as she had always felt, as protective as if he had been a son and just as worried. None of the other old souls in the street had a son half as attentive as this one.

'I've got some nice soup, if you want some,' Margaret said. 'But whether you do or you don't, I think I'll just have another of these,' and the pain in her chest, that premonition of tears, eased with the sound of liquid.

'No I won't have another, thanks. Two's plenty.'

'You're joking. We haven't even started. One more?'

'No, thanks. Look, do you mind if I leave you to it? I think I'll just go round to her place and see if she's in. It's not like her . . .'

'Sir, Geoff, it's just like all women.' Ryan was upset, more to the point, enraged. He'd seen sir home to find no one there at all, not even a burnt meal or a cup of soup, just a scarf on a chair to show she'd visited and left sweet all else behind. Man could not live on a waft of perfume. The answerphone had been blinking and winking like some creature with a cast in its eye and no sign of a lit fire or a petticoat. Welcome home our conquering hero, amen. Ryan, who could stand anything but another man's discomfiture at the hands of a woman, placed the patched, black-eyed hero in his motor and shuffled him off elsewhere. In his own experience, if you were late, you might as well be very late and very pissed. The later you left it, the more relieved they were to see you and the anger was the same after two hours as it was after six.

'All right. Listen, I'll take you there. Then I have to go, OK?'

'Yes, of course. You've been very kind.' There was a strange chill in this return to formality. Bailey never lost control, whether punch drunk or plain drunk, he could be colder and more dangerous than black ice and all of a sudden, Ryan did not envy Helen West, whom he liked and admired, if only she'd learn to behave like a woman.

They pulled up outside the large old house which contained her flat. Ryan knew the route from the pub, the way he always did. Even though he lived outside London, he'd knocked around it like a cabbie. From the door of the pub, turn right, cut down Legard Street past the football stadium, left at the park, over the lights and into respectability. Not exactly Ryan's stamping ground, but Bailey was familiar with it, because the woman lived there, God help him.

Ryan waved and revved the car even while sir was stepping out. Then, two doors down, he cut the engine, got out and walked back. Helen West had a handsome front door to her basement and the lights were on. Ryan stood in the darkness and watched sir ring the bell. 'Where were you, Helen?' he was saying to her as the door opened. 'Where were you? Couldn't you wait?' He watched the older man push inside, heard her words. 'I'm sorry,' she was saying. 'I'm sorry. Oh, what have you done? Not again . . .'

That was more like it. Ryan was glad about Bailey wearing a patch. Made him look hurt but still like a pirate.

He cut back up through Legard Street on the way to the motorway. What did anyone mean by late? It wasn't late at all by his standards. He wondered about stopping off on his way home. Down, boy, down: he remembered. Bramshill the day after next, be good and get home by ten. His wife knew better than to call that late. Swinging right, enjoying the speed and the sensation of righteousness which came from being sober, Ryan dimly recognized a familiar face in a car he passed, weaving its way through the double-parking of those dubious streets round the stadium. Do you know, he was thinking to himself, I thought I could predict the way this evening might go. I thought I'd get him pissed and I shall yet. He'd taken bets on it.

Rose Darvey had known exactly the way the evening was going to go, but she was still disappointed to find it quite as predictable as it was. There was a price to be paid for any escort away from the office. Exacted now and all for a ride in a beaten-up Ford Cortina, the best a rookie police constable could afford. He'd taken her to a pub for three rounds of drinks and three of crisps, then, more reluctantly, to a McDonalds, where they had sat in silence, munching the best of the menu under the kind of light which trans-fixed her into silence, and all as the prepayment for dessert. Rose Darvey, with her knickers round one ankle and the tights which had bagged at the knee now hidden under the bed where she lay in a police section house. With Constable Williams working his way between her thighs before leaving for the night shift, and making a great deal of noise about it. Oh, Rose, Rose, Rose, as if the name mattered while he still had his shirt on, thrusting between her legs with his face all trembling. She watched him, uninterested, as he towered above her. Her hands were on his thin buttocks, kneading as she might have kneaded dough: men were dangerous when roused, you had to behave as if you enjoyed it. Rose was stretched and sore: he was taking his time to the tune of her artificial groans and the scluck, scluck of the sound, while her eyes gazed at the artex ceiling. Just when she thought he never would, he finished and collapsed. Oh, Rose, Rose, Rose. Shut up, she thought, but she remembered to keep on stroking. Ten minutes later they were back in the Cortina, he on his way to work and her to bed. They went down Northchurch Street, where Rose knew Ms West lived, because she knew all those things. Lights on down there: I expect she's drinking her cocoa. Her eyes at this point were fixed straight ahead, like they were most of the time. Paul began to doubt her silence, but he knew better than to question his luck.

'Which number is it again?' he said when they were two miles beyond the stadium.

'Wouldn't you like to know?' said Rose pertly, the tights now more or less in place, but a disturbing stickiness between her legs. 'Just drop us at the corner, it's easier. See you.'

He obeyed, his mind elsewhere, building up his concentration for the night shift, wishing he'd slept more by day. She walked down the street slowly for as long as he was in sight and then she began to run.

Oh Lord, save me from admitting I am frightened of the dark.

CHAPTER TWO

The offices of the Crown Prosecution Service did not look any more dignified in the early afternoon than they did after dark, but Brian Redwood, lord of all he surveyed, comforted himself with the thought that the visual irritations were at least unusual. He had always wanted a huge office if only to reflect status, though he now recognized it was a myth since he was a king without a crown. The room he occupied was large enough for a potentate to sit like a pea on a throne at one end, but the splendour was that of a ruined Russian palace and offered all the comforts of a cave. When forced into these premises the year before, in pursuit of the ever-cheaper lease, Redwood could not believe his eyes and although his incredulity had diminished, the disappointment had not. It was all part of the humbling process and he was never sure whether that process was deliberate. The only feature of the building he liked was the magnificent railings outside, which surrounded the place on three sides, standing tall and close-ranked with lethal tips at the end of each elegant fleur-de-lis, a barrier against the world. Redwood vaguely approved of these as a means of keeping his staff in, rather than keeping others out, defying the truant and the escapee, but he hated the rest of the building. He was an unmemorable man, one of the grey brigade, uncoloured by humour but far from stupid. He had never found problems with the letter of the law, which was why he had chosen it, but human beings were a different matter.

On this afternoon, he was conducting an exercise in better communication with his professional staff. An excruciating management course had informed him this was not only long overdue but imperative, since staff morale was his responsibility. In vain he had tried to explain that no single chief marooned in a building like this could remove the dust of ages and make the indians happy unless he increased their wages. The response to this from above was derisory: he was supposed to win their hearts and minds and make them tolerate the intolerable. The end result was monthly meetings for the lawyers only, held at tea-time. They sat in his room on a medley of chairs, and ate the jam doughnuts he had paid for out of his own pocket. Redwood had a very old-fashioned idea of a treat and did not see why a waste of time should be expensive.

They were supposed to discuss, in mutual confessional, those cases which troubled them, which is what they did, more or less, among themselves, ignoring Redwood, whose gaze meanwhile travelled round the walls. High ceilings with broken mouldings, big, panelled doors so thick with a dozen layers of shiny paint the panels had all but disappeared. There was a large and ugly open fireplace from the 1890s obscured by an electric equivalent from the 1950s, now defunct. Gas pipes ran up the wall, again redundant since the newer radiators stood side by side with the old. It was a room of many additions with nothing taken away except what might have been beauty. He almost broke his fingers each time he tried to open one of the huge sash-windows which rose from near floor level to above his head. He was uncomfortably aware that below his feet and over his ceiling, there were rooms in this colossal warren of a building he had never even seen. On arrival, it had taken him three days to find the lavatories on this floor and even now, he took a different route each time.

Smoking was not allowed within his personal domain, and Redwood noticed with obscure satisfaction that Helen West was not only fidgeting but looked as if a strong gin would be preferable to weak tea. He regarded her with his customary mixture of grudging respect and awkwardness. She had changed, recently. Before, she had always seemed to campaign for them to be aware of the possible innocence of those charged with criminal offences, but now she seemed obsessed with their frequent inability to prove guilt. At the moment she was keeping them all entertained with the story of a man named Logo.

'Well, he came in, suit, tie, the lot, looking the soul of poverty-stricken respectability, and, oh yes, I forgot, clutching his Bible. "I brought my own," he said sweetly and bowed to the bench. He listened to all the evidence, asking only the most pertinent questions, as if he'd been representing himself all his life.'

'He probably has,' said Dinsdale, laughing. Helen was accompanying her saga with a number of gestures. He, too, had seen Logo before and he anticipated the perfection of Helen's mimicry.

' "Excuse me," he says to the mother of the first witness, "but your dear little daughter did not complain that I had touched her in any way, did she?" "No, she never," the witness concedes. "I only offered her sweets, as I offered them to others?" "Right on," says the witness. "I did not accompany my offer with any kind of lewd gesture?" Witness puzzled. "What's one of them?" "I don't know, madam. I cannot really define what I could not do, but I thought that was what I am accused of." Oh, he's so horribly articulate. "I'm afraid, madam," he says finally, "I only followed your daughter from the school gates because she was alone and crying, because I was concerned for her, and because she so resembles my own daughter, who I've lost." He had the witness in tears, feeling guilty. And the bench. He's sort of naïvely ingenious. Then he told us how rough the police were, showed us the handcuff burns and no one dared point out they weren't recent at all. Everyone ended up turning somersaults to be nice to him and then when he was acquitted, you know what he did?'

'Yes,' said Dinsdale. 'He sang.'

'Exactly,' said Helen. ' "Abide with me, fast falls the eventide. The darkness deepens; Lord with me abide . . ." He's got a beautiful voice, but he knew the limits, so he stopped after verse two.'

'I know,' said John Riley, the only church-goer of them all.

'Swift to its close, ebbs out life's little day;
Earth's joys grow dim, its glories pass away;
Change and decay in all around I see;
Oh, thou who changest not, abide with me.'

His fine, bass voice finished on a cadence of embarrassment and he looked down, blushing. A pin would have dropped with a clatter in the silence which followed. Redwood stirred uneasily. This was really too much for a man who preferred others to remain inhibited.

'You see what I mean?' said Helen, breaking the spell. 'You can't cross-examine a man who sings hymns like that. Nor can you get across that it's the fifth time he's been caught prowling. You know his first speciality, years ago? Being found on enclosed premises. People would turn round in some office block he used to clean and suddenly, he'd be there. Now he's a road sweeper. These days he tries to lure dark-haired little girls to go with him for walks in graveyards. And he knows how impotent we are. He never actually does anything. Am I the only one who finds him so sinister?'

'He shouldn't have been prosecuted in the first place,' said Redwood angrily. 'Not if the evidence was as slim as you suggest. What were you thinking of, Helen? What's happened to your judgement? You're becoming a persecutor!'

It was an old joke, persecutor, prosecutor, the best he could do to make it seem as if he had listened to anything other than the singing, but Helen rounded on him without any humour at all.

'Of course there was evidence!' She stopped and blushed. 'There was at least half an indecent assault. I mean he was pretty persistent.' A smile began to emerge at the corner of her mouth. 'OK, point taken. He didn't actually touch her. He says he's driven mad by football. Like a werewolf by the moon.'

'What's half an indecent assault?' Dinsdale enquired.

'A decent one,' said Redwood, 'and now if you don't mind, I mean if that's all . . .' He had done his duty. They took the signal and rose simultaneously with relief. The meetings were a strain, the room was stifling.

'Helen, would you wait?'

Dinsdale paused at the door, ready to come back as Helen remained where she was. 'Oh, it's all right, man,' Redwood barked. 'I'm not going to tick her off, it's about something else entirely. No need to be so protective, she doesn't need a witness.' He wondered, not for the first time, how it was Helen acquired her legion of allies. But once Dinsdale had gone, Redwood wished he would return to save him from being alone with her. He coughed with the hollow sound of a man looking for his place on a page, unable to stand a silence, but wishing to postpone speech. He waited for the door to close. At least the doors here closed with a weighty quietness, unlike the windows which rattled like thunder.

'Helen, I could do with your help. Rather a delicate matter and I don't know how to handle it.'

She looked at him sharply, waiting for irony, remembering that Redwood didn't send people up, only brought them down when they were not looking. Perhaps it was a genuine plea from a man helpless when faced with the complexity of emotion, envious of her own insouciance in the brash, prison corridors of life. She decided to give him the benefit of the doubt. He coughed again and searched for a handkerchief, abandoning the quest in the desire to begin so he could finish. He often referred problems to Helen and he was ashamed of it.

'Rose,' he said ponderously. 'Rose Darvey.'

Helen was instantly defensive. 'She's a great girl. Clever, should have more responsibility, works like a Trojan, early morning, late night—'

'It's the late nights I'm talking about,' he interrupted.

'Why? We should be pleased to have someone like her. I thought you said she could go out, see more trials, take on more. I know she isn't exactly polite, but who's complaining? She's rude but she's keen . . .'

'How very apt, both rude and keen. I'm glad you see her as that. So does the Chief Inspector at the local nick who has particular responsibility for the welfare of his youngest police constables in the police section house up the road. He came in to see me.' Another cough. This time he found the handkerchief, looked at it, uncertain whether to blow his nose, but increasingly certain what to say. 'Rose has been through the whole division like a dose of salts. She's out with one or other of the bachelors every night. She has favourites, but it all seems to depend which shift they're on and their consequent availability, otherwise one's as good as another. I asked the doorman downstairs and he confirmed there's a lad in half blues out there every evening when she leaves. What's more, I happen to know for a fact, she's changed her address in the year she's been here and we've only got an old one on the file. The Chief Inspector's worried: he says the section house is in a state of riot. Youthful jealousy, all that. Could we have a word with her? Oh Lord, what do we do?'

He spoke with the weariness of a man who has lost sight of youthful lust and jealousy; on that account alone, Helen sympathized. She was silent. Redwood went on.

'The CI is politely concerned because he says he's got six young bloods on one relief who are at one another's throats, though God knows why, they don't apparently have to compete for her favours, which are priced at roughly three drinks and a packet of crisps—'

'You mean that's all they offer,' said Helen angrily. 'Mean bastards. They aren't badly paid.'

'I mean that's all she seems to ask,' said Redwood. 'The Chief Inspector says of course there's nothing new about the situation, girls will be girls and boys will be boys, but they haven't had a man-eater from the Crown Prosecution Service before. Doesn't exactly engender respect from the constabulary for our service, does it?' he finished lamely.

'And what did you say to the Chief Inspector?'

'I said I wasn't responsible for the private lives of our case clerks, or lawyers for that matter.' He looked at her meaningfully. Helen's ongoing love affair with a police officer was still the subject of comment. 'I asked him if he had had a word with the lads themselves, since it takes two to tango.'

Helen, approving of this response, nodded.

'But he was insistent,' Redwood went on. 'Would someone have a word with our Rose? Well, it can't be me. She'd spit in my eye.'

'And in mine,' said Helen.

'But you seem to get on with her best.'

'Best doesn't mean well. How can I stop her, if this is really what she's doing? Perhaps I wouldn't want to, perhaps she's having fun . . .'

'I doubt it,' Redwood volunteered with surprising wisdom. 'I doubt it very much. I've always thought the height of sexual pleasure lay in monogamy.' Helen looked at him in one of those rare moments when they understood one another. He was not, after all, a man devoid of compassion and he did have daughters. 'I'll think about it,' she said. 'If you don't mind me taking her under my wing rather more than I do, perhaps we could offer her alternative stimulus? Like better quality work? prospects of promotion?' Redwood winced and smiled wanly. Helen always exacted a price.

He watched her get up to leave, recovering her shopping as she went. Only Helen West, always in a hurry, would be shameless enough to dash into a meeting late, armed with groceries, as if she was trying to make some kind of point. He forgot she had come in from outside and it was a long haul to her own room.

'You look as if you're about to feed the five thousand,' he grunted.

'No,' said Helen, suddenly embarrassed by the weight of what she carried. 'Only one. But I need a wife.'

The groceries bounced against her legs as she wandered down the endless corridor to Room 251. What on earth had possessed her to stop at a market stall and buy kilos of fruit and vegetables when she still had to do the supermarket on the way home? Oh yes, my turn to apologize for being so mean yesterday; my turn to cook and I hate cooking, why didn't I just say we'd go out? But, poor soul is a bit embarrassed about being seen in public with an enormous black eye which I wasn't qualified to kiss better.

Tapping down the corridor over the lumpy carpet, rustling as she walked, Helen forgot Rose Darvey. Rose could wait until tomorrow. Waiting, like everything else, until Geoffrey Bailey with his black eye (worse this morning than the night before) had gone.

The clerks' room was only three enormous doors down from Redwood's office, but he visited it as rarely as possible. The red light for the ludicrous goods lift winked in the gloomy corridor. Helen passed the room where Dinsdale and John, the one as extrovert and charming as the other was shy, kept one another company. Three of the case clerks, Rose included, gathered by the door, drawn by John, who had carried on singing. Helen paused in passing, drawn as they were drawn, not only by the sound, but by the glamorous Dinsdale who was not like the rest of them at all. There was nothing of the misfit, for a start: he bore all the signs of privilege, private money, charm, humility and a way with words. Everybody loved him. Even Rose, which meant he had passed the acid test. To Helen Dinsdale was a divine problem: the thought of him made her go pink, remember her age (five years older than him), and also remember Redwood's remark about the joys of monogamy. As Helen watched, prepared to join the fan club, Rose detached herself from the group and sped off, running for the telephone, her spiked hair waving and that plait swinging against her neck. Helen plodded behind with her own prosaic shopping of which she was faintly ashamed. Bags of potatoes and fruit made her feel she had traversed the loop between youth and age: they diminished her into nothing and she quickened her step down this endless corridor in the shadow of the girl. Helen found herself standing outside the door, listening to Rose answering the call, looking for some sort of confirmation of what she had just been told about Rose and the police boys, uncomfortably aware that she had not really questioned anything Redwood had said, not shouted, Where's your evidence that our most promising non-professional is as promiscuous as a rabbit? Knowing she had not argued because she had not been surprised. Helen often worked late. She knew that Rose never left the office alone.

Rose's voice sang with irritation as she held the phone; it was an inflection carried on a draught from another huge window. Helen's belief in the imperviousness of youth fled. 'Listen,' Rose was saying, 'listen. You either fucking turn up or you don't. If you don't, well forget it. Sod you.' It was clearly milder than it might have been. Rose was speaking through gritted teeth, controlling herself. 'What do you mean later?' she was saying. 'What use is fucking later to me? Oh, I might be in a pub. Oh, Crown and Anchor, somewhere like that. You'll have to look, won't you? Bastard,' was what she hissed, putting the phone down. 'Bastard, bastard, bastard.'

It was already dark outside, darker than black velvet, darker than the charcoal with which Helen drew her odd but often accurate depictions of faces, and that was all Helen saw through the window as Rose looked up and spied her own reflection. Rose's face on the old glass bore wavy lines of a childish and unattractive fury, but the look as she spun round had changed to one of cunning.

'Oh, it's you. Well, I don't mind people hearing me mouthing off.'

'You're quite entitled,' said Helen. 'As long as you weren't talking to the Attorney General. Wouldn't do your career much good.'

Rose barked with laughter, her sharp little face alight with it and becoming animated into that of a different, more malleable creature until she stopped abruptly and looked at Helen assessingly. Helen could feel the scorn for the depressing bags of fruit and vegetables. Such luggage would never weigh down Rose Darvey or make her consider there was ever a time in Helen's life when she too might have lived on gin, tonic and crisps, a *modus vivendi* she still often craved.

'You look tired, Miss West. Why don't you come out for a drink with us after work?'

Helen was amazed, gratified in a way. Whatever the hidden motive, there must surely be in there some expression of approval which she needed in her present insecure frame of mind. But before she could think, she was stuttering the negative, raising the polythene bags in a helpless gesture which made her feel older still. Apples, oranges and potatoes, God help me.

'Rose, I'd love to, but I can't. Got to get home, food shopping, you know . . .' Rose did not know. Too late, Helen found herself making excuses for a refusal which could have been both warm and gracious but sounded merely lame. The moment in which she could have established some intimacy died in the speaking. Rose turned back to her desk, fiddled with the phone, showing no sign of disappointment, shrugging.

'No problem. Forget I asked.'

'Another time . . .'

'No, forget it. Only an idea. But listen, while you're here, can I ask you something?'

Perhaps the chance of mutuality had not fled after all, but Rose was businesslike. 'You know how I keep track of all the case papers in a notebook? And then who's-your-face puts them in the computer every day with all the dates for the remand hearings, so we know where everything is, and which dates someone's got to turn up to court the next time?' Helen was ashamed to say she did not really know, deliberately ignorant of the way the office worked. 'Well,' Rose continued, 'someone keeps nicking the notebook. You've got the untidiest room. My sodding notebooks haven't wandered in there lately, have they?'

It was spoken like an accusation, so unnecessarily aggressive that Helen had the fleeting suspicion Rose somehow sensed that she had been discussed in critical terms and was defending herself in advance. Or maybe it was her response to the mildest of rejections. 'I don't think so. Why should I have them? Does it matter, as long as it's all gone on the computer? That's the only record we need, isn't it.'

'Oh, you are stupid,' said Rose. The other five girls were clattering back, yawning, reaching for hats and coats, grinning at Helen. They were all so much nicer than Rose and so much less complicated, she thought with the rise of a familiar irritation. Rose's back view and her overbright hallos to her mates had the same effect as a dismissal and Helen took the hint. Rose had a shining charisma and energy in her which defied the brash rudeness; she would find someone else to go to the pub. 'Night!' she yelled, rudely, and then with a last, pitying look at the unglamorous bags, added, 'Have a good evening.' Suddenly her pretty face split into a grin. 'Listen, you can always wow a man with potatoes . . .'

I wish I was like that, Helen thought later, still wondering what strange and guilty fit of domestic conscientiousness had led her to purchase the vegetables. There were some days in which a weary stupidity seemed to take over and she was easily mesmerized by a shop or a stall. I wish I was nineteen and careless, energetic and about to fall in love, adopt a new career, go out giggling and screwing men every night, although not perhaps the rookie policemen from the section house with their fresh and pimply faces. Geoffrey Bailey had once been one of those, and the thought stopped her in her tracks as she struggled from the bus and into the supermarket. The thought of Bailey did not bring joy: it brought instead a dull weight of anxious dread and a feeling of guilt.

Geoffrey Bailey was not by any manner of means a vain man, but his own embarrassment at the public vision of his beaten-up face made him feel uncomfortable. He should have been too old to care, and as Ryan had said, 'You were scarcely an oil painting to begin with, were you, sir? Who do you think will notice?' Ryan did not quite do him justice. Bailey's appearance was never less than dignified. He was long and lean with a face of surprising asceticism for a man who knew how to handle himself in a fight, although the lines betrayed an age well beyond forty and a malnourished youth. Ryan had also been heard to say that Bailey got promoted because he looked so good in a suit, and that was not quite fair either. Ryan could not understand his master's obsession with fairness and conscience in a world which was supplied with neither. Bailey looked impeccable and unyielding in a suit, frightening to some, unless he was decorated with the comic effect of a black eye above. The eye throbbed with the foolishness of its own existence and Bailey had endured quite enough teasing for one day. The rest of him smarted for reasons quite unconnected. Helen West was his lover (he hated the word mistress, which implied an element of financial dependence and there was certainly none of that), and he had been gratuitously unkind to her the night before. It did not matter that

31

the unkindness was mutual, but he had called her unreliable, selfish, self-absorbed. There were other epithets, far more extreme, from which he had refrained and the guilt was for things left unsaid, for the pathetic failure even to have a proper row with pots and pans flying. It had ended with mutual apologies and witch hazel placed on his eye by Helen, using all the kindly and remote consideration of a nurse. Today had begun with promises of killing some fatted calf to celebrate his departure which he suspected she viewed with as much relief as sorrow. The guilt had inhabited his day and led him to the supermarket which he knew, by instinct rather than information, she would visit on the way back to her place. Her turn to cook.

He yawned. Your place, my place, no place to go. He was never in the right place to find the shirt which went with the tie. He might as well shack up in the back of a caravan in the middle of a field, that was what he had wanted to say the night before. I do not mind any of this, Helen, but could you please relinquish just a little more of yourself than you do? I admit being born forty-five years ago with the expectation that a woman might cook my supper for life; I have shed that hope and did not particularly like it when it was offered, but I would indeed like it if you occasionally volunteered, although I cook far better than you. It becomes the yardstick of what we feel about things, this business of shopping and feeding. Nor can I rid myself of a notion which you have proved absurd, namely that a woman should be soft and have an interest in babies by the age of thirty-five. You accord with none of my expectations. I love you dearly, but there are times, especially latterly, when I have to say it in order to feel it, and you do not say it at all. You have become brittle, my dearest, the sugar spun hard, but I cannot speak too loud, because ten years ago, before I recovered my compassion, let alone my sanity, I was as hard as nails.

Guilt for things unsaid had him standing in the light outside the supermarket against the backdrop of a dozen brazen advertisements, 'Nescafé! 10p off! Jaffa oranges! 20p!' Absently, fond of oranges, fonder still of tangerines which reminded him of the Christmas they had just had, he went indoors and selected oranges, grapefruit, apples, potatoes. At least he would leave her with some supplies.

He saw her behind aisle one (soaps, detergents, bleaches, toilet rolls), already overburdened with a briefcase and three white bags of bulging plastic. Even in this cruel light, she was beautifully distinctive. He saw her first in the television monitor which hung above the door; his height allowed him to see above the corridors of produce, and he had thought, Darling, you could never rob a bank, you are so unmistakable. A big wide forehead, with that faded scar disguised by worry lines, the thick, dark hair pulled back into a slide which could not quite contain it, and the face which had always reminded him of some exotic dancer blessed with oddly imperfect beauty and enormous eyes. You could not even guess her nationality with those saturnine looks, and here and now, despite the casual elegance of her fine, swinging coat, you could not guess the authority she held. She looked lost. She stood at the counter labelled, FISH! paralysed with uncertainty. Supermarkets did this to her. On a market stall it was different, but here, she failed to function. In an instant, he understood her better, loved her better, though the liking was still in doubt. He saw that she had bought vegetables and so had he.

People looked at her, without her ever seeing, he noticed, but they were not drawn to a man with a black eye as he went his aberrant way, tipping all he had chosen back on to the fruit and vegetable aisle. He looked like a thief who had abandoned the expedition, a reprobate who could not pay, and he felt a fool, for being ludicrously tidy in his replacement of what he knew she had already bought, putting back potatoes with potatoes, fruit with the same breed of fruit, plastic bags where they belonged. Bailey, who was willing to bet she had selected worse produce from her stall and paid more, replaced his goods with an element of regret. Then he walked up to where she stood, still immobile. The red coat crumpled as he placed his hands around her waist and whispered in her ear.

'Fancy a night on the town, then? Take you away from all this? Man with a black eye, asking for you.'

She did not move, leant back against him.

'I never go out with strange men,' she said. 'I stay in. Do you want cod or plaice? I can't even spell the others.'

They might answer to their names, but he doubted they could spell them. At ten past ten, Sergeant Morgan examined the relief for night shift, E division, King's Cross. They paraded for duty in whatever shambolic order they chose and not for any other purpose than his counting them. You didn't brief them these days. Although the sergeant would have liked it to be different, half of this relief were probationers, rookies from the country with accents you could cut with a knife and as far as he could see, scarcely a good one among them. He was grateful he did not have to examine their consciences, but counting them was easy. Out of ten, three were missing. Those present, who had come via various routes to work, could not explain the absence of the contingent from the section house.

Sergeant Morgan sent the oldest constable, PC Michael, all of twenty-four, a handsome pugilist with a broken nose, and a temperament of surprising gentleness until he approached a fight and even then he seemed able to control his scarred fists. Michael was of a size which looked ridiculous in a panda car and the bulk of him made the door of the section house appear small by comparison.

Inside, PC Michael could smell the conflict although the place looked as empty as a closed shop. Late turn, the two-till-ten shift, were still on their way home, while early turn, who would work from eight till two tomorrow, were all still out on the town. Following a nose for blood, Michael broke into a run up a flight of stairs where the sounds of violence were now unmistakable. A hoarse yelling, grunting, the noise of falling furniture, a slow dancing of malice-filled steps, the vicious sounds of bone on bone and a cry of enraged pain led his progress. There was a bedroom door ajar through which the central light swung drunkenly from a low ceiling, casting a beam like a moving flame on the scene beneath. He could see a stereo system smashed, a cheap bedside lamp in fragments. In the far corner, illuminated as the light swung back, a wardrobe door hung on its hinges, supported from falling by the slumped figure of a slight youth with his left hand shielding his eyes, the other arm outflung to the edge of a rumpled bed on which sat a girl with spiky hair, balled into the furthest corner. Her knees were clasped to her chest and her hands were over her ears in an attitude which suggested both fear and indifference. Centre stage, two young men in half police uniform, with navy serge trousers beneath blue shirts, one ripped but both still buttoned, wrestled and punched with the savagery of fighting dogs. 'You cunt, you bastard.' Guttural, meaningless insults, as ineptly delivered as the blows which nevertheless made sounds of bruising flesh.

They were equal in weight, size and hatred, but neither had half of Michael's disciplined bulk. He stepped towards them, crunching over broken glass and seized each rutting youth by the collar. He took a fistful of stiff cotton shirting in each hand, twisted it, yanking the material against each throat, and with this purchase, braced himself and flung them apart. One staggered backwards against the wall, his head striking with a sickening thud, the other reverberated against the wardrobe door, falling half across the crouching youth and the girl, who shrank further away. In the silence of panting breath, Michael noticed that she held her skirt over her naked loins and on the floor, in the brief moment when the light swung back, he saw a tracery of lace underwear. The room smelt strongly of sweat, fish, cooking meat; a stench of smells, with the last scent of blood carrying the taste of iron into his mouth. Gradually, the light slowed its wild arc and the faces became clear.

'Parkin? John! Williams! You clowns! Will you wash your faces now and report for duty? Or you'll catch it.' The radio on Michael's belt crackled: they all remembered who and what they were, moved in a dream of automatic response to orders. In stumbling from the room, all but the boy crouched on the floor, whose room it was, cast a look of venom in the direction of the girl on the bed. PC Michael glanced at her in sheer dislike and left her there. It was only on the way back he felt sorry for his behaviour. At half-past ten, Police Sergeant Morgan convened the night-shift parade again and shouted at them all, innocent or guilty, including PC Michael, for repeating the cock-and-bull story he had been told, designed to exonerate them all. Michael stared straight ahead with his mild eyes; the rest were silent and resentful. Third from the end, the smallest of the relief, PC Williams, displayed a swelling eye, now pink, soon to be purple. He kept his mouth closed to relieve the pain of a broken tooth, but he could not prevent himself crying like a baby, raising his fist to his swollen mouth to prevent the shameful sound of a boy whimpering.

'I knew you wanted steak really. You could have put it on your eye, then I could have cooked it.'

'Bit like getting a dog to bury it in the garden to tenderize it. You have the sort of ideas to encourage a vegetarian. Did you read that one in the book?'

'Fish is good for you. Isn't it? Protein without fat? But think of how they catch it, all that thrashing around—'

'You could do with a bit of fat. Slender's one thing, being thin, another . . .'

'Now look who's talking. You look as if you could snap in half.'

'Well, if you want to try,' Bailey said. 'I'm all yours. Be gentle with me, though. I'm not a well man.'

Helen laughed, like the old days, when she had first sat on the worn but brilliant colours of his junk-shop sofa and admired the barrenness of his walls. She didn't even think of the journey home, the cold outside, the balcony cat which had sat on her pristine blouse and made it grey without any comment from either of them. Even then, he had been haunted by the vision of keeping her thus, a fixture in his life instead of this ever-moving, ever-tantalizing target. He supposed a woman as handsome as this, as kind but as definite as this, was bound to be this way. Bailey could no longer distinguish between the deficiencies and the necessities of their existence, could not see where they should go from here, only where they had been. He was humbled by the conclusion which had formed over the last twenty-four hours and found it difficult to articulate. Helen might have been relieved at the prospect of his enforced absence, but he did at least now know that she was not the only one. He was relieved too, even though she was in the crook of his arm, dressed in nothing but a shawl, her small athletic limbs bare beneath, enough to make a man forget his pain, the absence of dessert and the dry fish. Clinging to him, but with so light a clinging her finger's touch had all the weight of a feather.

'I forgot,' she said, deliberately drowsy. 'Do they let you out from Bramshill every weekend, or once a fortnight?'

'I don't know,' he replied, restive with the lie. 'I'll only know when I get there tomorrow.'

'I'll miss you,' she said, simply. Nothing more. He was not sure what he had hoped for. Remembered the hymn singing of his childhood. Oh, thou who changest not, abide with me.

Down the hill, far beyond the wilderness which was in turn far beyond the reaches of the football stadium, lit by arc lights still although the crowd was gone, Rose Darvey ran. She bore in her stride nothing but the encumbrance of her short skirt, her brutal shoes, a quantity of vodka and the dizzying effect of a light bulb swinging across her eyes. She knew she was pursued, knew she should not have stopped once to hide and howl quietly, should have known better than to give way to her fear of the dark. The car lights hit her full beam on the corner: the man who pursued her had gone round the back. She shrank into one of the hedges which skirted the tiny front gardens. Waited. A car door was shut carefully, with the deliberate movement of someone who was preoccupied. She breathed easier. Then footsteps came in her direction, hesitated, moved past with unerring pace, stopped, came back. If he had slammed the door, she would have maintained her hope: she was accustomed to such sounds, but the quiet precision made her want to scream. 'Come out, will you?' A voice equally careful, but harsh. 'I know where you are. Come on out. Don't be silly.'

When she moved, though, obeying him slowly, he caught his breath. He had expected a hard-bitten face and saw instead the beautiful eyes of a haunted child.

CHAPTER THREE

M rs Mellors reached out her hand and stroked the head of
the blond child who stood in front of her as they waited
for the bus. She did so because she could not resist it. The child
shook her head as if to dismiss a troublesome fly, then clapped
her hand to her golden locks as the stroking continued, turned
round, ready to be angry. When she saw who it was she grinned
instead, the toothless smile of a six year old who had lost the top
set of milk teeth early and was waiting for their replacements.
She was an ugly little cuss, apart from the hair, a screamer and
yeller, the kind Margaret Mellors particularly liked because there
was something in Margaret which always applauded a talent for
noisy hysteria. She didn't want to emulate it and besides, it was
too late now to change the gentle habits of a lifetime, where the
only vice was two drinks a night when she got the chance, but
she still had an artless admiration for those born rowdy. Her
own extraordinary patience with awkward children was one of
many reasons to explain her popularity with the young parents
in Legard Street. Yuppies did not live here. The newly partnered
who started their dynasties in these tiny houses were not those
who could employ nannies: they catered for their broods and their
mortgages via more hazardous routes. There was the occasional
father at the primary school gate, but mostly it was a question of

babes in arms being ferried hither and thither by mothers grey with exhaustion.

Margaret Mellors had never advertised the fact that she would willingly look after any of the children with all the skill of the apple-cheeked grandmothers who featured in their books but not otherwise in their lives, but such news did not need to be shouted. In the last four years which had marked both a vacuum in her life as well as changing fortunes for the street, news of her willingness had spread into a kind of fame and her house had become inundated with children. Only now she was stroking that irresistible blond head with a tentative touch, because she had sensed a slight shift in attitude towards her from the mothers of children like this. There had been a perceptible if slow alteration in their willingness to leave children at her house. At first, Margaret thought it was all about the onset of winter and the deep suspicion held by all these young people for the old-fashioned decrepitude of her spotless abode, but she had come to recognize it as something more. The disparity of the lives somehow made the grapevine of unwelcome gossip appallingly slow, as well as inaccurate, but still Mrs Mellors was being sent to Coventry by those who needed her most.

'Hallo, Margaret! How are you? Say hallo, Sylvia, will you please. Nicely.' The warmth of the mother's greeting made Margaret relax and the acceptance of the child gave her a feeling of authority. Whatever it was that had blighted the reputation of her own home, it was not herself. No one despised her bird-like body and her clean, talcum-powder smell. She hoped not, but in a way she would have preferred it if the opposite was true; if only they did not all dislike poor darling Logo so much, and if only they could realize that the lies which framed him were utterly and completely unfair. Talk about screamers and shouters, he was certainly one of them, but essentially a good boy, despite the Bible and the singing, if only they would see it. The problem around here was they were all so busy.

'Hallo to you too! Where are you going then? Shopping? God save us, you won't have much chance, will you?' Margaret's hand was still in the child's hair, touching the delicious warmth of the neck lightly. She knew when not to irritate and the child did not resist, squirming happily before she came to rest straddled over the old woman's leg, resting against her stomach and her stick, biding her time for attention.

'You haven't been round to see me lately, have you?' said Margaret, brightly. 'Are you going to nursery school now?'

'Yeth,' said the child.

The mother shifted her weight from one foot to another unhappily.

'Well the truth is, Margaret, she's supposed to go, but half the time they can't have her, so it only works out to two mornings a week, and the rest of the time she drives me round the bend. I take that much time off work and I'm only part time as it is—'

'Why don't you send her to me then?' Margaret asked mildly, looking away from the woman and peering down the street as if she had just seen something worth close examination. The child began to hum loudly, then set off round them both in close circles, making the dangerous noise of a wasp.

'Oh, do shush, sweetheart,' said Margaret. The child shushed and came back to rummage in Margaret's half-full shopping bag with noisy rudeness. Margaret did not protest, while the mother looked at her big, calm face, at odds with the little body, with something like hunger.

'Look, Margaret, I'd send her into you like a shot, but you must know I can't, not with that man next door to you. You know what I mean. Is he really your son? People says he's your son, you're both so . . . petite, but he doesn't look like you. Well anyway, if it's true, and someone told me it wasn't, I don't mean to be rude but I can't send Sylvie into you with him hanging around the place, can I?'

'Why ever not?' Margaret asked, stupidly.

'Don't you know? You must know, surely?'

But the look on Margaret's face confirmed an incredible level of ignorance of anything to Logo's detriment. She clearly did not understand that there was anything more than the merely indistinct vibrations of embarrassment which Logo attracted from his neighbours. For pinching the odd spade out of a garden, Margaret thought defensively; for looking through their rubbish bags like the scavenger he was. He was only a little bit crazy, poor Logo, and nobody likes anybody who carries a black Bible around with them, the reverse of a talisman. This wasn't a wicked neighbourhood, but it was godless. Margaret braced herself. If he looked like the son of hers who never was, Logo was her problem: she certainly didn't want him to be anyone else's.

'No, he isn't my kin, but I've lived next door to him and his family, when he had a family, for nigh on twenty years, so I know him better than anybody, you might say. It was when his wife and his daughter went off, you see, only a year or two since, that he went a bit barmy. You shouldn't take offence at him, he's all right really. Gentle, wouldn't hurt a fly, and he's been good to me, really. Ever so good.'

The younger woman's cross-examining glance was so sharp, Margaret thought for a second that the powder would be stripped off her own face. She always wore face powder, just a little, to correspond with the talcum on her body: she dressed and undressed in a shower of sweet-smelling dust and she tried to keep herself decent. It was her own compensation for age, infirmity, the bad hip for which treatment had never been successful, and as far as compensations went, it worked. Margaret Mellors, with her cake-like face, neat little frame and her almost edible gentleness, was never less than easy on the eye.

'Someone said,' the woman was saying, trying to keep the aggression from her voice, 'he's been arrested ever so many times. But he always gets off.'

Margaret rallied, she did not raise her voice because she never felt the need.

'Well, that'll be because he never actually does anything. He's always looking for some kid who looks like his daughter used to look, don't know what she looks like now, but that's what he does. Silly, but he does it . . .'

Her voice was fading softly into nothing. She knew as she spoke, with the child pulling on the shopping bags and dragging her sideways, that any attempt to explain or excuse the enigmas of Logo were useless. She had better try another route.

'Never mind what he does, it hardly matters,' she said. 'Anyway whatever gave you the idea he was ever in my house during the day? He does work, you know, after his fashion, but oh no, he's never in my place. Never. He's out with his trolley.'

It was almost the truth and she meant it to be the truth. She paused for dramatic effect. 'Never,' she added, with quiet emphasis, feeling disloyal as she spoke, but still determined. The child began to move again, re-creating the humming sound, but louder, until it became a kind of growling. The mother looked at her in alarm.

'I'm a dog, really,' the child announced.

'Of course you are,' Margaret murmured comfortably. 'Are you a big dog or a little dog? Only they make different noises. Wouldn't you be better as a cat?'

The mother's last defences were gone. Some persuasion had been necessary, but not much.

'Listen, if you could . . . Only I've got so much to get, and she's a nightmare round the shops—'

'Of course I'll have her if it helps. You just relax, you look a bit tired. Late-night shopping, isn't it? You'll be able to get a lot done. No need to hurry home.'

So Margaret Mellors had the company of hyperactive Sylvie for an hour or four in the dying afternoon. It hadn't strictly been a lie about Logo, she told herself. They did, after all, have an unwritten rule that they never went into one another's houses without invitation – never – but still the conversation left her uneasy, reminded her too much of things shoved under the carpet and best not brought out. His door would open with a kick, but something about the view from the window stopped anyone trying. And he was kept busy, she wasn't lying about that, cleansing officer he was called, she reflected with pride, that's what he was called. The Council wanted rid of him too: everyone picked on him, he said, but Logo remained on the equal opportunity pay roll, come what may, for a number of reasons. They liked an eccentric for a start and there weren't too many volunteers to brave the graveyard ghosts on his patch, even less to clear the rubbish after football, nor anyone else who came so much into his own for certain special tasks. They could raise him from the pubs where he was regarded as a singing-and-dancing mascot, though never quite a drunk. He would deal with burst water mains, drains in suppurating basements, the removal of a decade's worth of rotting rubbish: he would touch the untouchable with his bare hands; shovel up a dead dog or cat from a cellar, singing all the while. You didn't sack a wiry little man like that, whatever his timekeeping.

'Oh God our help in ages past . . .' Logo shouted, pushing the trolley. Big old thing, not the new-fangled plastic, double-binned variety, ergonomically, economically sound, he wouldn't have any, got the ole bin on wheels, hadn't he, suited him fine, but he'd fought for it. Despite the memory of that battle, the energy was low that afternoon and his feet in his training shoes were icy.

Logo took many of the opportunities his job presented for doing nothing, but he always noticed litter. Down in the gutters as he walked, some of last autumn's leaves were still half frozen from the morning frost, the slyest litter of all, unrecyclable, with nowhere to go, pretty at dawn but now becoming so much damp rubbish until the next night's frost would crisp them like toast, where the bugs and the slime slept easily until they melted and the smell came up. Logo liked that scent: he liked the earth when it was damp and stuck to his feet. He made his own timetable; lazy one day, industrious the next. Today he was finished with the graveyard: he could go home, but he didn't want to, he would rather sit on a wall and read his dog-eared Bible. He liked the stories.

'Have we not power to lead about a sister, a wife, as well as other apostles as the brethren of the Lord? Or I only, have not we power to forbear working?' he intoned, his voice a high enquiry as he went towards his street.

It had been one of those days when light had never properly featured at all; there had been nothing to the dying of it. Turning the corner, Logo saw the figure of Margaret Mellors retreating from him with her narrow back, dressed in the same clean, dun-coloured coat which went on from year to year with no pretension to style. She was in the act of reaching inside her bag for an orange which she then bowled down the street like a ball towards a wicket. A small child whooped, yelled, barked in pursuit of the orange until she waylaid it in her little fist, catching it like some terrier while it was still rolling.

'There's no need to bite it,' Margaret was calling. Logo saw the blond head in the intermittent light of the lamps. Watching with quiet intensity as Margaret threw the orange again, he became slowly aware of disturbing sounds. People gathering for a footie match. Beyond their road he could sense the traffic bearing down on them, felt from a distance the arrival of the first hordes. It always reminded him of flies descending on a carcass, but Margaret did not notice. He was trying to work out why she threw fruit for her charge; to tire her out, perhaps, you threw sticks for a dog and more edible things for a child, but his interest soon died. The creature did not resemble his own child, dark as a gypsy like him, run away a long time ago; she'd be a woman now.

Margaret called to the child and when she ran back, seized her firmly by the hand and led her up the street towards her house. Disconsolate, Logo remembered his icy feet and stood up and stamped them. He courted the cold, did not really mind it and the stamping was more ritual than necessity. He waited until Margaret was out of sight, then drew in a lungful of air and began to sing.

'Jesu, saviour ever mild,
Born for us a little child,
Of the virgin undefiled:
Hear us Holy Jesus.'

Keeping close to the walls, backing out of Legard Street, pushing the cumbersome trolley like a big old pram, he moved in the direction of the crowds which would throng the thoroughfares beyond. Looking for a small, dark child, with a headful of black curls cascading from the neck to her waist and streaming out behind her like the tangled mane of a thoroughbred filly as she ran away. From him.

Dinsdale Cotton thought Helen West was beautiful. He did not say as much, but the conclusion had been on his mind from the moment he had first met her. He could follow the present discussion with his brain all the more easily because it gave him a better opportunity to look at her eyes, hands, hair, legs in whatever order they happened to present themselves without quite seeming to devour her. He knew it was still far too soon to do anything else, that would be like spitting in public, but he planned it anyway, enjoying what he had for now. Besides the conversation was always worth while, even if they both chose to deny the undercurrent which flowed between them.

'Evidence,' she was saying. 'Come on, Dinsdale, why the hell aren't you doing this? Why me and not you, giving a lecture on evidence? How come I even got volunteered and not you, when you can talk the hind leg off a donkey and everyone knows I've never understood law at all? I only practise it. What do I say to them?'

He took a covert look at her slender crossed ankles, as she sat back in the beastly lounge of the Swan and Mitre, and decided he could look no further so he might as well entertain himself by intellectual effort.

'What you say always depends on the audience,' he said. 'And there's no audience, apart from a symposium of scientists, who do not want their information as simple as possible.'

'Just as well. I can't manage more than that. Come on, surprise me. Ten minutes is what I have to deliver, on the subject of, What is evidence? The audience being Justices of the Peace with nil legal training. Your starter for ten, please.'

Dinsdale sipped his drink, vodka in tomato juice, which did

not look at all effete in his hands. He removed an imaginary pair of glasses and shuffled an imaginary sheaf of papers on the rather dirty table.

'Evidence, my dears, is fact. It comes in the form of brick or cement. There are basically three kinds of evidence. The first is the most direct, say from an eye or ear witness to an event, the horse's mouth evidence. Then it comes, less directly, from those who follow on behind, picking up the pieces of the smashed car, testing the blood samples and the semen stains and who can thus say, this event happened. This is circumstantial evidence, although they are recycled bricks, they are the most certain of all. Evidence also comes from a number of unrelated facts which surround the victim and the defendant but have nothing to do with them, and this is the cement. They are little facts, positive and negative, which point to one conclusion. Thus, one witness hears a door slam at three in the morning, another sees a man in a street soon after; a third person mentions someone he met in the local earlier that evening who looked the same; a fourth mentions, by chance, a possible motive. By the smallest and most innocent innuendos brother betrays brother. A network of facts, individually irrelevant. You need this cement if you do not have enough of the bricks alone. Like bloodstains and fingerprints.'

'Confessions?' Helen asked, vastly amused. 'Are they direct enough evidence to make into bricks?'

'Oh, certainly,' Dinsdale said airily. 'Finest kind of brick, but in this generation, it has a tendency to crumble. What you must tell this audience, of course, is that the only evidence which can be used in the construction of a case is evidence that has been properly obtained. Thus if you make the defendant shit the brick, you cannot use it to build the wall around him. Will that do?'

'Certainly. But your recitation has taken precisely two minutes. What shall I do for the other eight?'

'Tell them stories. The taller the better. Another drink?'

Helen was about to refuse, responding to the automatic pilot-light which ignited inside her head some time before eight in the evening to remind her it was time to go home. Then she remembered there was no Geoffrey Bailey at his home or her own, hadn't been for a week. There'd been no trailing around a supermarket in her inefficient pursuit of their needs. The thought of her own relief brought into her throat an indigestible lump of

guilt which she decided to swallow. She might well love Geoffrey
Bailey, she was usually well aware that she did, but freedom
from the routines of the relationship, from the sheer time it
took to be with another, felt like a prize she had worked towards
for months. Especially if the privilege included sitting with a
man of Dinsdale's distinguished ease, warmed by his admiration
and his sheer ability to talk. It made a change from the barks
and grunts of familiarity.

'Well yes, why not? Aren't you due home, or something?'

Dinsdale shrugged noncommittally. Helen could not imagine
his life to be unaccompanied by less than a select harem, but his
domestic loyalties were his own concern and she did not have to
consider them. She did not, at this moment, have to consider
anyone or anything at all apart from the state of her digestion.

'Speaking of evidence,' said Dinsdale, returning from the bar
with a napkin which he used to wipe the table clean in small,
fastidious movements, 'is what I see over there evidence of anything
at all? Or is it a figment of my over-fertile imagination?' Helen
looked and whistled softly.

The Swan and Mitre was a pub with little to recommend it
apart from proximity to a thousand offices and a heavy sense of
age created by sherry casks hung above the bar. The grime was
unfeigned and the crowds stumbled their way through raucous
gossip in the artificial gloom. Smoking was mandatory: scores of
men and women had been released from work to indulge a number
of bad habits before retiring to the rigours of their homes. The
wooden booths lining the walls gave some scope for intimacy: for
the rest, the assignations were as public as a meeting in a telephone
kiosk. In one booth, selfishly occupying space enough for four,
prohibiting invasion by the cunning placement of coats which
made it look as if someone else was expected, sat Rose, flanked
by a young man. The size of him, the uniform shirt and the short
haircut betrayed him as a policeman or a security man or suchlike,
but there was no need for guesswork.

'Don't look so obviously, Helen, you do stare so. Is that PC
Michael? He of boxing fame?'

'I think so. Why shouldn't I look? My God, they're actually
talking to one another . . .'

'Well, so were we, it's a natural consequence of human
proximity.'

'Among others,' Helen said lightly, 'in which Rose is supposed to be something of a specialist. She's been looking very pretty over the last couple of days, have you noticed? More subdued, less spiky.'

'I thought that might have been your influence. You know, having a little chat with her, woman to woman, like Redwood asked you to do.'

'Asked once, then again and again, after more complaints and a fight in the section house. Yes I did try and talk to her, you know, Rose-is-there-anything-worrying-you? kind of thing, anything-where-I-could-help-you? But I didn't do much good. Quite the reverse, I must be losing my touch. I've never heard such a stream of insults in my life. No, that isn't true, I have, but not usually so fluent. The message was, Fuck off, leave me alone, you old cow, how can you understand at your age? And if Redwood wants to sack me, let him try. I made a tactical withdrawal.'

'Bloodied, but unbowed?' Dinsdale asked, smiling to show teeth which were admirably white.

'No, both bowed and bloodied. I wish there weren't such a thing as the age gap. I like her, I can't bear to see this brooding anger of hers, but she finds it impossible to like me. You can't convince her you might know what she means.'

'The effort was commendable,' said Dinsdale gravely, sensing a real humiliation. His hand on the now clean table hovered close to hers. The sight of it, pale, with its neatly pared nails, made her feel unaccountably lonely. The fingers tapped a neat rhythm, as if listening to some hidden music which was not hers to hear. Like the music which vibrated between Rose and her man, hidden but harmonic, cutting across the smog of the room to where they sat, the two adults. Helen thought she remembered what it was like, the music of romance, and felt older than Noah. Older than the sherry casks and just as deaf.

The pub on the corner of Legard Street and the main avenue which led to the football stadium also served sherry, but only if asked, with the request repeated several times. Their speciality was the kind of pie which, even when microwaved within an inch of its life, still challenged the digestion of a steam engine. The pie was held by the edge of the cellophane wrapper and it was not wise to examine the contents. Logo was indifferent to food and the pub was empty.

He ate his pie. It was burnt on the outside and chilly in the centre and did nothing to cure his hunger, but it made him feel bigger as he swallowed it. The concave stomach, knitted together in the middle by a scar which made him look as if he had been bitten by a shark, relaxed beneath the belted trousers. He belched, softly, looking round for an audience. The barman regarded him with marginal interest, less tolerant than usual. He was restocking the shelves for when the crowds came out of the stadium. On a night like this, during the silence in the middle of the two storms, he could do without Mr Logo, and if the bastard sang, he would pack him out of doors among the phalanx of parked cars, into the roar of sound which would reverberate as soon as someone scored a goal.

'All right, are you?' he said pleasantly and threateningly enough.

'All right,' said Logo. 'And you?'

'All right. Time you went home, isn't it?' He leant over the table, wiping the surface with a busy fussiness which betrayed watchful idleness and anxiety. Logo always leant over things without ever actually sitting down, the better to clear his chest for the next hymn, the barman thought, although Logo knew different. He found it uncomfortable to sit. The old scar was a wound known only to himself and some doctor who had long since moved on without his notes. The stitches were cumbersome, but they had been inserted in the middle of the night in a casualty ward without thought of future vanity, and they were old now, twitching in their wisdom to remind him not to sit with his small store of belly flesh curled into him, but always to stand proud, like a tin soldier who cannot bend. The barman made a mock punch in the direction of the old wound. No injury was meant – it was a playful gesture to underline a point and occupy the idleness – it was supposed to be friendly. But the reaction was absurd: Logo doubled up as if to pretend the punch was real, cried out in pain and lurched against the wall behind the now clean table. His arms were crossed over his abdomen and he wailed like a child. 'Aagh, aah, aah, please, please, don't. *Aagh*!'

The barman was unmoved. He did not care for the ulcerous pains of anyone who ate his pies; nor did he have to take hysterics from a little Bible-pushing creep like this.

'Oh go home, fuck off. I never touched you. Get out, Go on, get out, get out, get out!'

Logo, clutching his stomach, went out into the gloom without a backward glance. It had been warm in there, the pie inside him was warm enough and he had enough cash for another drink, but he went anyway. He took his litter trolley and its brushes inside from where he had parked it outside the door: it gave him stability as well as music as they went down the silent streets. Rumble rumble, wheels of worn rubber going round and round as if, in their bad design, they were as bewildered as he was himself, though he wouldn't have changed them for the world. The big trolley was good for a scavenger.

Home, don't spare the horses.

' "His roots shall be dried up from beneath, and above shall his branch be cut off," ' murmured Logo to himself, thinking of the barman, and then, self-pityingly of himself. ' "His remembrance shall perish from the earth and he shall have no name in the street." '

There was a great, sore-throated roar from the stadium as he passed; the streets were full of cars without people. Logo clutched the handle of his barrow and moved on, listening to the sound of thousands singing, 'Walk On! Walk On! You'll never walk alone!' feeling his Bible thump against his pocket, his feet warm now, as long as he kept moving. Which he did faster and faster, as far as the distant doors of his own house, no singing, no carrying on, nothing of the kind. He'd been a good boy, a very, very good boy; it was still early, so he wouldn't go in and see dear old Mother in case she was still trying to tire out that little blond brat playing hide and seek. Then he stopped, suddenly sober and cold.

Hide and seek inside his house as well as Granny Mellors', that's what it looked like. The lights were lit on his own ground floor, pouring from the frosted pane of his kitchen into the alley. He could not believe that Margaret had sent the child, that blond, naughty little thing, to play in his house, but that was the only explanation that sprang to mind. Unless the child had gone there alone, pushed the door open, entered to plunder and explore. He knew he was not expected home before eight: he rarely was, but for Margaret, for both of them, especially the child, to assume his absence, felt like a violation. He quietly laid down the trolley and tiptoed to his door.

Little Sylvie's mother was further up the road, trying to fight her way through a barrier of parked cars, three deep, no room for a leg in between. She was late to begin with, stopped at the Tube because of a football fight, then the bus stopped for the same reason. All transport became coy on football nights. She was panicking a bit but not greatly until now. She knew Margaret would take care of Sylvie but everything seemed to take longer and longer, and the child was in Margaret's house. She had tried to phone, but there had been a queue, so she hadn't done and now it was half-past eight. Never mind. She click-clacked down the road, on the long walk from the Underground, wondering when her husband would be home, looking forward to that, and then halfway home, at the back of her head, she heard the child screaming in the way only her own child could scream. She felt it in her bloodstream: the pain in her chest like swallowed razor blades as she began to run, stumbling with shopping. She ran and she fell down in the dark alleyway between Margaret Mellors' and the house alongside. She was sure, from the distance, she had heard the child scream: she could feel it. Crashing through the broom handles which struck out from a rubbish cart in the alley, knocking her hip and all the shopping against the brickwork, she pushed into Margaret's house without ceremony, still hearing screams. *Where are you? Where are you, my love?* She was panting with the effort, but there she was, Sylvie the tyrant, in Margaret's arms, in front of the television.

She was lying there, the next best thing to unconscious, with her arms around Margaret's neck and one of her feet twitching. There was ravelled knitting at their feet, a jumper sleeve poking from a bag, the child clutching rather than resting, and the mother was jealous. Then she saw the merest suggestion of tears at the corner of the old dear's eyes. Oh, she must be tired, the inevitable price of rendering Sylvie so quiet. But for all the reassurance of the scene, despite the comforting smell of powder, oranges, cocoa and the bright light, the mother could still feel something pulsing in her veins. She threw a couple of pound coins on the sink, made effusive thanks and removed her child with speed. Sylvie was sullen, almost catatonic, her little feet making leaden sounds on the lino of the kitchen floor and the passage outside.

Only when she was inside her own door, did the mother recall that the trolley against which she had collided on her way in had not been any sort of obstruction on the way out. It had been a bit like a pram. The memory flitted through her mind in a brief and inconsequential passage.

'Come in, Margaret, why don't you? Every other bugger does. All your friends.'

There was his whisky on the table, dusty from passage in the trolley, now out of sight in the yard behind. Logo's skin was as ashen as the dust on his shoes. He had taken off his jacket, revealing the drab, worn, black clothes he bought from second-hand shops, and Margaret had time to wonder how it was he always managed to keep up the appearance of being clean when his clothes were so ingrained with dirt.

'Listen, Logo, I'm sorry, I'm really sorry. Oh, she's a trial that child, she really is, but I thought she was tired out, and then I gave her something to eat, and then, I sat down, dropped off, I suppose, and she was gone. I was calling to her, thought she was upstairs in my place, and soon as I knew, she was upstairs in yours. Come on, you know you only have to push the door. So I'm sorry, but you shouldn't have done that. Wasn't her fault.'

He turned his big eyes on her.

'Done what?' he questioned. 'Done what, exactly? She done nothing. *You* did plenty.'

She sat heavily, exuding her clean dust, making a whoomphing sound, which was part chair, part a sigh of exhaustion. She settled herself into the chair and curled her fingers over the ends of the greasy, cloth-covered arms. She showed no signs of tension, but looked as an old woman might look after a doze, adjusting herself into the realms of dignity as if she hadn't been caught napping. Or been frightened.

'Oh don't be silly,' she said comfortably. 'All the poor thing did was wander out of my place when I dozed off and wander into yours, she can push the door as well as anyone. She turns on the lights, 'cos she's just about high enough, and has a look around. Then I came and found her, but by that time, you'd frightened her to death, you daft bastard. Why did you have to do it? Flapping your hands at her like that, was it a game?' She spoke as she always did, never raising her voice or changing tone. She could have calmed a herd of wild horses, and out of the corner of her eye she watched him relax and hand her a grubby glass, half-full of his precious nectar.

'I don't know,' she continued, in her grumbling, placating tone. 'All the years I've known you and I've never been upstairs in your house. Wouldn't want to either, looking at the rest of it. Never did have cause to go further than the kitchen. All the best parties are in kitchens. Where everything happens. Kitchens. About the only important room in a house. Yours could do with a bit of a clean.'

She stretched out her legs to prove her point. 'Ooh, this is nice,' she said, raising her glass to him with a well-rehearsed wink. 'Very nice.' She was choosing not to notice how dirty the glass really was, but whisky would save her from the germs, and she wasn't frightened of them anyway. You swallowed them as an infant and you were therefore preserved for six generations. Bleach and disinfectant featured in her own home, but she never really expected it to have the same dominion in another's.

If she was frightened, and she was, severely frightened, she did not show it. Margaret had kept from her husband the knowledge of his own terminal illness for two years; and she had always played games with children, so she knew how to pretend. She did not tell Logo that she had followed Sylvie into the house, not once but twice, had gone upstairs the first time and into all the rooms until she had found her hiding. Sitting in apparent ease now, it seemed better to say nothing; it was cold, so she drank. Two glasses a day, and she loved him as ever, but now, she was beginning to see what the neighbours meant. The child had been terrified: it wasn't fair to do that to a child; she felt ashamed of him.

Geoffrey Bailey found his room on the third floor. Inside his locker was his own bottle of Scotch, from which he poured a large measure into the tooth mug. Nothing else was his own, of course, it was provided by the Establishment, which left him the freedom of the guest to abuse it. He rubbed his thinning hair as he looked in the mirror. He could colour it purple in here and no one would notice. The smile faded: he had been surprisingly well fed for a canteen service, as he had been the night before. He might nip out to a pub with Ryan later to watch his black eye fade. The swelling seemed to diminish whenever he smiled, which was often.

It wasn't even late, half-nine of a Thursday evening, and he was pleasantly tired, stimulated by learning.

He could be going home on weekend leave tomorrow, he had that option. On balance, he thought he wouldn't.

It wasn't a Rest Home, but it was a rest. And it was Ryan's turn to buy a round.

CHAPTER FOUR

The panda car cruised down Legard Street rather faster than usual. It turned right at the end and began a dizzying circumlocution of the streets, left, left, right, right, a progress which seemed to owe nothing at all to the military precision of a prescribed route. It sped down Seven Sisters, looking neither left nor right, in search of the nearest exit which would take it round the back. There was no point pausing here in a car with a stripe down the side: observing the ladies of the night had to be covert or not at all. The punters might not notice a train bearing down on them, but the girls doubled up and disappeared into the black of the road itself, leaving male faces staring out of car windows on the third, desperate time round.

The policemen in the panda car looked straight ahead. It was an unacknowledged fact that neither was interested in finding anyone whose behaviour would necessitate arrest. Even after an hour and a half, they needed another five minutes with one another to formulate a conversation which was as necessary as it was difficult. Both of them hoped it would be brief. Past Seven Sisters, where the unsuitably shod women had run like athletes, sharp right, to the back of the still-lit stadium, all gone safely home, the car radio silent to their mutual amazement, the moment now riper for a talk, although neither could be described as a talker.

'Shit, I don't believe it, nothing's happening, nothing at all. Football out, all gone, nothing. Is it always like this?'

'No.' Police Constable Michael was less reticent than most, which still made him, on matters emotional, very reticent indeed with his fellow man. 'It's usually different, but it's early yet. We don't break till twelve, pubs aren't shut yet, there's no telling.' Suddenly he pulled the car into the side of the road, wound down the window and fished in his pocket for a packet of fags. The car rocked as he explored.

'Whoops,' he muttered, checking the brake, still fishing as his huge body arched against the wheel, the better to dig into his back uniform pocket. 'In here somewhere, everything is, everything's always the wrong end of your bloody trousers.'

The youth beside him rocked with mirth and the ice of awkwardness melted into something like slush. The cigarettes, when finally produced, came in the form of a battered pack of ten, all squashed and so pathetic in appearance, it was difficult to fathom what they might achieve. Probationer Williams, a lad from Wales, did not really smoke at all, once a year, Mum, but this would be an exception. His mouth hurt still, especially when he laughed.

'Looks like my cock on a good day, this does,' said Michael, staring at his cigarette, bent in the middle, a poor, pathetic thing, held between his fingers by the filter, smoke drifting drearily from the other end. 'Needs rewiring. And what's the matter with you then?'

The youth to his left took a drag on his fag and trembled. He was a good-looking lad, Michael thought, but he'd be useless in the ring where you couldn't let nerves show, awful. Might be just as bad if they had to get out of this car and show muscle to a group of youths on the other side of the stadium, fresh out of the football match and the front door of the pub, all crazy shouting and wanting to slap.

'Look,' said the youth, breathing in the fag smoke which clearly made him as sick as an over-rich cigar. 'Look, about the other night . . .'

'What night?'

'The other night, you know, whenever it was. God, ages ago, at least a week. Well, I thought you were all right. You know.'

'Oh, that. Never mind about that. I wasn't going to tell, was I? Why should I?' Michael became almost belligerent, chewing on the cigarette rather than smoking it. 'Might have been different if you'd hit her, but you'd none of you done that, and no, I don't want the story.' Williams was puzzled. He'd expected Michael to want to know how it started, and there he was, only thinking about the girl. Michael threw the half-done cigarette out of his window. It hit frozen leaves and remained lit. He turned his head and watched in wonder. Fire and ice, ice and fire, neither capable of extinguishing the other. Informed by strangely exquisite and painful moments of the last few days, he noticed everything with peculiar anguish. Trees, leaves, rubbish, the detritus of life and nature had all assumed some poetic status, but he was still what he was before. A kindly and loyal man with a better brain and greater heart than most of his colleagues, but still a policeman, whose greatest loyalties were his fellows. Only now he had other loyalties too.

'Bit daft, wasn't it?' he said softly. 'You lot, fighting. You took quite a thumping. How did it start?'

'You can guess, can't you? That bloody girl. I heard, through the wall of my room. Brian screwing her, God he makes such a noise, like a pig. I'd heard her voice first, then the sounds of it, and well, I saw red, because she'd been doing the same with me the night before. And with the others, but I didn't know that then. Cow.'

'All using your rubbers, I hope?' said Michael paternalistically, wincing all the same despite the calmness of his voice and wishing he still had the cigarette for his fingers to fondle. It was quite true he had not needed to ask about the origins of the section house brawl to find out what had happened, but he had needed this verbal endorsement. Suddenly he relaxed.

'So, I gather you'll have taken her home once or twice?'

'Once or twice,' the other muttered.

'Right, you can show us where she lives then.'

'Pardon?'

'Where she lives. Which street, which number.'

'I can't,' said the youth, surprised. 'I can't because she never let you take her to the door, did she? She'd say, "Drop me off on the corner," and I was late and Oh . . . ! I see.'

The respect and the gratitude which had illuminated his face earlier, disappeared and he looked at his companion shrewdly, attempted a laugh which emerged as a yelp. 'Oh, I see. You're on to her now, are you. Picking up the pieces. God, you—'

'Bastard,' Michael finished for him helpfully, starting the engine. 'And yes, maybe I am, but not in the way you might think. There's a difference, see? I'm not screwing her. Now, show me the corner where you dropped her. So I know if it's the same place as mine.'

His mind changed smoothly with the gears. The man beside him sat silent and defeated, waiting for the radio to give them work and dispel the gloom of jealousy.

Rose sat in the window of the second-floor flat she occupied with two other girls. She had been waiting all evening to watch the car go by. Not any car, but this particular car, with the white paint and the crowded wall of bodies on the inside. *Watch the wall, my darling, while the gentlemen ride by.* She'd learned that poem in school, taught by some silly old fart who was trying to get across to them that all speech had its own rhythm, but no one she knew talked like that. She was idle in her badly lit bedroom, watching her face in the mirror, over which there was the only light she was willing to use. Even a presence behind half-closed curtains was not something she wished to advertise. The street outside was peculiarly silent: the cold had driven all revellers and would-be visitors indoors. From the window opposite came the eerie neon light of a television.

Rose moved across the room whenever she heard the sound of an engine, then she moved back to her mirror, where she watched her own face, without vanity, and let her thoughts meander. At times, she made play with shadows, using her fingers, creating on the opposite wall through the unattractive spotlight, the shape of a rabbit waving huge ears with an obscenely large tail, the edges furred, the thing making gestures all by itself. It was almost compulsive, this nervous habit she had, creating, when the light was right, these not unfriendly little images. But all of a sudden she was irritated by the twitching of the clownish shadows, frightened by the life they assumed for her own distraction. Slowly she uncurled her hand and used it, coupled with the other in a voluntary handcuff, to wave itself goodbye on the opposite wall. Her spread fingers now resembled the wing of a huge bird flying away across the sun: she made the wings move until the thing, half sinister and half exotic, blocked the light completely and made her afraid.

Then she heard the sound of another engine, familiar without being tantalizing. The shadow play had calmed her: she moved to the window without haste, knelt and put her chin on the window-sill with the thin curtain behind her head. She was rewarded by the sight of a panda car, not speeding but cruising, a face on the passenger side looking out and looking up at the windows like some mother looking for a lost child in a department store. Dimly she recognized the face, withdrew her chin until her nose was level with the window, and giggled a little. Then she raised her whole head and turned it obliquely as the car stopped two doors down, the opposite door opened and he got out. She stole one lingering glance at his size, standing in the street with his breath on the air like mist, looking back towards his car door before looking up to her. She watched, with palpable pleasure, the straightening of his clean, pressed uniform, and then she was gone, scrambling across the floor with the curtains concealing her, towards the light-switch.

There was silence for a minute, then the doorbell sounded into the vacuum of the empty first floor, without response from the second. The two girls with whom Rose shared the upper storey were out: otherwise, they would have asked anyone in, especially uniformed men. Rose waited until the buzzer echoed away, then heard the sound of footsteps crunching on frost, a large body colliding with the dustbin and the general shuffle which heralded departure.

Back at the window with the light out now, she saw him adjust his jacket again before he climbed into the driver's seat. She tried to make herself laugh. Bet you always do that, you silly big twit, she said to make her lips move, but when the car edged away, she could only feel the pain of grief, so sharp she was tempted to bust the window with her fist and yell, Here I am! But the impulse passed without the grief passing too. She had come home from the office in a taxi and made up her face in case he found her: weeping would disturb her looks, so instead she turned on the light, and, crouching in the corner, began the shadow play again.

'Does he love me?' she asked the rabbit. 'Could he ever possibly love me? Can it happen so quick, just like that? Oh, please . . .'

Her bedroom was festooned with soft toys; they sat in vigilant rows along the wall-side of her single bed, allowing little space for herself. She had a frilled pillow case, frilled bedspread and a clutter of other possessions. The whole effect was somewhere between a boudoir and a toy shop.

There was a crash from downstairs, a clattering of steps and voices which led to their cramped quarters. Cheryl had the largest room since she had found the place first and, with great self-importance, furnished a deposit through the bank where she worked. The others had smaller rooms, all off a tiny lobby which led to a smaller kitchen. They had chosen to relinquish communal living space and not double up on bedrooms for reasons which were obvious but understated. In case they got lucky, as Cheryl put it; with a man, she meant, but in fact the other two had never got lucky on the premises or anywhere else yet: they were hard working young, full of ambitions and romantic dreams, and not inclined to promiscuity. As flat-mates, they had embraced one another through mutual need and the columns of the *Evening Standard*, but this was not the same as friendship although it passed for that between Mary and Cheryl. They went out together in the general direction of pubs and discos and presented a politely united front against Rose, because Rose was odd, secretive, not quite like themselves, and although she cleaned up the mess they made in the kitchen without complaint, the habit was not exactly endearing. There was nothing as keen as dislike. The regime worked, after its fashion, better than most.

Rose heard them lumber into the kitchen, then one to the bathroom on the landing, where they always locked the door quite unnecessarily since none would have invaded the naked privacy of the others, unless desperate. In which case, Cheryl kicked the door, Mary knocked and whined, and Rose simply waited. She liked this aspect of their forced intimacy least of all, and kept her cosmetics, her washbag and her towel along with her life in her own room, but now she remembered she had not quite honoured that self-imposed rule this evening in their absence, and she groaned. She should have done that test in the morning, like it said on the packet. The groan and the realization coincided with a kick on her door. Cheryl, friendly, concerned and voraciously curious.

'We're phoning out for a pizza. Do you want some? And what's this doing here by the lav, then?' She was holding aloft the self-testing pregnancy kit, clearly labelled on the cardboard frame which enclosed a small tube.

'You got something to tell us?'

Rose shrugged. It was too late now.

'I dunno. There's three versions. One says I am, another says I'm not and the third says it isn't sure to make you buy another test. This one isn't sure, but I think I am anyway. Yeah, I'd love some pizza. Tuna.'

They sat in the kitchen which could scarcely hold the three of them and a telephone at a small table. Mary phoned for pizza, looking at Rose out of the corner of her eye with the same expression as Cheryl. The discovery of the pregnancy kit precluded any talk about work or the weather; they were looking at her as if examining a strange animal in the zoo, with a mixture of reverence, curiosity and only slight distaste. As near-miss virgins, they'd sort of assumed she was too, and they wanted to know what actually happened to get you otherwise, blow by blow, thrust by thrust, what it felt like. They wanted to ask all that before the pizza arrived and made everything all right again, but Mary and Cheryl were beginning to understand it was not quite possible. Cheryl, more street-wise, opted for making light of it. She hauled a can of beer from the fridge and offered it round. Rose shook her head.

'Trouble is with sex,' said Cheryl, mournfully, 'nobody will ever actually tell you. What to do.' They both looked at Rose, half challenging, half beseeching. She grinned.

'You just don't do what I did,' she answered, making it sound rueful, as if the act in question was entirely isolated. All right, so she would tell them, make them laugh by lying all the way, anything to harness enough tolerance to help her deal with the molten anxiety which seemed to have taken the place of her blood. Anything to postpone the evil hour of wondering what to do.

'Are you in love, then?' said Mary, with her staggering naïvety.

Rose sniggered uneasily. Going downstairs for the pizza, she wiped her eyes and her nose on her sweater sleeve and hoped they would think she was only laughing herself to death.

'Don't tell me you're in love, then.'

The younger constable was recovered enough in the canteen after midnight to inject into his own voice an element of jeering. He winced as the scalding tea hit the tender spot inside his mouth and he thought briefly of an impending visit to the dentist. PC Michael was making notes with assiduous attention to detail on the subject of the juvenile they had just arrested at the back of an off-licence, more hopeful than wicked, he thought, a very quiet night.

'With her. That Rose, I mean,' the young one persisted, gratified to see beginnings of a dull red blush colouring the skin of Michael's placid forehead as the other bent back to his writing. The same blush might have been present, but unnoticed, in the car. It gave Williams the upper hand.

'Oh, I shouldn't think so,' Michael said. 'I don't know about love, do I? But after you lot were kicked into touch last week, I thought about how nobody was looking out for what happened to her, she was just chucked out. So I kept an eye open ar.d then I saw her, a bit later, running down a road she was, I mean really running as if she was in dead trouble. She saw the car and she hid, in a garden. So I fished her out, and took her to where I showed you I dropped her, got her number at work. I was just sorry for her that's all. She might be a scrubber, but she's only a scrap.'

The young one sniggered again and straightened his face. The tea was more comfortable and the cold outside was uninviting. He wanted to prolong the story and his own advantage. Michael's qualities often had the effect of making other men feel mean.

'Sorry enough to see her every night last week?' Jeering again.

'Yes.'

'I reckon that's love then. You must be mad. You've broken all the records.'

It was here somewhere, among all the other records of her life and that was why it was so hard to find. By foraging among old chocolate boxes kept in the big dresser in her living room, Mrs Mellors gave herself ample opportunity for distraction, since each box out of the five was like Aladdin's cave. There were her wedding photos, dashing wartime economy, a borrowed hat she recalled as if it were yesterday and a corsage the size of a bush. Penny-pinching then, pound-pinching now, nothing altering. No photographs of children followed: they wouldn't have bought a camera for years after and there was little enough to record. Mr Mellors being Mr Mellors, herself working in a school as a dinner-lady, moving into this house and him getting another job with the council, a foreman dustbin man in the days when a foreman was something powerful, and yes, yes she had been proud of him, but not of the constant struggle against dirt and smell and men who cared about neither, and about him sometimes reproving her for her inability to have babies though he tried every night, and about her never knowing until much later, when they were past it, that the failure was not hers but his, and never saying anything.

All that took more than an hour, the second box, almost as long, the third, longer.

In here were letters, not just invitation cards, birthday cards, Christmas cards, old keys (she could never throw away a key, you never knew with keys), photos, bills, pieces of ribbon, brooches from Woolworth's, pieces of lace, hatpins (ouch, her finger caught a point, but the wound was bloodless, memoryless), ornate buttons waiting for a rainy day, but only letters. There were postcards, from the children she had looked after, and a bound volume, of messages, cards, childish and adult scrawls from the Logos. Because life had begun afresh with the Logos next door, a whole new, fifteen-year chapter which covered the last years of Mrs Mellors' working life, the illness of her spouse, his death and the decline of the family next door into this one weird little eccentric. The Logos had marked the most productive era of all, when, in her fifties, she had felt, at last, as if she had acquired some family who would honour her, and did, oh they did. Logo the road sweeper (Mr Mellors had got him that job when the office cleaning failed), then his wife, then the child, all babes, all incompetent, waiting for a granny like her. But you never quite knew your neighbour, even when you thought you did, even when it sat in your kitchen eating your grub and weeping its heart out over some tale you knew even then was half truth and it wasn't your business to question. There are no truer contacts than blood, thought Mrs Mellors, putting on the kettle to unseal the envelope which years had resealed. Blood's thicker than water, thicker than glue, but between husband and wife, what is there? Some sort of flour-paste only made permanent by kids. So, among all the postcards, there it was, amongst all those childish letters from that little girl whom she and she alone had taught to write and read like a true grand-mother because no one else was going to do it, there was the final missive from next door's wife, that hapless, silly woman with the sweet smile who could not cook or clean and had let her daughter become Margaret's own. Mrs Logo wrote a lot of notes, always asking for favours; wrote this one as if it was not a sin to break a person's heart.

Dear Mags,
I'm ever so sorry, but I'm going now. I know I said to you things weren't right, but I didn't know how wrong.

The writing was bad, even though Margaret had read this script a thousand times, in scrappier missives which asked, Will you do this? Will you do that? Always in a feather-brained rush.

I'm leaving him, I've got to, I can't say why.

Why not? Margaret had howled at the time and was still howling now.

I'm taking Enid with me, we're going to my cousin in Scotland where I can get a job and everything.

A job? Feather-brain could no more earn a living for herself and a dependent daughter than fly over the moon.

I'll write when we get where we're going. Please don't tell Logo when he gets back, he'll go mad. Or should I say madder. And don't ask and don't interfere, I do know what I'm doing, honest. Will write, promise, so will Eenie.

Margaret had abided by her instructions not to interfere and not to speak, as discussed with her invalid husband, both sticking to the habits of a lifetime, he the one-time soldier, herself the soldier's missus, non-complainers both. She obeyed and watched as shortly after the delivery of the note, she saw Mrs Logo exit the house carrying a fibre suitcase and pulling the door closed behind her. There had been something jaunty in the carriage of the little woman on her escape, so that Mrs Mellors had assumed not ill-treatment, but the existence of another man, and she had never doubted that assumption. The daughter was behind her, carrying a school-bag, and it was only she, whom they called Eenie, who looked back, waved to nothing but waved in a sad desperation and hesitation which had made Margaret want to run after her and shout from where she stood. The fibre suitcase carried by the mother was old; it expanded on one side but failed to expand on the other: the weight of it was less cumbersome than the bulk. And so they had gone, the two of them.

More weeping in the kitchen, and the yelling of, Why, why, why? from Logo over weeks, while Margaret had listened, not said much while she kept looking at her own stairs and wondering if this were the night her husband might die. After some days, Logo reported his wife and child missing. The police came and searched their house; enquiries were instituted, but she never wrote, that silly bitch of a wife, and Margaret never said how she had seen them going down the back alley in the middle of the afternoon with the fibre suitcase which did not expand properly, because it was so etched in her memory she could not have given it words, and because she had been trusted and that meant she was bound by a promise.

'Why?' she muttered to herself. 'Why? How could they just go?'

You never know your neighbour. So her man had died, she had lost her substitute child and grandchild, and Logo had gone about howling, searching the hills and dales of North London, convinced he would find, if not the wife, the darling daughter. Poor, poor soul, with the police picking on him ever since. Her heart had gone out to him, she respected his privacy, believed and pitied him, never intruded, same as always. If it hadn't been for Sylvie, she might never have gone upstairs in his house, not unless he had fallen ill and he never did that.

But this evening, following Blondie, tut-tutting and still playing games up Logo's stairs, feeling cross with the naughty child, she had stopped in her tracks on the top landing. Facing her from the corner of his bedroom, spartan, bare of the superfluous, not a frill or a flounce like the rest of this house, was that fibre suitcase. As it had been, still crooked. The suitcase of a wife who had left with it and who, according to him and everyone else, had never come back.

Margaret separated Mrs Logo's letter from the rest and put it in the drawer where she kept knives.

Helen West was rummaging in the kitchen. From time to time she eyed the telephone, not quite wishing it to ring, but somehow resenting its silence. She had willed the fridge to yield exciting secrets but after her own time-honoured fashion there was nothing inside but a jar of pickle, one of dead mayonnaise, butter, rock solid, a lettuce which was brown to the point of liquefaction and six suspect eggs. I have no rules, she said to herself, no rules at all. I feed like a soldier on the retreat in some frozen waste and I have grown as thin. I like being a renegade: I forage in shops rather than buy. Is this the life for me? It took ten days without Geoffrey (two phone calls, one too many), for all the old regimes to be re-established. Through the very thin veneer of her domestication, acquired only through contact with men, the way they were supposed to acquire similar habits from women, she was emerging as an alley cat.

Though truth to tell, the scrappy eating and total lack of cooking which had featured in the last ten days, during which time she had passed the supermarket with two fingers raised and no potatoes to rub her shins as they strained at polythene bags, owed only as much to retrograde eating behaviour as it did to a strange feeling of nausea. The eggs eaten late were committed to the sewerage system so quickly it was as if they only lived in her digestion on borrowed time. They were unable to pay rent, these eggs, like most other foods except crisps, sharp, artificial, savoury tastes, or items of sickening sweetness. And she was thinner, definitely thinner: the waistband of her skirt that morning had hung loose: halfway through a court case, she had risen to shout some reply and found the skirt had swivelled round, back to front, crumpled and out of shape. That small incident vexed her.

She stood in her kitchen, admired for its warmth and flair like all her other rooms, the product of a hundred junk shops encouraged into interesting life and a little out of control. 'I love this old dresser,' Geoffrey had said. 'I love your old, cracked, unhealthy enamel sink, your mugs from the wedding of Charles and Di, and I love the ancient carving knives which came from car-boot sales, but, my dear, they do not cut.'

She was hungry and sick, sick and hungry. Three, four drinks with Dinsdale and the mastication of nibbles with all the nutriment of air, and she ran for the bathroom with its old and beautiful tiles, pictures on the walls even in there, only to be sick. What is this? she thought, raising from the basin to the mirror a face which was horribly pale. What the hell is this?

Helen West, arrogantly accustomed to health, an avoider of doctors when possible, rummaged in the cupboard beneath the mirror for something to settle this intestinal riot. Bisodol, Rennies, Nurofen, aspirin, every hangover cure under her sun. A pregnancy kit about a thousand years old which her hand nudged and knocked to one side in search of something efficacious enough to allow eating without retribution later, but the fingers stopped of their own accord and dragged out the unopened box as she squatted back on her haunches, rocking with the shock of her own conclusions. When was the last time she'd had the curse? And when last had she and Bailey celebrated the one thing they always seemed to get a hundred per cent right? His house, her house, something usually missing. You weren't fertility plus at thirty-five, but age was irrelevant to an egg.

Helen got her coat and made for the street. Dammit: she craved the produce of the Chinese takeaway; she would have it in any event, and she could not stay here with her own thoughts.

Outside, the night was peculiarly still and stiff with an icy cold which formed her breath into puffs of vapour, so cold, she immediately wanted to turn back inside, but driven by her own hunger, she did not. The frost which had formed in the darkness of dawn and melted in the afternoon, now drew exquisite patterns on car windscreens like some exotic artist. From the great distance of a mile or more, she heard in the stillness the great roar of an enormous crowd. There was no sound the same: the sound of the mountain moving to Jehovah. Helen stopped, chilled to the marrow by that distant roar of the jungle lion waiting to get out. Then the cars started again: the lights of the main road hit her eyes. The sickness had passed.

Oh Lord, do not let me be afraid of the dark.

CHAPTER FIVE

R edwood was often asked to give lectures – to new recruits, to
clubs, to Justices of the Peace. They were good for his profile,
so he did them when he could not farm them out.

'The mandate of the Crown Prosecution Service,' he was fond
of beginning in a good, loud voice, 'is to prosecute without fear
or favour, according to the evidence, those who break the criminal
law. Evidence is supplied to us by the police. It is we who decide
what to do with it.'

He made the process sound civilized and eminently streamlined.
What he did not say was that his own office was drowning in paper.
They were more vulnerable to paper than they were to heart attacks.
The paper would kill them first.

'Our office is computerized, of course,' he would say, remembering not to cringe. So it was, in a manner of speaking. The computer
received information and dictated the next move for every case:
they all had pathetic faith in it without any understanding, but
it did not obviate the necessity for portable paper to go to and
from courtrooms and barristers' chambers, fraying in a dozen sets
of hands, often without a duplicate, until finally it was filed in the
vast areas of the basement where Redwood never trod.

'Because of the confidential, incriminating nature of the material
we keep, we do, of course, take great care with security . . .'

Even he had to wince at that. By security, Redwood meant the high railings with their lethal spikes, the assiduous security men they had by day and the lazy character they had between seven in the evening and the same hour next morning, and also at the weekends. He came from an agency, it was cheaper. Redwood hated the building so much, he couldn't imagine anyone wanting to get in. Only a fearless child could climb the railings. It didn't occur to him there was any need for better security.

'Rose, any chance I can have tomorrow's paperwork by one o'clock? Like I asked earlier? Only I'd rather not come back this afternoon.'

Rose raised a harassed face from the files she was marshalling into piles, in date order, each like a rocky monument on the floor round her desk.

'I dunno. Doubt it,' she said rudely. Helen felt her temper rise. The link between her worries and her sense of humour was proving tenuous, the thread of it not only thin but frayed. She made a last effort.

'Please can you find me tomorrow's files? Surely it isn't too much to ask?'

Rose was embracing a bundle of six to her bosom, and she dropped them abruptly, turning as she did so. She was shaking with tension, but it looked like a gesture of petty defiance.

'Rose,' said Helen with warning in her voice, 'I really do have to go at one, and I might not be able to get back. Can you sort tomorrow's stuff for me now? Please?'

Rose turned to face her, livid with anger. The spikes of her hair, subdued of late, seemed to rise round her head like the defensive spine of a hedgehog.

'And supposing other people have to leave early too? Supposing there's no one else to do their fucking work and the computer's screwed and silly cows like you are asking for the moon? You can fuck off. Your bloody files are in here somewhere. Either find them your bloody self or come back later.' She kicked one of the heaps with a booted foot and the files lurched sideways, but Rose had not finished. There was an impulse to malice she could not resist.

'And while I'm at it, don't you come this holier-than-thou bit with me ever again. You and Mr Cotton, both with an afternoon off each? Good, isn't it? What's it to be then, your place or his?'

Helen wanted to slap her: Rose was waiting to be slapped, but something in the insinuation raised an inhibiting twinge of guilt. The files toppled in slow motion as Rose strode from the room. The other clerks watched from their tables and desks in a deathly silence. Helen breathed in and out slowly. She stared at the window where she had seen Rose's reflection two weeks before and saw only her own, paler and older face. With the others as an audience, she knelt on the floor and began to go through the papers, looking for those which bore her name, seething but still using her eyes. For the moment she hated Rose to the same degree the girl seemed to despise her in return. Perhaps that was why none of the clerks helped her, but let her grub around on the floor, humiliated. If they'd offered, she would have refused.

Redwood came into the room, as uncertainly as he always did for fear the clerks might bite him or reveal his failure to remember most of their names.

'Who was shouting in here? I won't have it . . . Oh! Helen, what are you doing?' She looked up from the floor with a fiendish grin.

'Looking for a contact lens, sir.' Sir was inconsistent in his observations, but there were some details he never forgot.

'I didn't think you wore lenses.'

'I do now. Was there anything in particular you wanted?'

'That shouting . . .'

'It was me.' He beckoned her out of the room with evident disgust, poised for a reprimand. From beyond the door, Helen heard the buzz of voices no longer suppressed, cutting through her back like an icy wind.

In the lavatory, Rose Darvey sat and gulped. Trained as she was in several aspects of self-control, she had long since mastered the technique of crying while remaining silent. You held your nose, so that the effort of breathing through the mouth somehow suspended the rising of the noisier sobs. Putting her hands over her ears also encouraged the silence which had always seemed so imperative when she cried. She sat with the door locked, trying one method after the next, while large tears ran down her face and made a mess of the make-up so carefully applied in the spotlight over her bedroom mirror. She couldn't make shadows in here: it required a light without a shade. She had bitten her fingernails down to sore stumps, another reason for habitually playing with her hands.

Granny had placed some bitter solution over them once to make her stop: it had worked temporarily. Granny, Granny, help me now, please help me now, where are you? The vision of Granny somehow increased the size of the hairball in her chest: the effort to make no sound felt like a thistle lodged in her throat. Granny, she thought. Got to try and see Granny. Granny could help. See Granny and do something about this bloody baby, before I go mad. Can't tell Michael, just can't. He'll never love me.

'Rose?' A timid voice. 'Rose? You all right Rose?' A plaintive whine from one of the others sent to enquire. Rose was her colleagues' heroine; she made them laugh, she knew more than any of them and was afraid of no one. 'Rose, come out of there, will you? Only we're worried about you. Come out, please.'

The plea in the voice made her freeze for a moment. Come on out, darling, and no harm will ever befall you again. Rose dropped her handbag on the floor, rummaged inside for her make-up bag, the old protector. She made a loud noise with the toilet roll, tearing it, blowing her nose with unnecessary violence, scrubbing at the ruin of the mascara. The same voice again, though not so wheedling, assumed less reminiscent proportions. It might be all right if she just carried on without too many cracks in her armour.

'Rose, are you all right? Talk to me, what's the matter?'

How she despised the tragedies of the ladies' lavatory; why did she come here when she could have hidden in the nice, warm womb of the basement? She gave an exaggerated sigh.

'Of course I'm bloody all right. Just get me a vet. I need putting down.'

The voice beyond the door giggled in relief. Same old Rose, their leader. And which one of you, Rose thought, as she ran her fingers through her hair to encourage the spikes she had been subduing because Michael did not care for them much although he never said so, which one of you is fiddling the computer then and stealing the files? Which one?

Margaret Mellors sat in the doctor's waiting-room at twelve-thirty, wondering who would go in next. She knew her own turn in this never-ending queue had been delayed for an emergency: she had been asked if she minded, which was an unusual courtesy, and out of habit, she had said, 'Of course I don't,' but she did. She had lost her faith in medical expertise when Jack had been dying, but she had never ceased to regard doctors as God. Even if they did not know what made a sick man sick, they surely had the last word over many things, police, fire engines and madness. They told you what to do and they gave orders to multitudes, and that was why she was here. Margaret never thought of her own long-delayed treatment, six weeks' wait for every appointment, the wilful continuation of her own disability while she waited one year, two years for a new hip; she still saw a doctor and smiled as if he or she could alter the world, and she still gave up her place in the queue, composing in her mind a series of apologies for being there at all.

'I'm sorry to bother you, but . . .'

'Yes, that's what I'm paid for. How can I help?' A strained smile from a young woman who had listened to her fill of winter casualties. Carmen something, her name was. Margaret preferred doctors to be middle-aged men, they were better fitted for their deity, but why oh why did she never ask, and why did she feel so wretchedly tongue-tied? As if her pension was charity and this white-coated waif a grand inquisitor.

'Well, I wondered . . .'

'Let's have a look.' She had a look, tutted, wrote on a pad.

'It's been a long time, hasn't it? You'd better go back and see the consultant . . .'

'Actually,' said Margaret, gathering courage in the panic-stricken knowledge that she would be out of the door in thirty seconds if she didn't, 'I can live with the stick. It was something else.' The doctor smiled encouragingly, sat back, unoffended by this oblique approach.

'It's my neighbour.' Having got this far, Margaret could only continue to blurt it out. 'I'm worried about him. He hears voices. He sings a lot and he told me yesterday his favourite place was the graveyard. He's mad you know, well, he's always been a bit mad, but now he's madder. He frightens the children.' The patient smile of the doctor was fading and Margaret's message was fading too: she could not bring herself to say Logo was dangerous, correction, might be dangerous.

'How does he frighten the children?' The doctor's voice was sharper.

'I don't know. He chases them I think, he's always looking for his daughter . . . They keep taking him to court, but nobody ever asks me.'

'Well, the police know all about it, then. Does he have a job?'

Margaret nodded. The white coat relaxed visibly. 'They must know about it too, I suppose. Have you spoken to the police?'

Margaret leapt, as if the doctor had spoken an obscenity. 'Oh, I couldn't do that. I wondered . . . I wondered if you could send someone round to him.'

'Well, Mrs . . .' she looked hurriedly at the notes, 'Mellors . . . I just don't think I can do that. He wouldn't come in and see me, would he? No? I didn't think so. Are you sure he's registered with this practice? Well, you try and persuade him to come in, will you? Only it has to be voluntary, or not at all. Look, I'll put you in touch with Social Services, see if they have any ideas.'

No, they did not, and yes, he was getting madder. Banging about in his own home these last three nights, weeping and wailing in his kitchen. For the first time, Margaret had hopes that he would get arrested again, and attract some attention. She met patience without comprehension whenever she complained, but then she was not quite telling the truth, and when invited to exaggerate the eccentricities she described, she could only minimize them. One thing she understood clearly was that there was no provision for those in the limbo land he occupied of the half mad, half dreadfully sane, and there she was, a second–class citizen, an elderly woman, part disabled but smelling sweet. They looked at her as if madness was contagious; until she began to think it was.

She did not, could not, tell anyone about the suitcase.

Margaret Mellors trudged the dim route home on a grey afternoon, promising herself she would light a fire. Down the alleyway, the last light already fading, she wondered how anyone could endure the cold without a fire. The landlord had blocked up her own years ago: with Logo's help, she had unblocked it and the thought of that and all the firewood he brought her, made her feel guilty. When she opened the door, there was a letter on the mat. First-class post, such extravagance. The writing had a vague familiarity. She turned the envelope over in her hand, postponing the excitement until her hands began to tremble and she put it to one side while she lit the fire. When the kindling wood began to crackle, she tore open the letter and read the single sheet within, flushed with pleasure and the light of the flames. 'Oh my dear,' she kept murmuring to herself, 'oh my darling dear.' Four years without even a note, and her darling writing now, oh, my dear. She found it difficult to let go of the letter: it simply could not be consigned to the hidden boxes of other letters, it had to remain visible as a constant reminder of its tidings. With great reluctance, Margaret finally placed the letter along with the other in the drawer where she kept her kitchen knives.

That way she could look at it again and again.

At six o'clock on Friday morning, someone rang and rapped on the grim doors of the old hospital. The bell sounded in the night watchman's room where he locked himself in with his TV and the phone every evening and all day Saturday and Sunday, neglecting to patrol since he found the confusion of stairs, corridors and ludicrously insecure exits peculiarly eerie: there were rumours of a ghost. Nothing here but paper anyway. Nor did he obey the stricture to note in a book the names of members of staff who sought entry outside office hours. Sometimes they came late at night, especially the fraud teams on the first floor, forewarning him by telephone so he knew to be by the door as they sped in and out with armfuls of forgotten files required for the next day, but it was rare for anyone to arrive so early in the morning.

The person on the other side of the door, stamping feet in the cold, smiled, waved an office pass and disappeared upstairs with all the swift ease of total familiarity. The watchman shrugged and fell back to dreaming of breakfast.

Three floors up, a feminine, well-manicured hand turned on the computer. There was no code for entry into its realms of information introduced by the surge of power. The hand tapped out in quick succession the serial number of a file already retrieved. The fingers shifted the burden of paper, deleted the last line from the screen which described a date of trial and the necessity to warn witnesses, and added instead, 'No Further Action: Withdraw summons . . . Defendant now deceased.' For the next file, the hands simply deleted the whole text. For the next, the finger paused and the hands massaged one another, still cold. A fastidious piece of destruction. Redwood was right: software made life easier. Then with equally neat footsteps, the person concerned went down the innumerable stairs to the basement to take an alternative exit, shoved up a sash-window down there, next to the boiler room, humming. There was less chance of being remembered if one did not pass the doorman twice.

★

Helen West, trying to think of other things than the constant queasiness, dredged her memory for nicer times. Thinking of cases at 3 a.m. was reminiscent of counting sheep and often worked, but at the moment it hardly sufficed to blot out the other thoughts which had surfaced from nowhere with alarming speed. Such as where, among the clutter of her colourful possessions, she would house a baby, let alone a child? These reflections, passing through with dramatic speed, induced sensations of panic which nothing could cure, so she rose, showered and encased her hot body in cool clothes. Normality, the continuance of life as it was before, danced before her eyes like a tantalizing vision.

Helen caught sight of her face in the newsagent's window as she waited for a bus, and that was normal, with the eyes and nose still in the same place. But she found herself standing back from the crowd, avoiding contact as if there really was something, for once, worth preserving from crush or contagion. She did not like herself much. Then she thought of Bailey as a father.

Squashing into the seat next to her was a young woman, pale and enormous, balancing her workday bag on the rock of her pregnant abdomen against which her coat strained. Helen made more room and stared ahead. Like a person counting sheep.

The graveyard was never closed. There was no need, despite the disturbing tendency in recent years to steal the stone angels. The late-Victorian church stood like a monument to disbelief, the small congregation rattling inside, but the graveyard took the corpses of faithful and faithless alike into soft earth which turned easily on the spade in summer. In the absence of a creed, internment in consecrated ground often appealed more than the queue at the distant crematorium. Logo could see benefits in both and did not much mind. He could clear the leaves as easily anywhere, but he found the graveyard rewarding and he liked the fact he knew so many of the recent names. There were dead flowers, souvenirs of the children from the junior school beyond the gates: and among the earliest, forgotten tombs, were Coca-Cola cans and empty cider bottles. He liked that. It added a little something to the place and confirmed his own usefulness.

Fifty-five years old, still young in comparison to these dead with their lead-etched names on stone. Logo felt healthy. He had loved this site as long as he had known it. By eleven that morning, there was a misty sun, glowing rather than shining behind the blanket of grey sky, giving a diffuse light which created no shadows but warmed the ground. Logo always marvelled at the gravediggers, stopped to watch them now. They dug in sequence along preordained lines with little space allowed in between each grave. Raw January, post Christmas, was the busiest time of year and their method was always the same. No measurements, rulers or spirit-levels, they dug out their troughs with automatic precision and no more modern conveniences than huge, sharp shovels, but they grumbled about the frost. The earth here had been turned, freed of rubble and thus softened, but the task was still hard.

The regular shovellers were unused to an audience: people tended to stay away, but there was the occasional macabre eccentric, Logo the least favourite. His interest bordered on the unhealthy, his jokes were vile and his habit of beginning the funeral service even while they dug was unnerving.

'Asses to ashes, dust to dust. If the Lord won't save you the devil must,' he quipped, squatting on his haunches beside them.

'Oh shut it, will you, Logo,' said the younger man.

'All right,' said Logo. 'I'll sing if you insist.' His voice passed over their heads, defeating the sound of distant traffic.

'Spare oh God, thy suppliant groaning!
Through the sinful woman shriven,
Through the dying thief forgiven,
Thou to me a hope has given . . .'

The older man turned round, raised a hand. Logo stopped his singing.

'If you don't shut it, Logo, I shan't be able to give you a cigarette.' He was more diplomatic than his companion.

'Who's dead this time?' Logo asked cheerfully, accepting the bribe.

'I don't know. Why should I?' said the gravedigger. 'I just get the message, dig one. A new one, I mean. Which means, don't dig up an old one to put someone in on top. Might be anyone. But I tell you, there're bound to be two or three more in the next fortnight.'

They never seemed to know for whom they dug, or care for whom the bell had tolled. They were as immutable as the graveyard itself where the gravestones were practically identical from one decade to the next, no innovations, no plastic, only stones the same shape as always with the same words and sentiments. The richer or the guiltier of the mourners had marble, but it all went grey in time.

'Why do you say that?' Logo asked with his birdlike curiosity.

'Say what?' The gravedigger had forgotten his prognostications about local death. 'Oh, I just know. It's Christmas kills them. Their families, probably. Bugger off, will you!'

Logo obeyed, not in deference to commands, but because he so wished. His boots scuffed the edge of the soft earth the diggers had displaced and he left his footprints with satisfaction. Look where I've been, he told himself. Look where I've been.

He set off on the day's perambulations with his trolley, the cumbersome old brute, obscurely satisfied, pausing by another grave several rows back and saluting a headstone which commemorated the death of an Angela Jones four years ago. He had known Angela, nice woman from Legard Street, died of cancer you know, a shame, and her only ninety-four, the bane of her relatives who had moved to another city to get away. Logo chuckled, oh, he felt youthful today. From beyond the road at the left gate, he heard children going to school, the end of the Christmas holidays signalled by their shrieks and yells. Logo sat on the grave nearest the gate. He felt for the Bible in his pocket, but did not take it out, determined to stay still until they had all gone indoors. He quoted, out of context, the way he always did, those chunks of the Bible which stuck in his head without rhyme or reason. Logo took no lessons from the Bible, only told himself he did, but isolated verses were merged and burned into his mind.

' "I will send wild beasts among you," ' he droned quietly, ' "which will rob you of your children, and your highways shall be desolate. And the flesh of your daughters shall you eat. And the sound of a shaken leaf shall chase you, and you shall flee as fleeing from a sword, and you shall fall where none pursueth." '

As the sun rose further, an effortful sun only waiting to retire without grace by midday, and the clock in the magistrates' court showed ten-thirty, John Riley, Junior Crown Prosecutor and new to the game, rose to his feet, his small height almost obscured by the pile of paper in front of him. He had command of the daily list of the drunks and disorderlies, those soliciting on Seven Sisters, those burgling the night before, and all those remands postponed from previous dates for the preparation of papers and defences before a full hearing in either the magistrates' or the Crown Court. John waded through, bobbing up and down as the occasion demanded, gathering confidence as he went. The magistrate was fierce: speed by advocates was the only attribute rewarded by a grim nod and the sort of smile imposed on a corpse by a mortician. Finally, they had dispensed with all the two minute appearances. 'Drunk, Your Worship, shouting and screaming, fourth offence in six months.' 'Anything to say?' 'Nothing, your Honour.' 'Ten pounds or a day, take him down. Next? Get on with it, Mr Riley, get on with it.' The Clerk of the Court, second only to God, shuffled to signify a pause.

'Mr Balchin next,' she said sweetly. John felt for the next volume. Balchin, the name rang no bells even on the inner ear. His hands dug through the remaining four files, no Balchin. 'Where's Balchin?' yelled the magistrate to whom delay was a mortal sin. Balchin stood in the dock, a smart businessman in a shirt which gleamed through a sober suit below a face of fleshy success. 'Trial adjourned until today from December, plea not guilty to driving with excess alcohol?' said the clerk, questioningly. Balchin nodded, anxious, but presentable. All eyes fell on the prosecutor, waiting for him to begin as he rose to his feet with all the steadiness of the drunks earlier in the list.

'I don't seem to have any papers,' he said lamely. 'May I seek an adjournment? We don't have the witnesses—'

'I object to that,' said the defendant mildly.

'So do I,' said the magistrate. 'Mr Balchin's third appearance in this court and the Crown Prosecution Service still not ready? How often do you want him to come back, Mr Riley, hmmmm? Case dismissed. Next.'

John sat, flaming red, scrambling for the next file and the chance to redeem himself. It was twelve o'clock and the day was suddenly long. Mr Balchin, businessman, left the court house and raised his eyes to the sun in quiet thanksgiving. Then he walked round the corner to his parked BMW, patted the shining roof in reverence and climbed in, to return to his business which so depended on his ability to drive. God had been good today. It was worth the thirty pieces of silver which had changed hands.

CHAPTER SIX

'Pregnant and happy? Fine . . .'

The advertisement Helen and a million others saw daily on
the Underground, showed a late-teenage girl with a curtain
of perfect hair falling across a pensive face of model proportions.
Her elegant neck was dressed with a single line of pearls. A
well-manicured finger rested on her white teeth in a gesture of coy
indecision, as if trying to decide which chocolate to pick next, like a
princess merely troubled by too much choice and a heavy night
sleeping on a pea. 'Pregnant and happy?' said the advert. 'If not
. . .' Beneath this there was the telephone number and address of
a clinic. The urine sample burning a hole in Helen's handbag
had been decanted into a miniature whisky bottle for lack of any
other receptacle. She did not know which embarrassed her most.

Standing in line on the escalator first thing on a crowded
morning, she passed the serene face on the poster and felt a strong
desire to rip it, but she was born onwards and upwards to the air
of Oxford Circus. She did not trust the pharmacist's pregnancy kit
and did not like doctors. This was also the first time in her life she
could recall responding so directly to an advertisement and that
was irritating, too. Although the nausea had faded after thirty-six
hours, it had been replaced by a kind of grim elation.

The cold was muffled by the crowd who swayed away from

the fetid warmth of the Underground, filtering through cars and the buses which disgorged even more people into the shops. On a day like this, Helen hated to leave the claustrophobic but volcanic warmth of the Tube.

The women she noticed most were those with the smoothest faces, *en route* to the make-up counters to sell promises through the medium of their flawlessly counterfeit cheeks. Her own face was comparatively bleak, but she was jauntily dressed in a scarlet jacket, tight black trousers, red shoes and a scarf of vivid stripes. Helen West, supporting her own team.

The family non-planning clinic was above other premises in the wide backwaters where the huge department stores gave way to the environs of Harley Street, with its shops full of medical supplies, private dentists and wholesale pharmacists scattered among esoteric restaurants and the head offices of the rag trade. The plate-glass windows of one of these flanked the nondescript door at the side, which led in turn up four flights of ever narrowing stairs past small, locked offices on each floor. The air grew cooler, more rarefied and, as she turned the last bend, developed into an antiseptic smell of cleaning fluid rather than medicine. Worn carpet, an electric heater and mismatched chairs in the waiting-room said the rest. None of the other three women, perched on these uncomfortable chairs and staring at the surrounding walls, resembled the princess on the poster who had drawn them there. Least of all Rose Darvey, sitting apart, in a state of defiant misery, chewing her pigtail.

They were the last people each could have borne to see on the opposite side of the road, let alone a place like this. The hostile nature of their surprise was felt even by the other two girls who waited, booted, spurred and disguised for some verdict on their lives. Helen had the feeling she was old enough to be everyone's mother. Rose looked away in disgust while Helen presented her fee and the whisky bottle to a receptionist whose drabness belied a personality ecstatic with *bonhomie* and a whispering voice of solicitude. Rose spied the label on Helen's bottle; stress, worry, the million reflections which were steaming through her head at a hundred miles an hour, all emerged through her mouth in a great, barking laugh which turned abruptly into a cough, then a series of violent coughs which almost brought her to her feet in her effort to breathe, before she slumped back in the chair and slid further down on the polished seat, still gasping. Helen took the empty chair next to her. There was no need for explanations: all that was obvious.

'Sorry,' said Rose. She looked as if the giggles of tension would consume her. 'Something I ate. Swallowed the wrong way.'

'Swallowed? I bet you wish you had,' Helen murmured.

Rose's coughing resumed a new note of yelping. This time she put her hand over her mouth and leant forward as the coughs slowly came under control. Helen patted her back, with a balled fist to take out of this stray solicitude any hint of intimacy. She stopped as soon as Rose sat upright.

'Keep that up, will you, and you won't need anything else. You'll give birth on the floor. Twins,' said Helen helpfully. Suddenly the whole situation was ludicrously funny. It couldn't have been worse if she'd sat in line with the wife of a lover.

Rose was off again. 'What a game,' she gasped between breaths. 'What a game. A whisky bottle, I ask you. I bloody ask you. Miss bloody West.'

Helen's expression became severe. 'Well I didn't drink it, he did. Present from Malaga, that little bottle. What do you think I am? Cheap?'

They were suddenly doubled up in their scarves, snorting and laughing like schoolgirls in church.

'Ms Darvey!' The receptionist called Rose's name, suddenly officious.

'Christ,' muttered Rose. 'Oh God, this is it. What shall I do?' She looked desolate, childlike as she began to stand wrapping her coat around her, wanting to delay, drawing a deep and painful breath.

'Listen . . .' she said, and paused.

'Listen,' said Helen, 'when you've finished, will you wait for me? Please?' Rose nodded, her eyes turning towards the glazed-glass door of the other room, to the received wisdom, the result of the test, the possible kindness and advice. It looked, she said later, like the entrance to an old-fashioned lavatory. She went like a prisoner to the gallows, turned at the door, pulled a face and waved.

Helen wanted to weep, on both their accounts.

Sitting inside a small cubicle with a counsellor, listening to the murmur of other voices, Helen found the need to weep became an actuality positively encouraged by the woman who told her with a no-nonsense sweetness that she was not pregnant, not this time and what was her reaction to that? Time marched on, did it not, and if she had not wanted this crisis, had she considered more effective means of birth control? She found herself accused somehow, of a lack of self-respect, an indigence about her own life, a laxity of purpose, a constant ambivalence. Or so she took it to be, having levelled these same accusations at herself over the last two days with all the sure-firing action of a rifle. Mixed in with that was relief (life could now, after all, go on as before), and a grief of such proportion it made her speechless, nodding and smiling and saying, thank you, thank you, you've been very kind, but let me out to smash things and scream and speak to someone else. For the five terrible minutes of the interview and the passing over of leaflets and wishes of good luck, Helen forgot Rose Darvey, but that was only temporary, because what she most wanted was to think of someone else, anyone else.

Waiting in the foyer with ill-concealed impatience and a smile on her face which could have lit a coastline, Rose gripped Helen by the arm and propelled her to the door.

'Come on let's get out of this place. It smells.' Rose led a race downstairs, making in her progress the maximum noise, saying nothing until they reached the pavement, where she leapt across the threshold, flung her arms in the air and yelled, 'Yeah! Yeah, yeah, yeah!'

'Does that mean you are?' asked Helen, her own responses dulling her perception of this display. Rose stopped and laughed out loud.

'Pregnant? Course it doesn't. It means I got it wrong and I'm not, I'm not, I'm *not*! God, I feel better. Christ, you've no idea what it's been like, awful, thought I'd die . . . you've no idea . . .' Then she stopped, looked at Helen apologetically, still unable to suppress her own smile, and her expression of dawning comprehension. 'What am I talking about?' she said. 'Of course you know. I mean, you wouldn't be here if you didn't know. Sorry. Only I never imagined . . .'

'That someone my age had a sex life?' Helen suddenly found herself able to laugh. Rose's state of joyous liberation was infectious: there was something oddly comforting about her present embarrassment and an overpowering desire to talk.

'No, no, I didn't mean that, not really . . .'

'Yes you did. Are you going back to work, or are we both playing hookey?' Helen asked. 'Only I want a pint of coffee, and then I'll tell you the story of my life if you aren't careful. Come on.'

'I'll buy you a coffee,' said Rose magnanimously, hugging herself.

'Too right you will. You owe me an apology, but if we can find a bottle of wine, I'd rather have one of those.'

'I know where,' said Rose, tapping the side of her nose in mock wisdom. 'Follow Rose. God!' she shouted again. 'God, I feel great!'

They didn't drink. Despite her much-vaunted knowledge of West End drinking parlours, gleaned from young policemen (and Helen heard more of them anon), Rose's wisdom proved deficient on the availability of booze outside regular hours and there was no need for a drink while each felt strangely high. Helen made a phone call to the office, on behalf of them both, announcing their absence rather than deigning to explain it. Then they went shopping. The mood of confidential euphoria lasted for several hours and left in the wake of all its conversations the sweet scent of friendship and a large bill.

They looked like mother and daughter, small, neat and dark, chattering like sparrows.

'Have you got any kids, Geoff?'

For once, the diminution of Bailey's Christian name which had been standard procedure for the length of his long career, failed to irritate him. He sat not in the college bar, but in a pub not far from the precincts. To his left was Valerie, the detective from West End Central, on his right was a local woman who happened to be a friend of hers, and opposite them both was Ryan, grinning like a fox who had managed to marshal a flock of hens into a pen. It was early Friday afternoon and lectures had finished for the day. 'Playtime,' said Ryan, ushering sir towards his car. At first Bailey had assumed he was being offered a lift back to London, but the detour was scheduled and he found he did not mind in the least. It was Valerie's divorced lady friend who was asking him about kids, a gentle probing into his background. He normally resented personal questions of almost any kind, but mellowed by the ambience of an oak-beamed pub, a succession of pleasant faces and the sensation of being liked, he did not mind at all.

'No. None. My wife and I had a child, but it died when it was a baby. We never knew why and we didn't survive it either.' As soon as he had spoken, he wished he had not. Such a statement contained an invitation to pity which he neither courted nor felt he deserved. Bailey's failure with his young spouse so many years ago, his ignorance in the face of that misery of hers which had turned into madness, his failure to keep or cure her, still haunted him. It had haunted him through the several liaisons which had prefaced his fragmented existence with Helen, whom he loved profoundly, although he did not mention her name in this company.

On his first pint, he remembered the optimistic phases of his life as a truly single man, after the second, he remembered his age and ordered a whisky; but the euphoric sense of freedom did not pass, it intensified. Oh yes, he was bound for home this weekend, but there was no harm in the delay. And there was always next weekend. The woman on his left laid a light hand on his arm.

'I'm so sorry,' she said with the same quickness of touch. 'It must have been terrible. Mine spend most of their time with their dad, but I'm glad they're alive.' She removed her hand as imperceptibly as she had placed it, a nice woman, called Grace. Ryan rose to get another round. They all laughed and offered him money, a sensible confederacy of classless, adult friends, who all knew about life and spoke a common language. Ryan was delighted by the passivity of his master. They might convert him yet.

The afternoon faded again, with its usual lack of glory, until school came out. Logo had parked his trolley in the graveyard, so ungainly no one would steal it or even play with it; full of bits and pieces lifted from skips, an old chair to be cut into kindling for Margaret, his whisky, his Bible and a couple of other things he didn't want shown the dim light of day. It was some distance from the school gates but, despite himself, he went to watch. Then, again despite himself, he chatted to a girl he had watched before, dark as himself, with old-fashioned plaits fraying at the edges, her thick curly hair not quite tortured into submission. She might have been a foreigner, most of them were, but she still looked like his daughter. It made him over-react.

Despite the anxiety, Logo usually found he got a buzz from being arrested. Ignorant of drugs, but not of the whisky he carried round in little bottles with all the silent glee of a successful smuggler, he knew that the sharp excitement of a chase was better than booze tingling in his veins. He was incredibly strong for his size without being swift, he could scarcely run at all, but he loved the brevity of his futile sprints for freedom, that fierce joy in the initial confrontation with the policeman, his neck bent like a penitent until they were off guard enough for him to pull away, giving himself just a small headstart because he always meant to be caught in a few yards. Logo's long, untidy hair would flap round his eyes as he ran, sometimes whooping and screaming enough to frighten the pursuer to a standstill before they pounded in his wake, and all to feel that last, delirious moment of surrender.

Thus it had always been, five or fifteen times, each time of the many he had been arrested, some gentle old hand with the fingers on his arm or, just as comfortably, some lone novice sent out in a miniature car on a call like this to a mere local nuisance, stepping out of his toy vehicle with grave self-importance, straightening his new uniform before they all ran a few steps of their ritual dance in front of their spectators who all but clapped. Both of them destined to get a little hot in the chase before Logo could compose his face into an expression of terror so pale he looked like a man in front of a firing-squad and they all went peacefully home to the nick where he would recover and protest his innocence, and then ask, sneering, Why did you never find my wife and daughter? That's how good you are, what have you ever done for me?

He should not have asked the child to step into the graveyard with him, nor told her he had something for her in his trolley, nor promised her a ride, but she was delicious. The cunning little brute smelt him downwind and said she wanted to go to the sweet shop first, so they did that instead and on the way, met her mother. The child screamed as if he had in fact touched her, although she had not been remotely anxious before, and the mother, screaming too, blocked him into the door of the shop, while someone called the police. Now Logo was at the end of the ritual, and there had been no gentleness in it, not this time, none of the usual contemptuous patience which had dignified the other occasions.

The rookie cop had grabbed Logo by the jacket after he ran, holding a fistful of shirt as he yanked him backwards. The frayed collar bit into his throat and he gasped for breath as an arm jerked his chin into the air. It was more than enough to subdue a man who wanted to be subdued, but the boy officer thought otherwise. The pressure on Logo's neck increased until he thought he saw stars, and it was then he began to struggle in earnest, kicking, hearing the satisfying crack of his foot against a shin, digging back with his sharp elbows, twisting like an eel, almost free, screaming as soon as he found the breath. He turned in surrender, but the sight of the other face frightened him more than the touch. Logo felt his elbows pinioned from behind, his still flailing legs kicked away and his body crashing to the ground, landing painfully half on one side. He screamed again as his arms were twisted up his back, the blades of his shoulders standing out like chicken wings, he felt something tear. The handcuffs locked around his crossed wrists. His fingers splayed in a futile agony of resistance. A radio crackled. Logo whimpered. 'Shut up, you bastard.' Logo's whimpering rose a pitch: he must have an audience. 'Help me,' he muttered, but all he felt was his hair held, his half-turned face raised and then let drop against the sharp gravel of the road, pressing into the surface.

The shock of that deliberate cruelty made him close his mouth against the punching, saving his teeth but not the kick to his throat. There was a numbness which was the forerunner of real pain, and when he opened one eye he saw his spittle in the dirt of the gutter and, inches from his face, the remnants of damp cigarette packets from a spilt bin. He felt he was on the level of a large dog turd and all his own litter, while the half-frozen wetness of the road seeped into his bones and his own blood and urine seeped back.

They were not saintly, the boys in blue, they always put on the handcuffs too tight, but they were not unkind either. They did not usually yank him into the back of a van and lie him face down as if he was a true man of violence. He knew later he had not imagined either the kicks to his ribs and one which seemed to connect with his face by accident, or the foot on his neck and the taunting from the officer who had arrested him. 'Bastard,' said the voice. Kick. 'Leave my balls alone, you pervert.' Kick. 'Going after girls, are we?' Kick. There were two others in the back of the van where he lay between the seats. He could sense their youthful disapproval in their silence; he reckoned they would save him if the kicking got worse, but not until it did.

The custody sergeant had time to stop and stare at a small, prematurely old man, wet and filthy, with one eye shut, blood seeping from his nose and forehead to mingle with the dirt and the snot on his torn shirt; a man breathing with an alarming, rumbling sound, a tiny, dilapidated creature.

'Take the cuffs off him for Christ sake.'

'He's very violent, sir.'

The sergeant looked at the oddly triumphant face of young PC Williams with a weary loathing, noting the absence of filth or even damp on the barely ruffled uniform.

'I bet he was,' he said heavily. 'Take them off. You!' he barked towards Logo. 'Sit down over there.'

The other two officers hung back, afraid to touch and anxious to be gone. Logo shambled slowly across to the bench against the wall and sat heavily. There was an argument, raised voices, which he heard without registering the words and then he was placed, with strange solicitude, in the cell he occupied now.

'My trolley,' he croaked. 'Look after my trolley. You'll get me sacked.'

'Yes. Anything to complain about?' Logo looked at the sergeant levelly.

'No.'

For that he was brought a blanket and hot, sweet tea, but he sat on the bench, weeping and seething, waiting for the doctor who would cure nothing.

It was all her fault. Everything. She had been his nemesis from the start, the black-eyed angel he had loved so much. Find her, bring her back, kill her. She had organized this; she stopped his very attempts to find her. The whole world blocked his attempt to find her. The cell smelled of urine which was not his own.

By tea-time on Friday, Margaret Mellors began to believe that life had taken a definite turn for the better. Yesterday, she had written a reply to her treasured letter. If she found it peculiar to send it to the address on the back of the envelope, an office called CPS something, which made her think of the gas bill, she did not dwell on it, and in the thrill of arranging a meeting, the mechanics did not seem to matter. The writing of the letter had been laborious: the posting of it had been a special expedition to the main post office, because she needed to believe the service for this missive would be first rate. That done, at vast expense, with a special-delivery sticker, Margaret breathed easier. It was also easier, she now felt free to confess, if several hours or even days could pass between her sightings of Logo. She had heard him go this morning with his dreadful rumbling trolley, and although visits home mid-afternoon were rarities, the absence was a relief. He might have caught her writing her letter and she did not want that at all. In her mind's eye, there was still the strong image of that suitcase upstairs; when she was braver, she knew she would have to go and look again, but not yet, please God, not yet.

Then there was the second surprise. A letter from the hospital, inspired by her visit to the doctor. Yes, she was still on the waiting-list, shouldn't be long, it said, might be short notice, it said. The impact of this news made her head swim: it meant that within weeks she might be able to walk as other people walked, behave as others of her spry age behaved, go further afield. Go to see Mabel in Croydon on the bus, go to visit Mary Cruft in Enfield, go to the house of George's brother, recently widowed, in Brighton. 'Help me,' said Margaret, fluffing her hair in front of the kitchen mirror. 'Help me get through this, there's a life out there, I always knew there was.'

There was also life indoors. The fire was lit. All the excitement had made her feel extravagant enough to coax her hearth to life in the middle of the afternoon, before dark, even. She settled herself with her box, to work out who she would visit in a month or two from now, who to tell the good news, and also to work out if the cure of her hip was going to cost her money if she lost the disability allowance which was currently helpful. Never mind, there were always children to look after and houses to clean if you were fit. She was knitting a sweater: she was always knitting something, making her hands work. There was a moment of doubt when she wondered if the operation was worth it, but the faith in doctors as gods and carpenters reasserted itself. The only worry was that Logo and child-minding didn't go together.

Then came the third delightful surprise to mitigate her money worries for the future. As surprises went, it did not rank with those of the last twenty-four hours, but it wasn't bad, in the scale of things.

Sylvie the hyperactive stood at the door, snivelling and clutching the hand of her father, who looked for all the world like a man leading a savage dog, while she in turn looked as if she had already bitten the hand which fed her many, many times. Sylvie did not smile until Margaret smiled, but she did not snarl either. When Margaret said, 'Hallo! How lovely to see you!' the child looked at her inturned feet and raised her father's wrist to wipe her wet nose, while the corners of her mouth turned up in some semblance of pleasure. The father let go of her hand hurriedly.

'I think I may just have some Smarties back here,' said Margaret without fuss. 'If your dad says you can, that is. My, you are a sight, you little rascal. What have you been doing then? Playing in a pond?' By some strange sleight of movement, the child's hand had become transferred to Margaret's apron pocket. Sylvie did not want to be here, but she liked it at home even less. The father let out a great, juddering sigh.

'Mrs M, it's very rude of me to disturb you, but . . .' He wiped a hand across his brow and tried to grin. The worry lines seemed impossible to erase and she felt suddenly sorry for his youthful cares. He was a handsome man, and you were never too old to notice that.

'It's my mother-in-law, you see. She came to stay last week, and now she's been taken ill. Very ill. She had cancer last year, we thought she was all better, but anyway, we had to take her to hospital today, and we've just been called in now. Got to go, there's a football match tonight . . .'

'She's going to die,' said the child matter-of-factly, and with a shade of satisfaction.

'Hush, you,' said Margaret without shock or rancour. 'Or no Smarties.' She turned her large, reassuring face to the father, put her hand on the child's neck, reaching for that small cranny underneath the messy hair where her touch could control the child. Margaret was suddenly firm. In the last twenty-four hours, she had become a person of greater consequence.

'Of course she can stay here while you go to the hospital. I hope your mother-in-law's going to get better.' They both knew it was a formal wish, but the words helped. 'Try and get back by eight, if you can. It's my neighbour, you know, he can be a nuisance.' There, she had said it, but she added the rider because she had no choice. 'If you can't don't worry. We've got plenty to eat. Would you like a cup of tea, or something?'

The man shook his head. Instead of words he made a vague salute and disappeared up the alleyway which he had told his wife he despised, but did not notice now. Behind him, he left his daughter, who went straight for the drawer which held the knives. Margaret stopped her. She took out the drawer and put it out of reach on top of the cooker. 'Silly,' Margaret said, with a note of authority the child had not heard before. 'Very, very, silly.'

It was the same syndrome as strangers on a train, a silly desire to confess which somehow did not diminish with the third stop for coffee. There weren't many shoppers in Oxford Street, post holidays and post sales. They could move freely from one mammoth department store to another. They smelt of the perfume counters where both had sampled in plenty, buying nothing but aftershave as a preliminary to the second coffee, but they were warming up to it. Helen joked to herself and to Rose that they were like two negatives making a positive. Rose didn't get the joke.

'OK. Who's the aftershave for? Your dad?'

Rose flinched, buoyant enough to recover quickly because it was only a send up. She was getting used to the fact that Miss West teased a lot, she rather liked it. It was better than being serious.

'My mum and dad split up when I was little,' she said quickly. 'Mum lives up north, dad died. No, the smelly stuff's for my . . . boyfriend.'

Helen stirred her coffee. 'Ohh, is that the one I spied you with the other day? The tall good-looking one with the nice face? Great big chap?'

Rose flushed with pleasure. 'Sounds like Michael,' she said. 'Yeah, that'll be him. Anyway, there hasn't been anyone else for two weeks and there won't be neither.'

'Is he as nice as he looks?' Rose blushed pinker.

'To tell the truth, Miss West—'

'Oh for God's sake, my name's Helen.'

'Well I can't get my mouth round that, Mum. I shall have to call you Aunty after today, but you don't meet your aunty in the pregnancy clinic, do you? Nor one of your bosses.' She giggled. They had both been finding anything and everything immoderately funny.

'My Michael?' She stressed the possessive with enormous pride, speaking as if she could burst. 'He's brilliant, just brilliant, that's what he is. I can't get over him. I can't get over my luck. When he touches me, I go all funny, but he doesn't try anything, honest. He treats me special. He says we've got to be friends before anything else and he wants to take me to places, show me things. Meet his mum!' Rose pealed with the laughter of delighted incredulity. 'But he knows what I've been like,' Rose continued, somehow assuming Helen knew too. 'He found me in the section house after all, he says he don't care who I've been to bed with before, as long as there's no one after. But I haven't yet.' She looked at Helen challengingly. 'Only you know what? I know he holds back. I know when he touches me, just holding my hand or giving me a hug, he goes all funny too. I can feel him trembling, you know. When he looks at me sometimes, I think I could die.'

Said in this fashion, Helen believed her. She ached for the

intensity of the other's feeling. All the world loves a lover and she was no exception. She felt a fierce hope that all the optimism would be justified. No wonder the result of the test had been so important.

'It sounds like a bit of old-fashioned true love, if you ask me,' she said gravely. 'Anyway, it has all the symptoms. But who was the one who might have put you in the club? One of the other boys?' Her desire for information was compulsive.

'Yeah, one or the other.' Rose was not quite beyond embarrassment: there was still a trace of it and more than a hint of reserve. She would only talk about what she wanted to talk about. 'I don't know why I did all that. I didn't even like it. Why did I do it, Aunty? You can tell me. All those blokes.'

'I don't know why any more than you do. We all do strange things and the daftest thing you did was not to take precautions.'

'Listen,' said Rose with all the old aggression, 'you can bloody well talk. What about you?'

'Yes, OK, but I'm an old lady and I did know where my bloke had been. I don't know why you were giving it away when you could have been making your fortune. Could be something like being afraid of the dark. Not wanting to go home alone. Something like that.' Rose looked at her in consternation.

'How did you know? How did you know that?'

'Been there,' said Helen promptly. 'And you don't have to pay for protection. Not that way, anyhow.'

Rose shifted uncomfortably. 'Yeah, I know now. Oh, I do love Michael. I really do. Nothing else matters. I can't see anything the same way. Nothing at all,' she added, fervently. 'Strange, isn't it?'

And I loved Geoffrey once in that delirious kind of way, Helen thought, and there are times when I still do. I hope he's home this evening. Rose sensed her preoccupation.

'Here, Aunty . . . you wanted a baby, didn't you? And here's me rabbiting on, but you weren't like me at all. Michael see, he knows quite a lot about me, what I've been like, but he couldn't have stomached a baby any more than me . . . Different for you, though, isn't it?'

Helen hesitated. 'I'd got a bit used to the idea, and when someone told me, No, you aren't, I felt as if I'd been robbed. Sad, furious, deprived, confused. Does that make sense?'

Rose nodded, but it didn't really. 'Listen, I'm sorry I made that crack yesterday about you carrying on with Dinsdale. I knew you weren't.'

'No, but I am tempted,' said Helen lightly. 'Who wouldn't be? You weren't so far off the mark.'

Each of them was lost in their own thoughts. Rose was looking forward to seeing Michael with a level of anticipation that gave her pain, but she was not going to tell him any of this. She wanted to shout. She was feeling hope for the first time that she could remember. Michael today, Gran tomorrow; she was fighting her way through all her shadows. Helen was pensive.

It must be age, she thought, where optimism was failing to triumph over experience and mistrust triumphed over everything.

'More coffee?' she asked.

'More shopping?' said Rose, shyly. 'If you've got time. Only I'd like a jacket the same colour as yours, only decent thing I've ever seen you wear, Michael would like that.'

'Did you know,' said Helen, 'that shopping for clothes for me or anyone else, is one of the greatest pleasures of my existence?' Rose grinned, cheekier than ever.

'Better than sex?' she queried. Helen paused, grinning just as widely.

'Not all the time.'

CHAPTER SEVEN

R edwood waited in the office until everybody had gone. No
one lingered on a Friday night and although he resented their
defection, his own staying behind was a self-imposed obligation
for which their absence was crucial. On a Friday evening Redwood
acquired nerves of steel and turned himself into a spy. He forced
himself to come out of his room to join the ghosts in which he
believed as much as the idle doorman, although Redwood, as a
man of logic, could not let himself acknowledge the belief and so
could not allow the fear to deter him. Like a ghost, he was licensed
to go wherever he wished at any time, but if he did so in office
hours, all those over whom he lorded it would know how often he
got lost. More to the point of his present subterfuge, they would
resent what he did in their absence – sneak around their desks, look
in the cupboards and cabinets, read letters, check schedules, investigate all those aspects of his domain which he should have known
about but was too ashamed to ask. He alone checked how many
times per annum each person cited a visit to the doctor or dentist
as the reason for an afternoon off. He checked by desk diaries what
people had done on those days when court finished at twelve and
they had failed to return before five. During the weekend ahead,
he would analyse all the information and work out how to use it
without revealing his source, thus preserving his reputation with

his superiors for effective, if unpopular, management. He called it keeping one step ahead. Helen called it something else.

The contents of Helen's room (all drawers open to the touch, had she never heard of thieves?), revolted him. It was hygienic but a complete mess. Helen West was the only one who had ever caught him at this game. With her own version of the thumb-screw, she extracted from him his promise never to repeat the exercise if she promised never to reveal it. One of them had been honourable about this deal: it was not himself.

There was an anglepoise lamp on her desk he rather fancied, if it would only go with the odd décor of his own room. There were three comic cards from Dinsdale Cotton, signed affectionately, plus cryptic notes in her diary about meetings. Oh, ho, ho . . . Redwood found himself chuckling like a malevolent Santa Claus. Then he had stayed even longer, still rejoicing, to read a set of notes headed, 'Evidence', ah yes, that lecture. Bricks and mortar, she was talking about, then she sidetracked on to the duty of the prosecutor. To sift and evaluate evidence, it said; to make sure no inconsistently sized stone was left unturned; to render the bricks and mortar with compassion; never to create the facts or deny them either; always to give the benefit of the doubt without allowing sabotage. All so much specious rubbish, he thought, fine-sounding crap, but could be useful next time he had to stand up and spout. Worth copying and she had such a legible hand.

He turned off the lamp, then found himself fumbling round the room, tripping over files, cracking his shin, stumbling, banging his wrist on the sharp edge of the filing cupboard she never used, preferring the floor. Why, oh why did they still have such savage furniture, full of lethal angles and poisonous metal? Pain made him incautious. Hobbling down the endless corridors, lit only by the red light of the goods lift which always reminded him of a dumb waiter in an old café, he was level with the photocopying room before realizing it was occupied, full of light and the clack-clack of the machine. Too late to go back now. He coughed and strode into the room, looking business-like. At the last minute, as darkness turned into blinding light, he remembered to shove the notes inside his jacket, from which they lurched, too heavy for the pocket, as bulky as a gun. Redwood was not built for stealth.

'Ah! Dinsdale! Late, isn't it?'

Dinsdale Cotton smiled his enigmatic, patrician smile, the lazy smile of the winner, which seemed to say, I love you, even when it didn't. He worked efficiently, like a man well used to a graceful economy of movement, retrieving documents from the feed tray with a flourish while the machine still clack-clacked out the copies then fell silent.

'Is it so late?' he said genially. 'Really, I'd forgotten the time. Actually, I'm glad to catch you. I was trying to help out Riley. Bit of a débâcle at court today. Can't really work out how it happened. Just running off a copy of the computer printout for next week, to make sure the thing isn't fooling us. It seems to write things off of its own accord. Or one of the case clerks does it. For what purpose, I don't know.'

'What happened yesterday?' Redwood asked for want of anything better to say. The lump of paper inside his jacket felt most uncomfortable.

'Well, the computer record on one of Riley's cases was altered by mistake to say no evidence offered last time, or the case was finished, don't know which. File put away, so poor Riley has no file, but defendant live and well, expecting to be tried, magistrate lets him go and we have egg all over face. No one could possibly mind,' he hastened to add with the same charming smile, 'except the defendant, who is not complaining, and the police who do not know since none of them was warned to attend court.'

Redwood slumped. Another crisis. Another example of how the office managed without reference to him. His shin hurt, but he could not say why, so he said nothing at all.

'No complaints?' he asked, hopefully.

'Oh no. Except from Riley.'

'Is that all? No publicity?'

'None.'

'Good man,' said Redwood fervently. 'Good man. Sort it out. Tell me next week.' Dinsdale nodded, still smiling as if Redwood had his approval in everything he chose to do. Unable to meet his eyes because of his own sense of having been found out, Redwood focused on Dinsdale's hands. They were rather like his own, small, feminine, unscarred as woman's hands were, awkward, soft little things, no good for holding a golf club. Redwood crept back down the corridor, into Helen's room and replaced the notes where he had found them.

★

The sergeant told Logo that he would be charged with assaulting a police officer, unless he would like to admit it and accept a police caution for breaching the peace. Predictably, Logo said no to the latter. He had recovered enough of his wits to remember that he'd liked the drama of the court-rooms as much as he had enjoyed his arrests up until now. The sergeant had looked at the collator's records on Logo with some anxiety: there it was, all the hand-written, locally known facts for police eyes only; a dozen arrests recorded, no convictions, mostly enclosed premises. The man had a talent for getting in, always said he was looking for his daughter or someone, otherwise he kept harassing children, harming none, a recent record too, nothing much before the last five years, never violent. Nothing to justify these livid bruises and that much blood. No broken bones, but injuries consistent with a beating, the divisional surgeon had said. Two paracetamol; fit to be detained, just. Whether the surgeon was drunk or sober, there was no fooling him. He cleaned Logo up and advised him to see his own doctor in the morning.

Then the sergeant told Logo that his trolley would be safely parked down his own back yard, if that was all right. Better than taking it back to the council depot and letting everyone there know he'd been arrested, wasn't it? Logo agreed. Telling this brought the sergeant the only real pleasure of his whole evening as he envisaged brave, young, PC Williams wheeling the trolley through the streets as instructed. Most likely it was the only piece of retribution the rookie would get – and there was more than one way to skin a cat.

Logo was offered a lift home, by different officers the sergeant hinted delicately, but the prisoner declined. The half-mile walk would be good for his soul and he went down the steps clutching the piece of paper which ordered him to report on bail to court the next week. Watching him go, the sergeant wondered if the bruises would have faded by then, considered it unlikely and was not displeased by the thought that he had done what he could within the parameters of well-established tradition. He hoped some lawyer would notice the gaps, but doubted they would. That was all he felt he could do.

Down the damp streets, coldly, Logo went, his clothes not quite dry and his body weak, sick and aching. Halfway home, he noticed something which made him laugh – the lit football stadium and the blocked streets. Friday night, special match, was it? So some bastard copper had been wheeling his trolley back, clanking with brushes, in the teeth of the descending crowds. Logo hoped they had jeered plenty. A modest attendance tonight: not the same density of cars or sound that signified a real gathering of the first-division tribes with all their war cries. There would not be the same level of chanting and he would scarcely hear them at home, unlike the other days when their communal breathing and gasping hit the windows of his house like a gale and drowned the sound of the television in a hundred living rooms. Logo tried to sing.

'Eternal Father, strong to save,
Whose arm doth bind the restless wave . . .'

The foot on his neck and the pressure on his throat made his voice sound cracked and the same mood of bitter self-pity which had sat on his head while he waited in the cell descended on him again. He needed to talk, he needed Margaret's soft, scented bosom in which to confide; he had to make a plan in which she would assist him to find her, his missing child. His daughter, find her and bring her home before the cancer of her loss affected all the extremities of his life and limbs. Love or revenge, either would do.

Lurching down the alley, he saw first the light of Margaret's door, then his trolley, upturned in the back yard with the contents spilled. He picked up the broken chair and threw it feebly, and when he bent over to examine the rest, smelt the whisky from the broken bottle and thought his head would burst. He knocked at Margaret's door, heard a scuffle inside, followed by a suspicious silence. The second knock was a good deal more aggressive. After another long pause, he saw her silhouette through the reeded glass of her half-glazed door, standing back.

'Who is it?' She sounded muffled, unwelcoming. In the near distance, he heard a ragged cheer from the football crowd.

'Me,' he said impatiently. 'Who else? Come on over, will you?'

'I can't,' she said. 'I've got a child here, asleep, Logo, I can't.'

'Well, let me in then. Open the door when you're talking to me, can't you?'

'No I can't do that either.' Her voice was firmer. 'Not tonight, another night. Or maybe later.'

'Let me in, you old cow!' he shouted suddenly. 'Just let me in! I need you, I need you . . .' He kicked the door hard with one foot, winced as pain jarred through his ankle. Her voice rose in reply.

'You aren't the only one who needs me. Stopit, Logo, don't be silly. I'll see you later.'

He kicked the door again, with the other foot, sulkily.

'Go away!' she shouted. 'Go away!'

The surprise of this unprecedented rejection made him obey. He lurched across to his own door, pushed it open and turned on the light to his dirtyish, cold kitchen. An acidic bitterness burned through his bruises. He had helped that woman rebuild her fire while he had none, he had brought home the kindling and sometimes stolen fuel even when he needed none for himself, the old cow. Logo switched on the electric fire with its two sparking bars and waited for the warmth to fill his bones with that cheerless heat. He huddled over it, tempted to weep and watch his tears sizzle themselves to death. Oh, they were all such turncoats, women, beyond redemption. Tempted a man with their bodies and their creature comforts and kind words and in the end gave nothing, took back all you had given with the talent of usurers, extracting the last drop of interest.

'Man that is born of woman is of a few days, and full of trouble. He cometh forth like a flower, and is cut down; he fleeth also as shadow and continueth not . . . Who can bring a clean thing out of unclean? Not one.' He was moaning, words came out by themselves.

Shivering still, he dipped back out into the backyard and in the light from his own doorway, found his Bible on the ground. It too, smelt of the spilt whisky, another desecration, but the damp solidity of the paper still gave comfort. He had never really needed to read his Bible, only to hold it and quote his disjointed quotes from it which memory jumbled into meaningless mantra phrases.

He went upstairs and found his daughter's school exercise books. Saw the handwriting of old essays and spelling tests, school projects all stored with the dismembered torso of a teddy bear in a drawer in his room. She had left so little behind. The central light in the room had no shade; neither did the lamp by his bed which shone on the immovable suitcase. Logo lay down, still cold, raised his hands in front of his eyes to examine the red weals left by the handcuffs, felt his grazed and grossly bruised face, wondering at its whole new set of swollen contours. God help me, even with these afflictions, Margaret would not let me in. A deep and dark suspicion began to haunt him. Then he looked at his hands again, more carefully, balled them into fists and punched them. Then hooked them together by the thumbs and began against the far wall, his game of shadow play.

What should she do next? What did a person ever do when they were waiting, especially if they were not used to waiting? Helen had found it thus when waiting for a jury to come back with a verdict, waiting for a case to come on for trial, the waiting time was useless, captive to expectation, a vacuum where logic and concentration were displaced by rage or anxiety. Waiting time was the only time in which she could ever acknowledge boredom. People waiting together grew close; people waiting for one another grew distant with every passing minute.

Helen was waiting for Bailey. The tersest of messages on her answerphone announced his presence which was more than half expected this Friday evening anyway. He could get away with a week, not with a fortnight. She had been turning somersaults in the last eight days and she had been shopping.

Shopping was always that mixture of excitement and guilt, but better than yoga in terms of total distraction. She and Rose had parted with genuine regret. Rose's boy would not keep her waiting, he would be straining at the leash. If ever Helen had flung a leash round Bailey's neck, now would be the time to pull it. Instead she was doing housework because he was very late indeed and she was storing up trouble like gas in a balloon.

The sound of his steps fell into her basement, with the loud tread of uncertainty. A car roared off into the distance with a joyous burst of power, not his car, Helen knew the sound, and not a taxi. Someone had given him a lift home. Maybe that little troublemaker, Ryan, who always found her lacking in female duties and judged her accordingly, Helen knew, although their mutual liking was as strong as the disapproval. Bailey hit the french windows at the front of her flat with a stern and well-controlled rap of his knuckles, which she ignored. Sober persons came in through the front door, having rung the bell. To hell with his short cuts. He rapped again. This time she relented and let him in.

'Sorry I'm late,' he beamed. 'Or did you get the message? Only we finished mid-afternoon, then we stopped off, you know how it is.'

She did know how it was, she had done it herself all too often. It was a hazard of both their lives, but she still remained stiff and unyielding in his large embrace. Bailey, who was normally so immaculate without the fastidiousness of perfume smells or perfect creases to his trousers, now smelt a little stale and beery. His hair was messy, his tie crooked from being loosened and hurriedly straightened, then loosened again and she did not want to investigate the source of the other scents he carried about himself, like nicotine, perfume, dog. He looked like a man who had spent a week camping and returned via a brothel, still pleased to see her.

'Did you forget your key?' she asked by way of a purely neutral greeting.

'Yup. Forgot everything. Shouldn't have let Ryan drive home either. Back to college! Must go on more courses! Lessons in irresponsibility! I can't tell you how nice it is, on one level anyway. Everything structured, even get woken up in the morning, good food. No decisions about where to go next, even after lessons, then Ryan makes them. How are you? Oh good, you've been shopping, something new. Lovely, I like it.'

Helen was washed and changed, two glasses of wine away from total sobriety. Part of the spoils of shopping were the tiny ear-rings which sparkled in her ears, very understated, she resented him noticing. Rose had not approved. 'You want great big ear-rings, Aunty, not them mingy little things,' but Rose had approved the steak and packeted salad, bought on the run with extravagant ease for the West–Bailey supper. 'More time for real shopping,' she had added, a distinction which Helen heartily approved.

Helen returned the pressure of Bailey's embrace without much of the feeling, deciding he was not really drunk, merely a little under the influence, which was the most he ever got since the stuff seemed to lodge in his bones rather than his brain. It explained the geniality.

'A drink?' she asked, over brightly. 'There's food too, of course.'

'Oh yes, oh yes. A drink first. Then let's go out to eat. I don't take you out enough. Oh my God.' He sat down suddenly, still in his winter coat, laughing.

'What?'

'I've left my car in Bramshill. Well, that limits my movements, doesn't it?'

'I'm not driving,' she added, flourishing the wine bottle and pouring him a glass, thinking of drunk drivers.

'Oh,' he said without rancour or comprehension. 'Never mind. Actually, come to think of it, I'm not very hungry.'

Helen thought of the mountain of food standing by and suppressed the desire to shout at him. 'I'll do something anyway,' she said, keeping her voice level.

'Great,' he grinned.

She couldn't bear to be in the same room so she made herself busy, action being the antidote to irritation, but when she came back to where he was, only minutes later, still ready to shout, Bailey's wine was drunk and he was fast asleep.

His coat was on the floor, lying at his feet like a dog. His suit was rumpled. Helen undid the loosened tie, tucked a blanket round him, neatly under his chin so he looked like a baby with an extra-large bib. With that image in mind she finished the bottle of wine and went to bed alone.

Rose Darvey's hand inside Michael's was warm. He was silent which she did not mind, since it was a warm silence and her hand was being held inside his pocket and she was more than glad to chatter. They were walking away from her flat. For the first time ever she was being collected from home by a man she adored to go for a meal out in formal fashion. The relief from the morning's anxiety and the day which had followed, had both been times of unholy joy, but this was the cream. They were late because they had lingered on this the first time she had ever allowed a friend across the portals of the upstairs rooms. The two other girls had been agog, they had preened before him, and in return he had been his usual, easy, friendly self, crowding the kitchen with his big male presence, while behind his back they had made exaggerated signs of approval to Rose, thumbs-up gestures accompanied by great rolling of the eyes.

'Did you go for that test?' one of them hissed as she crossed with Rose coming out of the bathroom door.

'Yeah,' Rose whispered back. 'Don't say nothing. It was negative, false alarm. What d'you think of him, then?'

The other put her finger on her lips, to promise silence. There was no envy in the gesture, only a gleeful solidarity. 'He's OK,' said Rose's friend, diffidently.

That had been the understatement of the year, Rose thought as she walked along with Michael. She was acting like a chattering celebrity, regal and voluble.

'Well,' she was saying. 'You'd never guess what happened to me today . . .' It was on the tip of her tongue to tell him how the day had started, but then caution prevailed. 'Well, I had to go up Oxford

Street, on a message, and guess what? While I was there, I met that Miss W., you know Helen West, the lawyer in our office I told you about, the one I said was a stuck-up cow, but she isn't really, not at all. So she buys me a coffee, well six coffees and a sandwich to tell the truth, and the two of us go shopping, just like that! Six hours' shopping, I ask you! It was easy.'

'Six hours!' was all he could echo. 'Six hours! Don't ask me to go up the West End with you, will you? Six hours! You must be barmy, but then I always knew you were a bit cracked.' It was said with light teasing and increased pressure on her warm hand, as they reached the car.

In fact there was little he could say or wanted to say; he felt like someone in an extract from *My Fair Lady* or *Singin' in the Rain*. There should have been a big band playing at the end of the street while he danced down it, singing and swinging on the lamp posts, throwing his helmet in the air, that kind of thing. A copper in love. The thought was laughable. He felt more disposed to laugh than to sing, and although he had never had difficulty expressing himself to Rose, he was short of words now. Michael was silent because he was entranced by her. She had greeted him at the door (the address, God knows, had taken a fortnight to prise from her), blushing through her make-up, dressed in black leggings and a longline jacket of red wool with a black collar. Her hair was slicked back against her head, and apart from that absurd plait the whole effect was just amazing. He had said so immediately and she had blushed further. There was about her a certain joy, a rich chuckling and the proud embarrassment with which she introduced him to her flat-mates. To know that he was responsible for that gaiety, that swift but steady metamorphosis from the sad and spiky waif he had picked from the damp garden of a damp street, made him giddy. All day he'd been counting the minutes, couldn't stop thinking of her any more than he could stop looking at her now.

There was one thing which niggled him, though only for a minute, as he ushered her into his car like a princess. Her bedroom, spring-cleaned, shown with shy pride, was full of traditional chintz, dolls, teddy bears, lace, toys, in so much contrast to the stark provocation of her usual clothes. Michael had seen and noticed the room of a child.

'I'm starving,' she said with enthusiasm. 'Where are we going?'

'Oh, not far, round about Finsbury Park. I should think you are starved, six hours' shopping—'

'Not too close to the stadium?' she asked sharply.

'Well no, pretty close, but supporters never go there, if that's what you mean. They only eat hamburgers. Why?'

'Oh I hate football, that's all. And there's a match, I know there is. I always read in the papers to see when there's a match. Anywhere. So I know to stay miles away.'

'Clever you,' he said admiringly. 'You should be on duty when they start.' He could not resist a little boasting. 'Go mad they do. The noise! We need ear-plugs, but then we wouldn't hear them thumping one another. Actually,' he added, honesty prevailing, 'it's not usually that bad. I don't really mind football duty.' She was silent: it was his turn to chatter. And the Greek place was dark and cheerful, half full, swagged with rich and tired velour which did not bear close examination, but half covered the windows from prying eyes and gave it a look of expense even before the waiters prostrated themselves for each visitor. Rose was nicely flustered. They sat after the table was adjusted three times, the candle and the flowers slammed back with the efficiency which gave the lie to the humility of the service. Michael held her hand over the darned, pink cloth.

'It's one of my locals,' he said simply, not quite explaining the explosion of attention. 'And I usually come in here by myself or with one of the lads. I just wanted to show you off.'

Her cup ran over. The waiter cantered across with another flower and a complimentary drink, but all she could do was look at the man who held her small hand in his big, warm one. If this was love, no wonder she had never known. It was almost too much to bear.

I don't know what's happened to me, Michael wanted to say. I just don't know, but I want it to last.

'Here, this is expensive,' Rose muttered, looking at the menu. 'Well quite expensive. You've got to let me pay some.' The challenge was back in her voice.

'No,' he laughed. 'When I take you out, I take you out, right?' She opened her mouth to protest. Years of fighting for survival had not bred a person of graceful acceptance.

'No, love,' he warned. 'Another time. When you haven't been out buying new gear for six hours at a time. Come on I, I know you get paid fuck all.'

'Do you call everyone love?' she asked pertly.

'No,' he said. 'Only little old ladies. And you. 'Cos I mean it.'

'Why?' she said seriously, looking down and playing with her flower. 'Why ever would you mean it?'

'I don't know why,' he said simply. 'I don't know if anyone ever does know why. I dunno why my mum loves my dad, but she does. You can't pick and choose. Leastways, I can't. I feel stuck with it, but it's a nice way of being stuck.'

Was it his imagination, or did her eyes fill with tears, either of petulance or sadness? Then she blew her nose, having fumbled in her handbag to look for an over-used scrap of tissue. Sophistication did not spread as far as her handbag. She was not a person to tease, he decided; she was as raw as a peeled onion and not like anyone else. Not at all like anyone else.

'So,' he said, returning to the topics which had been the staple and ever-effective subjects of their conversations. 'Tell me about work. When did I see you last? Day before yesterday? Seems ages. Let's have the *meze*, shall we, a bit of everything?'

Rose liked talking about work. He liked a girl who took work seriously and also knew a little about his own, that was a bonus.

'Well, there's something worrying me there. Can I tell you? Promise you won't tell anyone else? I wanted to tell Miss W. today, but it sort of never came up. Everything else did though.'

'Go on then,' he made a face at her. 'I'm all ears.'

'We've got someone fiddling the books, is what. Only I don't know who. Oh, not fiddling books for money or anything, just playing around with the computer, wiping off cases. So people don't know to go to court, and the magistrate chucks it out. We've had about ten, only no one's said anything yet and no one listens to me, I'm the only one who seems to have noticed—'

Michael snorted. 'You know what?' he said. 'Like I told you before, we got jokes on our relief about why bother going to court at all any more. Just wait for the CPS to lose the papers.'

'All right, all right,' she said defensively, her hand still in his. The waiter hovered but Michael dealt with him quickly, the boss without arrogance, smiles exchanged all round. How easy it was to unburden when your hand was held. Perhaps all burdens could be shed this way; she felt the beckoning of freedom. 'That's the whole point, don't you see? You just have to make a mess up with the papers and everyone thinks it *is* just careless, short staff, whatever . . .'

'While someone's taking advantage, and doing it deliberately?'

'Oh, I wouldn't like to think that,' she said hurriedly. 'I don't like to think that anyone in our office would do that. It's only cases about driving—'

'Why not?' he interrupted. 'Look, what's a licence worth? Hundreds? Thousands if you could get prison. Thousands? And the rest. Depends who you are.'

'I wasn't thinking it was for money,' she repeated stubbornly. 'I was thinking it was maybe for spite. But what I was really thinking, was that when they notice, they're going to think it's me.'

'Why?' he asked, surprised, although he half knew the answer.

'Because I keep the back-up records and they've gone too. And because I'm awkward, can't help it.' He nodded. Food arrived in quantity, dish after little dish, some of the plates cracked, but the contents delectable. They abandoned any other dilemma except which dish to attack first, but not before Michael had the last word.

'Well, if they blame you, they'll find out otherwise. Now you've got me, we'll sort it out. Listen,' handling her the hot pitta bread, 'I'm boxing next week. Want to come and see me?'

She had a mouthful, shook her head. 'Only if you win. I don't want to see you being punched.'

'Promise,' he said. 'I don't want to be punched, either.'

It was then that the face pressed itself against the window. A bloated red face with one eye half closed and the colours of tropical sunset beneath nasty, dirty, thinning hair. The figure beneath wore indecipherable clothes, brown, black, damp, funeral clothes and a grubby shirt collar, streaked with blood. A hand sheltered the eyes the better to peer inwards at the diners and their food. The face adjusted itself further to avoid the curtains, then flattened one cheek against the pane, making the expression of it lugubrious and exaggerating the swelling of the skin. Rose and Michael were in the corner window-seat, she had her back to the wall. Michael looked up, his eyes suddenly level with the eyes outside, inches from that terrible face, ghostly in the light from the framed menu outside. The eyes moved sideways, gazed at Rose, and Michael was uncomfortably alarmed, then violently angry. His first reaction was to stand up and bang on the windows, but it was tempered by the desire for peace.

'Here, Rose, love,' he said equably. 'You seem to have got a fan out there. Friend of yours?'

She looked up, he waited for the laugh, watched as the colour of her skin drained to a dull white. Michael had seen the same in people about to faint, but all she did was drop her fork and choke on what she ate. He leapt from his seat, round to her side, patted her back and waited for the coughing to subside. The man outside did not move.

For a moment, the two inside stared at him and then, most hideous of all, the face broke into a great, flattened grin, a hand appeared clawing at the glass beside the smile, then sketched a wave as the glass was misted by breath. Michael went outside.

He pulled the man by the shoulder, feeling the loose fabric slip over a knob of fleshless bone. A ghost. The man was still grinning.

'What's your game, mister? What's your bloody game?' Michael shouted. 'Fuck off out of it! Go home!'

Logo appeared to consider. In height, he reached somewhere about the middle of Michael's chest and he would have known a policeman at fifty yards, even in the fog. Restlessness had driven him back outdoors, but he was in no condition to run, fight, beg or face another arrest. Michael, too, remembered to conciliate.

'You should be at home, old man, not out on a night like this, frightening people. Go on, go home.' But he could not resist a rough push which sent the other reeling back a few steps, wiping away that smile for three seconds until it reappeared with his balance.

'All right, all right,' in a wheedling tone which irritated more than any sign of aggression. 'I was going anyway.' He turned with dignity and his voice came floating back. 'Tell her I'll find her. Tell her I'll go on looking.'

'Fuck off,' Michael muttered, watching until the man was out of sight. Logo, that's who it was, seen him before, poor old loony. That was all right: anyone recognized was all right. He shook himself like a dog, tried to get rid of the anger and returned inside.

The corner-seat where Rose had sat was empty. The waiter hovered, anxiously, with the next course on a large dish.

'Keep it warm a minute, will you? Where'd she go?'

The waiter shrugged and pointed to the back. He was used to alarms and squabbles and ladies hiding in the lav after too much retsina. Michael forced his way to the back behind the bar. She was standing against the lavatory door, holding the same piece of tissue she had produced before to press against her mouth, as if that talisman alone could stop the trembling.

'Come on, love. It's all right. Don't be upset. It's all right. He's only an old no good, lives the other side of the stadium, harmless old fart.'

She shook her head. He put his arms round her, began to lead her back to their table. She resisted.

'Come on, no damage. Come on, love, we've hardly started.' She mumbled something into the disgusting rag of tissue.

'What? Didn't hear you. Tell me what's up. Look, he only likes scaring people, that's all. I can tell you a tale or two about Logo.'

She took the tissue away from her face, heaved a large sigh to control the shaking.

'Don't bother, will you.'

Michael felt the huge wave of irritation for the wreck of a well-planned evening.

Bailey woke with a crick in his neck. The fire was out and for a long half minute he wondered where he was. In the house of the woman where he had spent part of his afternoon, not innocently, but no actual disloyalty either? In his own home? He looked down at his own long length covered by blanket, tucked firmly if ineffectively round his stiff shoulders, bunched round his middle and kicked away by his feet. A covered corpse which had managed to move.

Now he was in the present he liked the conclusions less than the confusion. He was hot and cold by turns, his hands sweaty, head chilly, and surely, she knew him well enough after three years to rouse him from a stupor and put him to bed. Wincing, he threw off the blanket and surveyed his crumpled suit in the soft light she had left on for his benefit. No doubt to stop him stumbling and waking her up. Then he looked at his watch, although he knew as he always did, roughly what time it was, just this side of midnight. There was no sound anywhere until he heard the faint rumble of the North London Line, vibrating to remind him.

Well he needed a bed and he needed more sleep, so he rose stiffly, took off his clothes and slung them over the chair, padded naked to the bathroom and stood beneath the shower. A warm body is always more easily forgiven than a cold one, he reflected, making as much noise about his scouring as possible. Deliberately noisy, clumsy in any event from fatigue and headache, knocking things over. She had dishes and jars in her bathroom where he had merely closed cupboards and soap, it was easy to make his presence audible. During the teeth-brushing stage, which he did with great vigour, splashing the mirror, he noticed a new brush by the side of the basin, wondered briefly, decided he was too tired to wonder about the significance of anything. Then padded next door. He slipped in beside her and hauled her close without any resistance.

'We aren't doing very well, are we?' he said. 'I've missed you. And I'm sorry I didn't say so.'

'So am I. So did I. Miss you.'

Silence. 'Tell me,' she said more distinctly, 'if we split up, do you think we could just be good friends?'

Silence.

'No,' he said. 'Couldn't we just be lovers?'

CHAPTER EIGHT

M argaret deliberately recited to herself the events of the last evening as a way of passing time and speeding the progress of the bus which went from the end of the road all the way to Oxford Street. Perhaps Eenie remembered the route, Margaret thought.

The night before, Sylvie's mother and father had come to collect her long after Logo had knocked, it was closer to midnight by the time Margaret offloaded one sleeping child. The mother was tear-stained: Granny in hospital was dying, she said, and Margaret remembered how nothing was ever quite as bad as the death of a parent. Not even a husband. Perhaps the defection or disappearance of a child was something worse than a death. Even with a clear conscience as far as Sylvie's safety was concerned, Margaret could not triumph in her contribution to it. Her sense of guilt was becoming permanent and she worried about shouting at Logo. It did not do to shout: it was not her style. Neither was the habit of hiding things from anyone, although to do so was one of life's clearest duties. So she had lumbered over to call on him after Sylvie went.

His house showed no lights and no sign of life. Margaret knew she could open the door, but ever since she had seen the suitcase, she had not felt the same. It was not Logo who made her frightened, it was the ghosts, so she went home, wondering how she would ever manage to rediscover that love for him which seemed to have fled. She would just have to wait for it to come back.

It wasn't even lonely without him: the day had been too busy, replete with the promise of what she was doing now. Debenhams, Oxford Street. Coffee shop, half-past four, Saturday, just as the crowds were clearing. She had got up last night, one more time, to look at the letter in the knife drawer to make sure she had the time right. If only she had never seen the suitcase, if only there was some way to talk without breaking any promises.

Debenhams had changed since Margaret had gone there first for knitting wools and sensible shoes. The present format of crowded escalators moving up past vast but cramped floors made her dizzy although she was glad they were not stairs. Holding on to the rail with one hand, juggling with stick and handbag, she felt she was being propelled into the sky by catapult and there would be no way down. She panicked. After four years, how would she recognize the runaway? Four years was enough for any young woman to change out of all recognition, but then she calmed herself as she managed to step off the last escalator with greater dignity than the first two. All she had to do was sit herself down and wait to be recognized; she knew she hadn't changed at all.

'Hallo, Gran.'

There she was, a beautiful young creature. Oh, what would she be now? Margaret, of course, knew to the day, one whole month beyond nineteen years. Still with that lovely skin under too much make-up, why do girls do that when they need nothing at all? Funny hair, not the long dark curls which had bounced in abundance on her shoulders, such a waste. Thin as a reed, skirt too short: a mixture of beauty and a ferocious little beast, standing by Margaret, towering over her, half anxious, half defiant.

'I can't get up so easy,' Margaret said. 'But give me a kiss. Oh, Eenie, sweetheart!'

With one bending awkwardly and the other raising thin arms restricted by the too hot winter coat, they clutched each other. 'Oh, Gran, oh Gran, where have you been?' said Rose with her face in the old woman's neck, breathing in that scent of sweet powder which brought to mind a range of comforts, closeness and discipline. She was not going to cry: there was no time to cry, and although her need was great, Gran's helplessness still made her obscurely angry.

'Listen, I'll get us some tea.'

'I'm paying,' said Margaret. 'You fetch it, I'll pay.'

'I could get used to this,' said Rose darkly, with a ghost of a smile, flouncing away while Margaret admired her ankles, dismayed by the short hair and the plait. Oh dear, oh dear, why couldn't the young be themselves, and why was she thinking of that now? Don't nag, Margaret, don't nag just because she looks like all the others, a stranger. But she was, a stranger.

'Shop tea's never the same.' To her horror, Margaret found herself grumbling when Rose came back having brazened her way to the front of the short queue. 'But lovely, dear. Here, take the money.' Rose opened her mouth to protest, shrugged, took the money. Now Margaret was peeved. Four years without a word and the child shrugged. Never mind. She was overcome with emotion, dazed with a delight which she had wanted to be uncritical, but wasn't.

'Eenie, you look marvellous, really you do. I've been all bothered since you wrote, been bothered and worried sick for four years, come to think of it. Why? I asked myself. Why? Did that little girl never love me at all? Was I so bad to you? What did I do wrong, Eenie, what did I do? Not a word from you, or your mother—'

'Oh, you neither?' said Rose with more than a trace of bitterness. 'You and me both then. I hate her. She dumped me. And I did write to you. At least twice.'

Margaret was only following slowly. 'Where did she dump you, pet?'

'I told you. With a cousin up north. One Dad wasn't supposed to know about. We were both going to go, but we went from Legard Street to a hostel and then she put me on a train. She said Dad would find her, but might not find me, so it was better that way. She just couldn't face going up north and getting a job, was all. I knew she'd either go back to him or off with some bloke she was seeing. That's what she did do, anyway, wasn't it? Went off? Her cousin said she never went home. I suppose that's why you didn't write either.' Oh Christ, what was happening? Why was this so snappy? In her confusion, her mind buzzing with letters and more letters, Margaret remembered the suitcase with sickening clarity. Oh, yes, Mum had come home, and yes, Logo sometimes brought in her post.

'Didn't Mum write to you then, after that? Not at all?'

'Not ever, but she never was a writer and she said she might not. Then I ran away from the cousin, who was weird and demented. I got a live-in job at a school, but then I always liked school, would you believe. Got two O levels and got paid! They were good to me, a convent school too, they saved me.'

Yes, Eenie had always liked learning. Margaret remembered a funny little girl, often withdrawn, accepting all those extra-curricular lessons she had given to a child whose parents had no idea how anxious she was to learn. She'd needed a firm hand, mind.

'Oh why didn't you come back, pet? The police came looking for you both. Your dad left it a little while, but he did report you missing.'

Rose looked at her with complete incredulity, eyes darkening with anger at the other's innocent partiality, forgetting all the anticipation of this meeting in its sudden sourness. All this time, and Gran still nagged.

'You don't know, do you?' she taunted. 'You just don't know anything. Of course he knew where Mum was! She'd always joked about where she'd go if she ever left him, to that hostel where you didn't have to pay . . . of course he'd find her if he wanted, only I don't suppose he was in a fit state, oh never mind. Anyway, it doesn't look as if he did want. It was me he was after. And I thought I'd killed him.'

Again Margaret did not follow.

'You nearly killed him,' she said sternly. 'He drives everyone insane, talking about you, asking about you. It's made him strange. You've got to help him, Eenie, put him out of his misery before it drives him mad. Come home for a bit. He's your dad, after all.'

'Oh Jesus, God! You haven't the faintest idea.' Rose gulped tea, shook her head and went on talking more to herself, so Margaret strained to hear, deafened by puzzlement. 'I've moved address twenty times. I don't know why I moved back so close to home; I don't know what it is, I hate it anywhere, but there's something about . . . something draws you back to what you know.' She looked at Margaret challengingly. 'I wanted my mum. I thought I might run into my mum. I want my mum every day. I wanted my mum.'

'Is that why you wrote to me after all this time?' Margaret asked humbly. 'Because you wanted someone? Your mum? Not me?'

She was irritated by the selfishness of the girl, loved her at any price, was hurt, confused, unloved. You never talked about yourself to the young: you only listened since that was what they expected of you, as if you had nothing to say. The meeting bore no relation to the cloudy script she had played over in her mind a dozen times, tears and copious huggings and reminiscences. All she wanted to do was stroke this strange, prickly adult and be held; remind her of her childish loveliness and the chasm of loss and memory in between. Instead, remembering the schoolgirl Eenie had been, she let a scolding note creep into her voice.

'You've broken his heart, Eenie. Your mother did and now you. And both of you broke mine. You haven't got anyone else but your dad. He loves you and so do I.'

The word 'love' seemed to sting Rose into a fury.

'I'm not called Eenie any more. And did Dad tell you what I did to him? I bet he did. You were always on his side. I bet he told you and cried all over you: he was good at that too. Why do you think Mum and I went that day? Why? You silly old cow!'

'Shh,' said Margaret, red with embarrassment at the noise. 'Keep your voice down. People can hear.'

'I don't care if people fucking hear. They can fuck themselves. Oh shit.'

Margaret was crying. Great gobs of soupy tears running rivulets down her powdered cheeks, dropping on to the formica table top. Heads turned. Rose glared back, stuck up two fingers in the air, then leant across the table.

'Oh, listen, Gran, I didn't mean that, I'm sorry, got a short fuse, you know that, I'm sorry. Christ, you've got me going too.' She scrabbled for a handkerchief, but the piece of tissue had finally died, so she used the stiff, unyielding paper napkin instead. It reminded her of something. 'Listen, Gran, don't cry, I'll make it up to you. Look, I bought you a present.'

'Four years,' Margaret was murmuring. 'Four years, and you shout at me.' With shaking hands, she accepted a carrier-bag, opened it uneasily. Talcum powder in a presentation box, the finest kind, her favourite, relatively expensive and saved for high days and holidays. A treat she had always demanded for birthdays and used sparingly for two decades.

'You remembered,' she said tremulously.

'I remember everything, don't think I don't. Are you all right to get home?'

They sat staring at one another hungrily. Other tables had resumed talking. The row had been dismissed as a squabble about a birthday present.

'Home? Why? You aren't going now! You can't, there's so much I've got to tell you, please, pet, please . . . I'm worried, Eenie, I'm getting frightened—'

'Not now, Gran, eh? I've had all I can take. We've got to do this in stages, you know, and I've got to go.' The powdered face was crumbling again.

'Gran, *please*. Listen, I tell you what. Same place, next Thursday, six o'clock. OK?'

'Why don't you come and see me?' Margaret wailed softly. 'Only I'm waiting for this hip, it's not so easy for me to get about—'

'I'm not going anywhere near Dad, Gran, I'm just not. Don't ask me why, you won't want to know the answer. And you mustn't tell him or I'll never speak to you again. Promise? You never broke a promise.'

'Promise.'

'Right, come on then, I'll take you to the bus.'

Margaret Mellors was paralysed by the briskness of it all. They were floating down the catapult and out into the street without another word. She clutched her handbag, the carrier-bag with the talcum, her stick and Rose's arm in alternate grasping movements as people pressed by them on the way out. Margaret kept saying sorry. The bus appeared obligingly and uncharacteristically as soon as they were outside in the breathtaking cold. She staggered, found herself assisted aboard, holding on to the rail, unable to wave with her hands fully occupied and that was what she remembered later. Watching Rose waving and smiling until the crowd closed around her and her not waving or smiling back. And not understanding anything at all.

PC Michael Michael, No 711749, turned up for late-turn duty as clean as a new pin. This did not reflect the fact that his Friday night out had gone according to plan, or that he was luxuriating in any kind of wellbeing. It simply meant he had had more time at his disposal than he might otherwise have had if all yesterday's expectations had been fulfilled. He had taken his girlfriend home to her flat instead of his own, at one a.m., which meant he had gone training at the gym the morning after, with time for his domestic chores as well. His mother would be proud of what he'd achieved in an hour on Friday, but perhaps not of what he had had in his mind. Wait till you find a good one, Michael boy, before you let her indoors. Wait till you find love, then go for it, his mother had said.

Well, he hadn't waited, in the virginal sense, but he hadn't exactly gone mad on wild women and whisky either. Saving and boxing had preserved him from much, and he thought he'd found love in Rose, an utterly gorgeous, bad-record, mixed-up kid, thrust at him by fate. Only he was just now realizing how fragile and complicated a plant love could be. No wonder Ma had said, Wait. She was only trying to ensure his survival.

His mum had been wild, so his policeman dad had confided in closet admiration, ever so wild. It hadn't stopped her being marvellous, the envy of other men, as well as other sons, and that was how Michael thought he knew the difference between what was real in a girl and what was shadow, but it didn't stop him wondering why it was all so difficult.

The late-turn relief was idle on Saturday afternoon, idle and fretful. No football, no major events to police, no major traffic breakdowns, in fact nothing to laugh about at all. Even shoplifters were kept indoors by the cold, although someone was bound to steal or have a fight at home after Saturday lunchtime drinking and the enforced proximity necessitated by the cold. Just now, there was plenty of room for friendly chat in the panda car, manned by three of them, for a change. Scope for that or malice, whichever came first. Even since yesterday, word had got around about Williams and Logo. For a man who had been seen almost crying on parade, Williams had a lot of image to build. He was trying as best he could.

'See that fight last night?' Williams was saying in the locker room. 'See that bloke get it in the third round? Whoom!' He was feinting blows at his locker door. 'Whoom! Down he goes! But he hasn't been done proper, see? Up he gets, and then the other bloke hits him between the eyes, then he really goes down . . .' Williams was dancing round the open door, pulling out a creased jacket. There was silence in the place, the silence of men resenting a lost weekend, towards a boy with something to prove. Michael sauntered by Williams' locker. 'Mind if I borrow a spare pair of gloves, Paul? Only I left mine at home.'

It was an excuse to look inside. Williams was too naïve to respond until he noticed the intensity of Michael's brief inspection. Then he slammed the door. 'Sorry, mate, gloves are off.' He walked away, humming loudly, but not before Michael had seen a vicious-looking pair of handcuffs, a bowie knife and two truncheons, one more than regulation and both more than he carried.

Plus a lot of mess. Michael shook his head and passed on. He had a sudden, disgusted sympathy with a frightened man like Williams. Last night, Logo had scared him half to death. He wished he had been more sympathetic, less sharp on the subject, with Rose. Love was as fragile as smoke, but at least his uniform was durable.

As Williams strutted on to the parade, twitching his shoulders and standing to attention ostentatiously, grinning left to right as if a grin assured acceptance, the sergeant thought he was a right nasty little toad, who fancied himself as well. Williams looked at Michael for consolidation of that view, but Michael refused to catch his eye.

'Something to say, Michael?'

'No, sir.'

'Will you lot stand still?' The irritation with one was expressed against them all. Michael felt a brief draught of bitterness for all the mores that surrounded him. He would have to give Williams a chance to get rid of his contraband before he suggested a locker inspection. All this, although he had no respect for the fool.

Patience waned as the car skidded from corner to corner. It could have been an afternoon rich with jokes as the grey sky winked through the windows and they were free of any of the gut-wrenching, silence-inducing panics. There was PC Singh, a steady constable of two years' experience who joked; Michael, with more than five years on the clock, capable of uproarious laughter, and Williams who somehow deadened the atmosphere and began the teasing.

'Still going out with that girl, Mick?'

Michael hated being called Mick. A Mick was an Irish hooligan on the terraces.

'Which girl was that, Will?'

'Ohhhh, now he tells me! Who was there first then, apart from half the Army? Who did you take with you to see if we could find out where she lived?' Michael had often regretted that. 'Has she let you in yet, know what I mean? Not saying nothing, are you? Suit yourself.'

They turned a corner at high speed, Michael driving as if the car was stolen so that Williams toppled over in the back seat. He recovered, sat forward and tapped stolid Singh in the front.

'Here, you know what? Our Mick here is going out with the biggest scrubber of all time. Only he likes his birds to have practice, see? To make way for the big one!'

114

The radio crackled with some meaningless message, a brief interruption. Michael's back was broader than most, but he was seething. It touched a raw nerve as he'd been thinking that maybe he should have known sooner in his brief, intense and so far celibate relationship with Rose that she would be as loaded with grief as an anonymous parcel left on a station concourse during a bomb scare. All that fear last night, all that talk about being followed. All those difficulties ahead, rocks sensed but unseen, feeling ashamed for wondering if it was worth it and if he had the bottle to cope with a girl who was half angel, half mess.

'Come on, Mick, you can tell us. What's she like?'

'You should know,' he said evenly. Then slammed on the brakes on the car. 'But I bet you don't. That'll be my privilege.' In the same moment as spying the open door to an empty, half-derelict house in a street consisting of many of the same, Michael had made up his mind and felt a keen exhilaration, the way he did before a fight. Of course he had the bottle. Of course he'd go back and see Rose tonight. Of course he'd wait however long it took to get through to her and make things better. Like his dad with his mum. If it didn't work, it didn't work, but it wouldn't be for lack of trying.

'Here, Will, get out of this motor and see what's wrong with that building. It wasn't like that yesterday. Looks like someone's broken in. Go on, get out and take a look.'

'What about you two?'

'Just get out. I'll turn the car.' Williams got out, whistling, and sauntered over to the broken door. Michael sped up the street.

'Are we ditching him, then?' said Singh hopefully. Michael grinned. The exhilaration of his own resolve was catching.

'Like I told him, I'm just turning the car. Slowly.'

When they got back, Williams was standing outside the house, businesslike.

'Contact the key holder, do we? No one about.'

Michael peered into the dark hallway of a small, old, terraced house. Council owned, awaiting renovation and waiting a long time. 'Looked inside, have you?' he asked. 'Squatters? Anyone in there been pinching pipes and fireplaces?' He knew as he asked it the question was futile because Williams would not have been further inside than a few steps out of fear of the dark stairs and any lurking presence, and because, despite the arsenal in his locker, the silly fool didn't carry a torch. Michael took his own from his belt and strode into the house without waiting for an answer. Singh followed. Williams came last.

'There's no one there,' he was saying lamely. 'I'm sure there isn't.'

The intruders were long gone. Dust danced in front of Michael's eyes in the dim light from a dirty window at the top of the stairs. The banisters had been removed, leaving drunken treads with traces of carpet. He shone the torch into the empty living room on the right where the ugly, twenty-year-old fire surround was still intact. In the back kitchen, there might have been a stone sink, he thought, knowing as he did the geography of the houses in these particular back streets better than the lines on his own hand. No stone sink, no copper piping either, but a smell of cat and mouse. Everything recyclable was gone. Michael retreated and went upstairs gingerly with each tread creaking under his weight. There was a pole of sorts which obstructed his entrance to the bathroom door and he pushed that aside, imagining he could almost hear the ticking of dry rot in a place like this, wait till he told Rose about it. Rose, he'd say, I've found our dream house . . . and they'd laugh. He shone his torch into the room where daylight was obscured by curtains drawn over a small window, bath gone, basin left. Yeah, love, he'd say, a real *bijou* residence. Michael squatted studiously to see if he could see if the removal was recent, looking for signs in the dust like footsteps in the desert, and then, the room came crashing in on him.

Something the size of a railway sleeper hit the side of Michael's head, felling him to the floor for the plaster to rain down on his back in sharp and blunt lumps while he registered nothing more than a vague surprise and no pain. Then stunned, but conscious, he was aware of footsteps on the stairs, shouting, thundering, and the light of his own torch, free of his hand, shining a futile beam into a corner. More noise, louder; then a silence full of images and a red glow behind his eyes.

He thought with great clarity, I'm going to miss boxing next week, the championship, now is that a relief or not? And I'm going to miss Rose tonight.

'I wish I knew where Rose Darvey lived,' Helen said to Geoffrey Bailey, standing at his kitchen door and briefly admiring the functional nature of all she saw, himself included. Hostilities had not been resumed, but the morning's sleep had been interrupted, admittedly late in the morning, by a phone call for Helen. Bailey had taken it, a man called some silly name like Dinsdale. 'Sounds keen,' he'd said wryly, handing her the receiver and watching her blush, very slightly, but still a blush on the pale, unmade-up face that Dinsdale never saw. 'His toothbrush, is it?' Bailey mouthed as she turned her back on him and cradled the receiver against her shoulder. She ignored him. 'No,' she was saying. 'Sorry, I'm fully occupied this weekend,' without specifying how she was occupied. 'Would have been nice,' she said to the voice on the phone, which Bailey found himself mimicking. Could I possibly speak to . . . ? Naice, very naice. No one at Bramshill talked like that. He also wondered how much of the conversation was for his benefit or the benefit of the man on the line who was obviously wanting her undivided attention. She had never mentioned a Dinsdale, which was suspicious in itself, since she could talk until the cows came home about everyone else they knew, especially if they had problems. Maybe this Dinsdale was the problem. Bailey told himself to remember that Helen did not play games, but then he was a policeman and knew there was no such thing as truly predictable behaviour. The phone call was not mentioned again. One of Bailey's duties, both public and private, was to keep the peace and treasure it.

There'd been some corny stuff, about come on over to my place, the vintage of a song he remembered and she did not, but she was easy to please today. The ceasefire, which had looked like remaining stable, almost broke when she slung his baggage to one side of her car and put some of her files in; had looked more fragile when he insisted on the supermarket and the dry-cleaners, and nearly cracked into ominous silence as he watched the way she drove. Still he was a man of iron reserve; he'd been driven by worse and at least she knew she was bad. In the afternoon, they went back to bed. Housewarming, he said. In the evening he embarked on cooking. She read some of her damn files, to make Sunday less depressing, she said, and after a while came to stand at the kitchen door.

'Rose Darvey? Oh, the case clerk you told me about.' He never forgot a name or an anecdote. 'Why do you want her address? She won't thank you for calling on a Saturday night.'

'Just a feeling. For one, I know she'll be lonely. Unless she's got the beloved Michael, of course, and that one's invested with so much great white hope he might not turn out to be Saint Christopher. I can't explain her. She's woman and child, all wrapped up. Street-wise and childlike. No parents. I was thinking of her.'

'You said "one". What was two?'

She looked blank, mesmerized by his activity.

'The second reason for wanting to speak to her?'

'Oh, that. I haven't got the right files. Or something's gone wrong. I noted in my diary a remand case for Monday, same court, asked for it to come back to me because I want to get the little bastard.' She launched forward and picked up an olive from the work surface of the clean kitchen.

'Tut, tut,' he said, sweeping her away with an evil-looking knife.

'But it isn't here. Now, I told you, both of us were playing hookey on Friday, but I went back for my papers. That file isn't on the list and it isn't with me.'

'Forget it. Tomorrow will do. We can go into the damned office and check. Open that wine, will you? Maybe the defendant's died.'

'Ha ha,' she said. 'Fat chance. Drunk drivers never die, if only more of them would. What the hell are you doing?'

There was the satisfying sound of emerging wine cork. 'Ooh,' said Helen, casting her eye over the open page of his cook book. The page was already stained with his preparations. Bailey was a good cook; something you learned from following the recipes and being bothered to buy all the ingredients without substituting something else to save yourself another hundred yards.

'One chicken, roughly four pounds, two large peppers, chorizo sausage, four ounces basmati rice, sun-dried tomatoes in oil, white wine, garlic, three ounces pitted black olives, sorry there's only one ounce now,' she added with her mouth full, '. . . cayenne pepper, three thousand other ingredients. I mean is that all, is that really all? What about the kitchen sink? And ear of bat and eye of toad? What do you have to do, apart from brown and chop and sauté and slop it all around and wait for Christmas?'

'Eat it,' he said, 'in about an hour. And don't be so morally superior about all things domestic. Especially cooking.'

She paused with a bottle of wine in one hand and an olive stone in another and nodded.

'Yes, I suppose I am, a bit. I don't mean to be, but I am and it must be irritating. And while I know I like it better cooked, left to my own devices, I'd probably eat the olives first and the chicken in a sandwich.'

'You always admit your errors of judgement,' he said, opening the oven door, 'to exonerate them and have an excuse for going on exactly as before. A bit like a Catholic going to confession. How long does that recipe say for cooking? If you can bring yourself to read it.'

'Geoffrey,' she said, still leaning on the kitchen door. All conversations were fine until one sat down, they were somehow better on the run. 'You know I told you about my day's shopping with Rose Darvey? Well, we met up by mistake yesterday morning. In a pregnancy clinic.' The oven door slammed shut on poultry magnifique. 'And?' said Bailey, even toned, busy.

'And nothing.' He wiped his hands carefully on a tea-cloth, with his back to her, before turning round. He seemed to speak from the middle of the kitchen sink, and she heard him from the distance created by her well-controlled, dim ache of misery and disappointment and the struggle to stop crying which had been the hallmark of the week.

'I have to go back to my course tomorrow evening. I think we have twenty-four hours.'

'So long?' said Helen, wanting to cry, hoping he noticed. 'Really that long?'

Walking was more difficult than usual for Margaret. It was as if the pain of her emotions had transferred itself to her legs and made her slower. On the way back down the street, having been spat out by the bus, it was only the ingrained force of polite concern which made her stop at Sylvie's home to enquire after the granny. Her sense of failure was intensified by the presence of a young stranger, attempting to feed Sylvie in the kitchen. Sylvie was screaming and kicking. 'I want to go with Mags!' she yelled, but it was not gratifying: it was all for show. The parents were out. The old lady had died, said the stranger in a murmur, there was a lot to do. Leaving offers of help and messages of condolence, Margaret withdrew.

No sign of Logo, but she knew he was there. She wished he would come and knock at her door, but she also wished he wouldn't. She couldn't contrive the expression of a lie, but she ached for the company, to talk about anything. Meeting Eenie had carried all her hopes for redeeming loneliness, but all it had done was confirm it. Margaret locked her door firmly. Later, she thought she heard the rumbling of his cart down the alleyway, but going in or coming out, she couldn't be sure. By that time,

Margaret was cocooned in her warmest night-dress and the luxury talcum had been used with great abandon. It was the best she could do for comfort.

Logo sat in his bedroom and played with shadows. His reflection in the mirror, showing a puffed-up purple face, told him he was ill; his wiry constitution told him he was not. He was not sure which to believe. He still could not sing, but he could croak and howl in a kind of triumph.

So. He had seen her and been driven off like a fox from the hens. Seen his Eenie child, fancifully named to remind his wife of the Ena Harkness rose she had once tried, in her usual, unsuccessful fashion, to grow in the backyard. They should have stuck to calling her plain Rose. 'Eenie' had soon been coined out of Enid at school. It was an ugly name, but it stuck somehow, as she grew ever more beautiful. A lithe, lissom, little thing with a bottom like a peach and long legs like a colt and all that glorious hair. When her mother had combed out that hair while the child stood still, temporarily mesmerized by the touch, Logo had watched, equally spellbound until the spell was broken by her energy and she twitched to move again. He would watch while the little body wriggled away with sinuous grace: enough, Mummy, enough of this being still. And then when Mummy began to go out, more often, as she grew bored with the child and the child with her, Logo and daughter would play together. Shadow play, she squealing and screaming with delight.

At first, only shadow play. And then less and less of the delighted screaming until she was silent.

CHAPTER NINE

Sunday afternoon saw the doorman at Helen's office let Bailey past the door on the merest flash of a warrant card, nodding Helen through on sight of a small plastic permit because it looked the right colour. 'You could have shown him your bus pass,' Bailey said, admiring but aghast. 'This place is about as secure as a football pitch.'

'Or a lunatic asylum.'

'No, far worse than that.'

'Don't tell,' said Helen. 'Everyone thinks it's safe. The railings, you know.'

No file, and no computer record of a file when Bailey found his way into the screen. No sign of back-up records in Rose's neat hand. Helen looked in the open book which contained each person's home address and phone number. Rose's was crossed out. 'Secretive, isn't she?' Bailey commented mildly. Helen was defensive.

'So? She may have reason, poor child. They may not have a phone.'

'All teenagers have phones. They live on the phone.'

Helen wasn't listening. 'I'll have to ask for yet another adjournment. Unless the court's changed the date, but it still doesn't explain why everything's gone from here. I could try the basement, but I don't know where to start, all that paper—'

'You said this would take one hour out of our twenty-four,' Bailey pointed out reasonably. 'So far it's taken two and a half. Come on, cases are lost all the time. You must be used to it by now.'

'No.'

There was that hard edge in her voice which he hated. 'Losing them fairly in court is one thing. Losing them through negligence is another. Let's go home. Your place or mine?'

'Mine. Ryan's collecting me later.' She grinned an apology.

'Good, we can have a drink then. With the steak. Just for something completely different.'

Not perfect, but functioning as a team. This time she didn't want him to go. Nor did he. Neither of them said so.

And by Monday, the briskness and the fury were back in business. Because Miss Helen West was a dozen times more persuasive than her junior colleague, John Riley, she managed to secure a two-week postponement of the drink drive case without papers. The expression of anger on the face of the defendant as he left the dock was one to which she was well accustomed, might even have sympathized with, if only he had not looked so sublimely smug before. Something was wrong; something stank with a lingering smell, sniffed but not forgotten, tucked away in the hurly-burly which followed. Two thieves, four burglars, one rapist committed for trial, a posse of football hooligans up for affray, five neighbourhood fights to be bound over, three arguments between prosecutor and the clerk of the court, one with the magistrate, but none with the defence, and Helen was out of there, back to the office at a canter. Racing up the stairs with a bright coat flying over funeral black, unselfconsciously elegant and consciously impatient with the world. On a good day, Miss West could move mountains. On a bad day, she blew up tunnels with herself inside.

There was no sign of Rose. Off sick, someone said, she'd phoned in with a cough. Helen paused only to hope that Rose was not really sick but having a lovely time with Michael. Her own work ethic had taken a battering recently, she wasn't going to impose it on someone with such a meagre salary. There was also a big distraction. Notices on desks. All professional staff to go to Redwood's office at four o'clock. Helen went out to find Dinsdale, merely for the effect of his smile.

'Panic attacks,' he said languidly, waving his own, photocopied notice. 'He gets them on Mondays.'

'What's it all about? He hates meetings.'

'Don't we all? It's all about missing cases. Something of the kind, anyway. You know that débâcle with poor Riley last week? No, you wouldn't, you weren't in on Friday.' It was said neutrally, but still made her feel like a defector who had left the family behind. 'Anyway, I told him about it on Friday evening, which he was quite content to ignore, but there's been a bit of a stink. Not from public authorities or the police, I hasten to add. Only from the solicitor who was hired to represent Riley's drink driver, but was sacked by the client before the last hearing, on the basis of the client saying, I quote "it was all fixed". The solicitor's furious at the loss of a private fee. He wants to know if it was "fixed". He goes to the same golf club as Redwood. That's what it's all about.'

'Drink driving?'

'No, suburban golf.'

'So what's this meeting for? Increased handicaps?'

'Something like that,' murmured Dinsdale as they dawdled towards Redwood's throne room. 'Sorry about the weekend by the way. I gather your man was back.'

Dinsdale could always make her blush. So did the mention of Bailey.

'Pity,' she said lightly. 'Another time, if your harem lets you go.'

The door to Redwood's room was open: the meeting was already called to order. This is my life, thought Helen, should I ever want to progress in it. It will owe all the success in terms of status to being good at meetings, attending courses, bullshitting selection boards. It will have nothing to do, as Redwood's elevation does not, with being a good advocate and a creature of passionate common sense. Nothing to do with falling over in the course of justice, spending days on your knees looking for paper. She looked round the room at the others, seeking a mirror to her frequent frustration. The set of gargoyles looked meek and expectant. Optimism shone on their little faces, all but Dinsdale, who had the serene look of the respectful, ever-amused, ever-removed cynic. Redwood looked as if he were about to embark on a witch hunt. Normal.

'It has come to my attention,' he began, portentously, 'that we may be losing files from the office.'

This opening was greeted with hoots of laughter, some loud, some smothered. Lost files, lost cases and causes and egg all over advocates' faces was not exactly news. It might have been ironic if he had not looked so thunderous. The laughter died away. Aren't you a little worm, thought Helen, who had laughed loudest of all. Redwood raised a hand like a vicar stressing a point in a sermon, a gesture both of blessing and cursing.

'Be quiet. Is this the way you behave in court?'

A long time since you've been to court, sir, we laugh all the time.

'Someone has been interfering with the computer . . .' again, more smothered laughter. It sounded indecent.

'. . . and emptying it of vital information,' he continued. 'About ten cases appear to have been syphoned away, quite deliberately.'

'The evidence?' Dinsdale's voice, calm and interested. 'Does the evidence point to a culprit?'

Redwood looked at him meaningfully, man to man.

'Yes, Mr Cotton, we have a very good idea, from purely preliminary investigations, I hasten to add. We have one absentee from the whole staff, one only today. Of course, the nonprofessionals are not at this meeting, they will have their own, and I think we may know who . . . The whys, apart from some kind of vendetta, have yet to be established. Obviously we cannot ask the persons who have managed to get themselves acquitted, and we don't want to involve the police who have no powers in these circumstances to do more than ask for voluntary responses . . .'

'You've got to try. Even if it's entirely off the record, you've got to try. I'll try, if you like.' Helen's voice. Riley was nodding. He was remembering his own drunk driver of last week, the smugness of the man. Helen was remembering hers of this morning. Bribery and corruption? Mistake? Redwood thinks he knows who. She knew in a flash which way this meeting was going.

'I needed you here to discuss,' Redwood was saying, 'alternative methods of record keeping. New forms are being prepared. To be submitted to me, each week. With your diaries.'

Helen remembered him looking at desks late on a Friday night. She found herself on her feet.

'You think it's Rose, don't you?'

'. . . She's off today, was off Friday, has refused to leave an address . . . knows how to work the machine, spends a lot of time in the basement . . .' Redwood was saying it like a litany.

'And is down with the lowest paid and the easiest to sack, so that's convenient, isn't it?' Helen was shouting. The others shifted in their seats with embarrassment. Redwood was shouting back.

'She's the only one who stays late. The only one—'

'With an attitude problem? OK.' Her voice had gone down an octave: Redwood was momentarily relieved. Then it rose again, not quite as high but still rising. 'What about her notebooks?'

'What notebooks?'

'You don't know? Well, they're the sort of thing you might collect on a Friday night, if you happened to be tidying up,' she hinted broadly. Redwood had the grace to pause. 'Anyway,' Helen continued, 'anyone can get in here. My friend got in here, yesterday; so did I, just by flashing plastic, all of us here know how easy that is, apart from you. And it isn't Rose. If it's anyone at all.'

Helen sat down to refuel. She wasn't finished yet. Dinsdale looked discomfited. 'Steady on,' he murmured in her ear. The proximity of his shoulder to hers was disturbingly public. 'Steady what?' she hissed, recoiling from his reservation. Now all she noticed was the perfection of his hands which she did not want to restrain her.

The room, with its draughts and floor-length windows, was alive with little sights and sounds. The wind outside, rattling those inside, the muted buzz of shocked conversation, Helen's red cheeks, Redwood's sudden, public paleness. So that was what they were, those notebooks, bottom drawer left, next to one of his feet. He could not move. He had amassed them on Friday-night perambulations without any notion of their significance.

'OK,' said Helen, conciliatory but ominous. 'No meeting with the clerks, no stones thrown without evidence, OK? And if there's a real suggestion of malpractice, the police can investigate us just as they would anyone else. And no more forms to make up for lousy security, all right? We're already sinking in paper.'

'Thank you,' said Redwood frostily. 'Now, unless, there are other comments, I suggest we postpone this meeting for a day or two . . .'

There were other suggestions. There was a chorus of complaints, a comparing of notes, a vote of confidence for prickly Rose Darvey, who treated them all with equal rudeness and served them well.

Dinsdale was silent, apparently vastly amused. Helen found herself irritated; all he could do was sit with one elegant hand fingering his silk tie. True to form, nothing emerged from the meeting; no master plan, no conclusions, nothing except an adjournment for a week and their silence requested. And Redwood's agreement that Helen West could keep Rose Darvey strictly at her own side, until the next meeting.

'That man,' she said, striding away with Dinsdale, 'needs a sign on the door asking you to knock so he has time to jump into a cupboard in case you ask him to make a decision.'

'Could you do better?' said Dinsdale lightly.

'No, probably not,' said Helen cheerfully. 'But it would be different.'

Cheerfulness to this degree often followed the catharsis of anger. It always made Bailey deeply suspicious.

Helen went to the clerks' room, casually. They were ill at ease, full of speculation and her grinning presence was reassuring.

'Anyone know Rose's address? Thought I'd send her some flowers.'

One of them gasped in astonishment; flowers for Rose, after what she'd said, but no, they didn't know. They all knew vaguely where one another lived, but names and street numbers, no. Helen phoned PC Michael's station from the privacy of her room, he would surely know where Rose lived, but Michael, she was told, was also off sick. The reserve officer was cagey, but a little verbal bullying and stressing of urgency revealed more. An accident, Whittington Hospital. Too bad if Michael didn't want visitors: if he couldn't worry about Rose, she must.

On Ward C, Michael Michael was sweating. My, haven't you been lucky, they said, if you'd been less fit, that beam would have killed you. But you've only got a hairline crack in your great big head, ha, ha, plus a face which would not look good in a mug shot at the moment, and a broken arm. No, you can't go home, not yet. The manic cheerfulness of doctors depressed him. He didn't feel lucky, he felt indescribably foolish. Flowers from Mum and Dad in Catford, fruit, food and forbidden alcohol from his relief, a trickling of cards so far, all with rude messages, winks and conspicuous attention from the rare nurses, a headache fit to blind and a heartache of worse intensity. What would Rose think? What had she been thinking? He could no more have told the wretched Williams, or Singh, or any of the others he knew well enough, to go round to Rose's place, knock on the door and give her a message. Faced with such a caller, she would think she had been placed back in the section house pot.

Michael persuaded a nursing auxiliary to try her at work. Not there, said the auxiliary, apologetic for not being able to aid the

course of romance. When told there was someone to see him, his
heart had leapt against his ribs, then descended.

The woman was slim, dark and smart, a professional-looking
stranger with a nice face, but she was not Rose Darvey.

'Don't worry,' said Helen, presenting a dozen white daffodils.
'This isn't a social call.'

When she left, he felt better.

Rose Darvey's mind had crawled up and down walls for thirty-
six hours. Late on Saturday night when the disappointment was
becoming terminal and she was sick with the cigarettes that her
body loathed but her misery craved, she was stationed by her
bedroom window when she heard a panda car cruising down the
street. By that time the bitter hurt was belly side up and beyond
logic. Oh, go on, she'd told herself earlier, he only half promised,
no more than that, and was not comforted, then the sound of an
engine sent her rushing to the light switch to turn her bedroom
into darkness. If it was him, she would be out, teach him a lesson,
make him worried; who did he think he was, that Michael? Half
of her knew, even as she resumed the watching by the window,
that she would never keep it up. That if he got out of the car and
rang the bell, she would fling open the window and yell at him,
or run down to the door, whichever movement occurred first,
but she could not have let him go. The other girls, with their new
friendliness, told her what a find Michael was. 'Yeah?' she shrugged.

They went out, she stayed in, couldn't bear to step out of doors
in case she missed him, waited in silence with her mounting anger
and misery. Gran was forgotten, except for a furious guilt about
how she had made a mess of that longed-for reunion, but then what
did she expect? She always screwed up everything, every bloody
thing. Rushing Gran home, so she could be back here to wait for
nothing but this agonizing pain, making her feel as if she were some
live specimen, with a spike through her head and a chain to the
wall, confined to the circuit of her room, tethered, pacing, wincing.

On Sunday she rallied, after furious dialogues with herself had
somehow induced a sort of sleep. She thought briefly of all the
reasons why he might not have arrived the night before. None of
them bore close inspection.

'Did he turn up? Mr Gorgeous, I mean?'

'Naa. He phoned though,' she lied. 'Extra duties, he said. Probably
a football match.'

'What, at the stadium? But they didn't play last night. At least I don't think—'

'What do you know?'

She cleaned her room again, singing to pretend she hadn't been found out and that within this little, expedient household she was becoming ever more the freak. Out to an off-licence with her much abused credit card to buy beer for the girls and enough booze for herself to induce a total anaesthetic. On Sundays, they went home to see mothers: complicated journeys to Crystal Palace and Neasden which made a trip to the Gulag sound easy, the way they described it. They would come back grumbling about nagging and trains while she died of envy.

Sunday, early evening, the phone rang. She launched herself towards it.

'Hallo, is that Rose baby? How ya doing?'

'Who's that?'

'Paul. Paul Williams. You remember me, surely? Police *Constable* Paul Williams. Thought you might like a drink.'

'Who was it you said you wanted?' She put on her haughtiest mimic, trying to sound like Dinsdale Cotton. The odious voice on the other end paused, briefly.

'Aw, come on, Rose, I know it's you.' He knew it from the diary taken from Michael's pocket as they looked for the address of his next of kin. 'What about that drink, then? Aren't Sundays boring?'

'Not that boring,' said Rose.

The room swam as she crashed the receiver back on the kitchen wall. Little shit. Cheap jack little shit with a cock like a thin banana. Shit on Michael too. They all did that. Passed you along. Left you wide open for your big daddy to find you, with your legs spread open on a slab. Get your knickers off, Rose.

Sunday night, bad coughing. Glazed over a TV film, beer, martini. Monday morning, decided she couldn't show this face to the world, wouldn't be able to keep up the façade and crack jokes all day. Lay down, got up, walked around, afflicted less by Michael than all the dirty laundry of her grubby little life and the self-disgust which went with it. Shadow play, distraction as the light fell and the condensation formed at the window, and she had nothing to do, the phone was silent and she felt dead. Shadow play, lying alone with the second tumbler of stuff, her back uncomfortable against all her teddy bears and dolls, her fingers making eagles on the far wall. Then a bunny rabbit with waggling ears. Then a house with a roof you could turn inside out by inverting your hands against the light. Here's the church, here's the steeple: open it up and you see the people.

'No, I liked the bunny rabbit,' she heard herself saying, nervously. 'Give me the bunny rabbit. Or the kangaroo, jumping, I don't mind.'

'You don't mind?' Daddy's voice. 'You don't mind? Here, feel this.'

'Don't, Daddy, please don't, don't, don't, I don't like it, please don't, Granny wouldn't like it.'

'Granny says it's fine, it's good for little girls, to look after their daddy . . .'

'Don't, Daddy, please don't. I'll scream, Daddy.'

'You wouldn't do that, now would you? What's the matter? It's only my little lollipop.'

'I don't want it, Daddy, I'll scream.'

'No you won't. Who'll hear? Just put it in your mouth. No harm . . .'

'I can't.'

'Yes you can. No, put it in the other place. You want Daddy to love you, don't you? Then I'll make you a bunny rabbit.' That sound of desperate breathing he made as they lay on his bed, she sticky, weeping.

And on, and on. The shadow play for two years: pain and soreness and itching and crying and never telling, in case she should lose him. Only her and Dad against the world. Then a pause for two whole years in which she could not quite stop looking round all the time. Then again, with a different violence when she was nearly fourteen, still a child, but old enough to know and to fight. Hit him with the kitchen knife. Trying to cut at Daddy's lollipop because she could not bear it any more, didn't care if she lived or died, carving a loop in his stomach instead. Blood all over the lino on the kitchen, that look of hatred on his face, Mum coming home.

Daddy said she tempted him, she was the devil. No wonder no one could love her. They would want to stone her, he had shouted, like they did in the Bible. Outside the city walls. Stone her to death and leave her there.

Rose came round, sweating. You could always relive being fucked by Daddy.

A shower of gravel hit the bedroom window. Small stones stinging the glass. Rose had been transfixed by her hands twisting themselves into shadows against the far wall which she watched like one waiting for an omen. She swung her feet off her bed as another shower followed the first. An alarming sound, one which should have had her hiding, but so novel in its peremptory summons for attention that hope sprang, then faded as she heard someone shouting her name. It came from the great distance of the street below. The voice sounded like something from the penumbra of the same dream, Gran's voice, scolding to make her achieve.

Down in the street, Helen waited for a response. She had aimed for the only window showing light and now she leant against the front door. When it opened fast, she stumbled and both of them swore.

'What the hell . . . ? What the fuck do you think you're doing, chucking things at people's windows? Oh, for Christ's sake, come in. You doing welfare as well as law, now? Come in.'

Once the foundations of defence showed cracks, it was easy to let them crumble further as long as a bedrock was left. Rose took Helen indoors because they had found each other in a pregnancy clinic and they both liked shopping. Tea was made. The kitchen was immaculate; somewhere in two day's meandering, Rose's small amount of surplus energy had taken a domestic direction. Helen opened the fridge to find milk to go with tea and found four cans of lager, diet coke, jam, low-calorie margarine, all the typical foods for three girls slimming or slumming.

'Now, Rose. What's up?'

The child shrugged, desperately relieved to see another face but trying not to let it show.

'If you're ill . . . you don't look too hot, can I contact anyone for you? Or will I do?'

'I'm not that ill. It's just this cough. No, like I told you, no one to tell. No mum and dad, no thanks.'

'Fine, but you might like to put your coat on and go and see your beloved if you aren't at death's door. He's champing at the bit, but leave it for half an hour, then I'll give you a lift. His mum and dad were arriving as I left, and he's a bit rocky. Are we talking about the same bloke? Michael.'

'What? Oh, him.'

'In hospital, you dope. Accident on duty, Saturday; something fell on his head, but part of the headache seems to be worrying about you.'

'Worried!' Rose burst. 'He only gives away my phone number and tells all his mates where to find me! Fat lot he cares!'

Helen considered this. There was something pathological about Rose's secrecy; Michael had hinted as much and it was obvious anyway. Takes one to know one, Helen thought. She knew about secrecy, but not quite to this degree.

'He didn't give anything away, at least as far as he knows. Maybe he rambled in his sleep, he was knocked out, see? Men never do have control over anything important. On the other hand, the lads might well have gone through his pockets. Anyway, he told me he couldn't send anyone round with a message, because you'd think he was "throwing you back in the pond". Does that make sense?'

It did. Rose's face was undergoing a gradual transformation, from pale to pink, from pinched old woman to glorious juvenile, until finally, she smiled. There is nothing in the whole wide world, Helen thought, quite as powerful as a beautiful girl, so powerful, it was as well so few of them understood it. As suddenly as she smiled, Rose slumped again. Not back to where she had been, but halfway up.

'I bet he doesn't really want to see me. He thinks I'm a mess.'

She pulled out a cigarette and lit it, grimacing with the coughing. 'And he's right, I am a mess. A right, fucking mess.'

Helen took this literally, quite deliberately.

'If I looked as gorgeous as you on a day's sick and a broken heart, I'd be out there dancing a tango.'

'Not that kind of mess. The other kind.'

'Look, do you think you could give me a clue? Just a small one, no need to go mad. Such as why you're so cagey about your address?'

Rose twisted her hands together, turned her fingers inside out. Here's the church, here's the steeple . . . She looked at them, funny looking mitts, and sat on them, fixing her eyes on the smoke from the abandoned cigarette.

'It's my dad. It's all his fault, no, all mine, in a way. He keeps looking for me.' The rest emerged in so sudden a rush it was as if she had recently swallowed an emetic. 'You see, what happened before I left home, with my mum, well I had a go at him. With a knife, as it happens. A big kitchen knife. We borrowed it from Gran . . .' Rose added inconsequentially, the voice trailing away, hidden in a lunge towards an uncomfortable drag on her cigarette.

'Oh yes?' Helen said conversationally. 'What had he done to deserve that? He must have done something.'

Rose was silent.

131

'I once bit a bloke,' Helen volunteered. 'On the arm, not the balls or anything, but it wasn't a nibble either. I was like a Rottweiler. I think it bled a lot, but then he was trying to kill me. I often wonder if he would have done it. Probably not.'

Rose's eyes widened.

'That's how I got this,' Helen continued idly, gesturing to the thin line of scar which graced the width of her forehead. 'So I reckon he did me more damage than I did him. I hate that boy. I wouldn't have bitten him for nothing, but it was the best thing I could have done.'

'Why?' Rose was incredulous.

'It made me realize afterwards that I wasn't a total victim. I wasn't exactly brave, but I wasn't helpless either. It's the sort of thing that stops you losing your mind.'

The tannin in the tea was as sour as the memory. Silence fell at the kitchen table.

'I thought you led such sheltered lives, you lawyers,' Rose said finally, a shade mocking.

'Sheltered? Oh yes. By and large I have, we do. Anyway, what had your father done?'

The barriers came down on Rose's confiding. Enough was enough.

'All right, as long as you know I'm on your side.' Helen put down her mug and grinned the grin which went from ear to ear. 'I mean, we'd better be friends, hadn't we? We're probably the only women we both know who go round knifing and biting people.'

Rose snorted with laughter and stubbed out her cigarette with an angry passion. She spoke only after she had ground it into a saucer and watched its demise with apparent fascination.

'My dad's looking for me 'cos he wants to pay me back. He writes to me. He writes when he finds out where I am. So far he's always found where I am, someone says or whatever. I thought it was safer in a way to come back closer, London's so big. Anyway, so far, it works. Go to work for a big office. I love that place: it's safe, you can get lost in it. Only I can't stand the dark anywhere else, and my dad wants to have me back and pay me back. I can't fight him any more. I can't.'

With the last, shivery smoke from the cigarette, the confidences had now ended along with the tea. Helen sensed a mere scratching of the surface but there could be no more talking without both of them having something to hold; tea, food, anything. No acting without a cue, no speech without props, something to do with the hands.

One more try as she got up and put the mugs in the pristine sink. 'Have you told Michael anything about this?'

Another mug crashing against the first, both of them standing, which made it easier.

'No. I sort of tried, last Friday, when I thought I saw my dad – I'm always seeing my dad, but then I thought, I've only just started with Michael, I can't, can I? Not about knives and all. Couldn't blame him, could you? Him being a copper and all.'

'Oh, I don't know. I'd say, just take a deep breath, you know, before you jump in the deep end. Got my car outside.'

Beyond the door, Rose thought, what an ugly, battered, old car with a twisted bumper, a few dents and winter filth an inch thick from the frost turned mud. Someone had written on the boot, 'Also available in red'. Rose saw this and another of her perceptions about the lifestyles of lawyers hit the pavement.

'Oh, something I ought to mention,' said Helen airily, fumbling with her car keys, using them on the door like a knuckle duster. 'There's a rumour about someone stealing files from the office. Probably nothing, but some people are having their jobs rejigged in a Redwood efficiency drive until they find out a bit more about it. So you're on court duties, with me, like it or not. OK?' The door yanked open as if it was yawning.

'Do you know,' said Rose, looking at the litter on the inside of the car with fascination, 'I didn't know Michael was working on Saturday. I thought he had a day off.'

'Listen,' said Helen, lurching them down the road, 'let me tell you something important. If you're going to hang round with a copper, get a copy of his duty roster. You've got to know when they're working. Otherwise, there's no controlling them at all.'

Rose thought, Miss W. looks like a funny monkey with a grin like that.

Oh Lord, make us not afraid of the dark.

CHAPTER TEN

The rain came down on Monday, Tuesday and Wednesday morning, driven by a buffeting wind, obliterating any view. The two days went by in a fight with the elements. There was a train strike.

Logo lay in bed halfway through the week, thinking idly about which of his half-clean clothes he should wear today. The texture of the sheets on which he lay reminded him of his own neglect since his feet lay in gritty socks on a gritty patch of sheet. He had never been so lazy in the days of Mrs Logo's sloppy dominance, but the abandonment by women had come to equal dirt and somehow, in the last three weeks, he was even dirtier. The Bible, through which he flipped for something to do with his cold hands as well as to search for passages to soothe his soul, was symptomatic of the change. The pages were as rippled as the surface of a pond and still smelt of stale whisky.

Deuteronomy, chapter twenty-two, verse twenty-three. 'If a damsel that is a virgin be betrothed . . . and a man find her in the city and lie with her; Then ye shall bring them both out into the gate of the city, and ye shall stone them with stones that they die . . . the damsel because she *cried* not . . .'

He flipped back through the wavy pages, some of them stuck, so that he could read one side but not the verses which followed, which suited him fine. It was the words he wanted, not the sense. Leviticus, chapter eighteen. 'The nakedness of thy father's wife thou shalt not uncover: she is thy mother . . . The nakedness of thy sister, the daughter of thy father or daughter of thy mother, or of thy daughter's daughter, even their nakedness thou shalt not uncover, for their nakedness is thine own . . .'

No mention of a man's daughter, or not as such. Maybe that was over the page. Logo laughed and twiddled his toes inside his socks. Then back again to Deuteronomy. 'If a man find a damsel that is a virgin, which is not betrothed, and lay hold on her, and lie with her, and they be found: Then the man that lay with her shall give unto the damsel's father fifty shekels of silver.'

He sniggered. *If* they be found . . . that was what it was worth. Logo swung out of bed and attempted to sing. The damage to his vocal cords did not prevent sound but there was still a temporary dearth of music from that source. While shaving, he looked at his face in the mirror with grim satisfaction and smiled at it. The left profile was the best to present to the magistrates this morning; it was every colour of the rainbow, ranging from a sick yellow to a violent indigo, one malevolent-looking eye half open.

' "And I will set my face against you, they that hate you shall reign over you: and you shall flee when none pursueth you," ' he murmured to his mirror where the specks of toothpaste, soap, and hair all but obscured his own image and hid the grubbiness of a once white shirt collar. He shaved in part, leaving patches of beard to add to the effect.

A grave had been dug in the graveyard yesterday. Ask not for whom the bell tolls. The diggers had waved Logo away but he lingered, looking at the fog while they ignored him but allowed him to eavesdrop. One of them was saying how the dead woman was from Legard Street. The detail lodged in Logo's mind as he waved to their broad backs and passed that other grave which he saluted in acknowledgement. The knowledge remained with him now as he picked up his bail notice, left the house quietly and took the bus to court. He didn't want Margaret ever since she'd shouted: she had joined the enemy.

The court foyer was full, but then it always was. Dense with smoke under the no smoking signs, floor pitted, plastic chairs full of draped backs in attitudes of nonchalance or anxiety. Many sat with their families, drooping under the pressure of the nearest and dearest before whom it was so hard to tell the truth because of what they would think. Logo was an old hand, absorbed in one amused glance the nagging and the embarrassment, the loneliness and the boasting. He always stood himself; no other position enabled him to watch the human tide of misery, fear, jubilation, bravado and sick jokes, twisting to observe each innuendo from his own slouched superiority. People were uncomfortable with those who would not sit.

Out of the corner of his eye, he saw Helen West, hidden behind paper, nursing an armful of files which she held against one hip curved to meet the load, swaying along like an elegant but listing ship and reminding him of a mother with a child which had grown too large to carry. As he saw her he remembered to avoid the challenge of the eyes, ducked his head right down to waist level and began a close examination of the fingers on one hand while the other covered his face. Looking up through his spread fingers, he continued to watch as she stopped at the door of court three, readjusting her burden, and although he knew he would not be facing a trial today, only a remand on further bail for a trial time to be fixed, and although he knew for once he was innocent of his trumped-up charge, he was unaccountably afraid. Last time he had seen her, she had been running scared, driving her car like a dodgem at a fairground, now she had eyes like melting ice. He kept his own down, skulking against the wall for cover, waiting for the bellow of his name.

After an hour of waiting, in which he recited in whispers the Bible passages which came to memory, plus the hymns he knew he could not sing, the fat usher, in a gown which reached the ground, called for him. He smiled at her, but she flounced away and let the swing-door flap back against him and his bruises even as he followed her bottom into the fray.

Somehow the lights in court were loud; stepping into the dock was like going on a stage where the footlights dazzled. All those present, clerk, magistrates, lawyers, shuffled paper for what seemed an eternity, only a few seconds, he realized later, seconds that seemed to last for an hour each. He could not assume an act, for once; he could not even look around and assess the weaknesses in his audience, gauge when to burst into song. Behind him was the public gallery, full of idlers looking for a thrill, curious witnesses, people sheltering from the cold, families. None of them was looking out for him: they never were until he entertained them, but all of a sudden, he had no energy for that, no inclination to play the holy fool. Then he saw Helen West's melting eyes upon him, saw the shock, the passing sensation of fear, and then the terrible pity. She was staring at his colours, this woman whom he had loathed through three trials: looking at him without fear or alarm, but with that dreadful, debilitating concern which was worst of all. The clerk yawned, spoke.

'Charged, assaulting a police officer, 31 Jan.' A mumbled formula of words followed. 'Do you plead guilty or not guilty?'

'Not guilty,' he croaked.

The clerk leafed through her diary, a large volume, held so close the pages crept up against her face. 'Remanded to 14 Feb,' she uttered. 'On bail? Valentine's Day,' she sighed with a highly audible breath.

Logo's eyes, shielded for the last hour, began to function again. Saw first but not last, Helen West. 'Wait a minute,' she was saying. 'Can we put this one back? He's charged with assaulting the police, what four days ago? No, five. I'd quite like some information on his injuries,' she turned, apparently panicking in her concern, to the girl who sat behind her. Logo could hear: the magistrates could not.

'This isn't right,' she said, pushing one piece of paper in the direction of the girl. 'This statement of facts doesn't mention injuries. Can you get me his custody record? I need to know how he came by that face.' Helen turned back to the clerk. 'Could we make a few further enquiries, please? Maybe Mr Logo could see the duty solicitor.'

'Sit at the back, would you, Mr Logo?'

He moved as the girl behind Helen West moved. An angular child with slicked-back hair he had noticed from his vantage point, before she ran from the court with the speed of a frightened cat. Logo knew her at once. He reached a hand towards her as she passed: they almost brushed each other, as close as a shadow, breathing in each other's faces. He sat silently behind the dock, looked at the scuff marks in the wood, filled with incredible jubilation. God was good to him: what was lost was now found. Found on Friday night; seen through a window, a dazzling vision of beauty viewed by the beast pawing at the glass. Seen now, sensed, smelt, dragged within inches by the hand of God. Logo did not resent his bruises, no longer minded that searing look of pity from Helen West, the look which deprived him of any power he would ever have to make her afraid again. Logo had just seen his daughter, heard her gasp and watched her run. Enid, named after the rose, making his thin blood race and his heart pound, the same ache of desire gnawing in his groin, the same fury, the same hatred. His daughter. He sat unsteadily, weak with joy.

The court scene broke into fragments. Ten minutes, please. Footsteps went by him in the direction of both doors; one downstairs to the cells, the other to the foyer, led by the big-bottomed usher, a crowd in search of coffee, cigarettes, clients. Logo stayed as he was, dreaming. Gradually, sounds of a muted conversation from behind the cell door, penetrated into his dreaming

'What's the point of putting it off? You say the arresting officer had no injuries . . . I *know* this man hasn't got the habit of violence, never has . . . and he looks like a punching bag, so who assaulted who? No one's even saying he fell over. No, I'm not going to run a case we can't win. OK, fine.'

Footsteps back inside. A slight smell of perfume. Helen West's cool voice.

'Mr Logo?'

As if she didn't know who he was.

'We'll be offering no evidence, this time.'

'That's good of you,' he mumbled, the emphasis of his irony lost in the croak. 'I came off worst, I can tell you.'

'Yes,' she said quietly. 'I think you did. Do you want to see a solicitor?'

'No.' Humbly. 'Will you tell me something, though?'

She paused, for once anxious to please.

'Does that girl, the one behind you in court, work with you?'

'Yes,' said Helen, surprised. 'In our office. Why?'

'Nothing.'

She did not stand close, he noticed. Either the unwashed hair on his head or the livid face deterred her, but he could smell the pity in the same way he could smell her cleanliness, and only the pity stank. He kept his head down: the footsteps went away and he heard the shuffling of paper, the hum of the air-conditioning and the people coming back. All of them but Eenie. His case dismissed, Logo did not linger in the foyer with the dead coffee cups and the overflowing fag ends. There was no point. He would never find her there.

Out in the fog he would find her. Vengeance is mine, says the Lord. Are you guilty or not, my child? Yes, you are the guilty one.

★

138

'Rose! What happened to you? Why didn't you come back for the rest of the list? How do you think you're going to learn anything?'

Helen West was extremely angry, but since she was also irritated with the nerves which arrived as soon as she doubted her own impetuous wisdom, the anger lacked force. In particular, fury against individuals could not be sustained for long, any more than she could sustain sulking. So what? Rose had been sent on an errand, had looked at her as if she had been mad to issue that particular order, had gone from the court, done the necessary in fetching the policeman responsible in double-quick time, and then disappeared. Did it matter? No, not really. Before that, she had been a perfect mother's little helper, interested and industrious, a luxury, if a mite hyperactive this morning. What infuriated Helen at the moment was not so much Rose's disappearance from half-past eleven in the morning until one, but her own reactions and abreactions to Logo. How could she ever have found him sinister? Seeing that messed-up face, and succumbing against all the odds, to that little cancer of pity she thought had died. All these times, knowing he was bad and dying to get him, only to throw in the towel at the first sign of blood. He'd be grinning and singing all the way home and she would be in trouble. Rose was shifty, staring at the wall, her skin whiter than the scuffed paint.

'Why didn't you come back?' Helen asked again, far less icily. 'Did you by any chance spot a friend on the premises?' She and Rose had been getting on well; a little teasing was allowed.

'I was sick,' Rose murmured, still whiter than paper. 'Very sick.' Helen was immediately full of concern.

'Oh, Rose, you idiot, what am I to do with you? Why didn't you say?'

'It's all right,' said Rose, shrugging, but without the more familiar insolence. She looked small, weak and defeated, a persona Helen neither liked nor approved. Her own anger was finally converted into puzzlement.

'Why sick? It can't be . . . You never did look after that cough, you've still got it, you make yourself sick trying to keep it down and you don't eat. For Christ's sake, do you want to go home?'

It was brisk enough to help. Rose shook herself. No, it did not do to hide in the lavatory, any more than it would have done now to go home, or anywhere else alone; better stay with the pack.

'I'm much better now. Sorry. Next time I'll send you in a message by fucking pigeon.' That was more like the usual Rose. Helen grinned.

Rose continued. 'What happened then with, with . . .' She waved a languid hand as if unable to remember the name, 'Him? Logo?'

'My *bête noire*? Oh, I don't know. Think I did the wrong thing as usual, offered no evidence. After all this time. But there's something so fishy about a statement of facts which doesn't mention injuries, not with a bloke who isn't violent.' Rose began to cough, violently.

'Are you all right?' There was a nod and the colour had turned from white to pink, a spreading blush of relief. Helen regarded that as a sign of health and a licence to continue in a self-indulgent vein.

'I mean, what do you think? Do you know, I've hated that little hymn-singing man every time I've come across him, but today? Well today, I just knew it was all wrong. He didn't assault anyone, he wouldn't, couldn't. He's just pathetic. And do you know what? He wanted to know where you worked. Another fan. I don't know how you cope.'

Rose looked up, between coughs, the pink complexion verging on a sickly purple. 'And you told him, I suppose?'

Helen had no reason for the lie, but it came forth unaided anyway.

'Course I didn't. You could have been the usher's cousin for all he knew.' Rose relaxed and Helen felt a sense of shame as acute as it was undiagnosed.

'What you need,' she said, leading the way, 'is some food.'

Bailey's palliative, she thought. He may know something I don't.

Margaret fussed. First she bothered and after that she fussed, a process which meant everything took longer, slowing down into a crawl of non-achievement. She would walk into a room, in search of something such as a pen or a piece of knitting, forget on the threshold what it was she had come for, see something in need of a dust, go back to fetch the duster and forget halfway back why it was she was aiming for the cupboard. Concentration on anything was limited to thirty seconds: she would end up with something in her hands, looking at it, puzzled, her sense of priorities shot to pieces. The condition repeated itself into a hundred meaningless errands, and endless dithering from room to room until the whole place became an ice rink of silly exhaustion. Should she seek out Logo? Her ally, friend, adopted son, whom she was betraying? Should she, on the other hand, deliver the flowers she had bought for Sylvie's grandmother, or do that later? Should she press her clothes for meeting Eenie tomorrow? Would that help? All day she dawdled, until the tiredness finally made for clarity. Take flowers to Sylvie's house. *Then* press clothes. On the way out or back, put a note on Logo's door, saying would he please come in for tea or something. Confine her shopping to the expensive corner shop today, simply because it was the nearest, even though each time she bought whisky in there, she blushed for shame. And oh yes, stoke the fire. Make the man welcome, mend fences. Hadn't seen him for days.

Once established in their right order, the tasks became simpler. One hour all told. The flowers were accepted on the doorstep with murmured thanks but without, thank God, an invitation indoors, even though Sylvie was screaming. Margaret was served her half-bottle of whisky by a woman who smiled as if she was dispensing lemonade, and at home, the fire burned briskly against the fog which had followed the rain outside. The note still pinned on Logo's door looked friendly. Five in the evening and the day still hers. Margaret felt suddenly at ease. What would be would be, with Eenie, with Logo, with all the world, now smoothed by the fog which took her back to a safer childhood. Fog and yellow smog in London, that sense of safety when you reached your own front door and banged it shut and waited for tea and argument. Far worse fog than this gentle mist which deterred no one from movement, but gave a gentle glow to the street lamps and made her imagine that each lit window hid a happy, laughing family behind itself. She was suddenly at peace, a great, grand peace.

I am resigned, Margaret thought, to the occasional sweetness of life. I *love* this room, but how I managed to clean it today, I shall never know. What a fuss, what a fret to be in, because of what? Because of telling lies to Logo, as if that mattered, lies are as necessary as breathing: they exist to keep us sane. Because of a funny kind of grief about Sylvie's grandmother, although I never knew her, because she is mourned and I shall not be. Margaret sat by her fire and chuckled. No, but I'm not dead yet. Give me my new hip and I shall move, and no, don't be fooling yourself now, that isn't what has stopped you, Margaret, it's your own silly willpower and being a coward and not wanting to look a fool as you sway along, but if you smell nice and look clean as well as cheerful, nothing else matters.

On that reflection, Margaret went for a wash and change of clothes. She could never change her clothes without washing first. She used Eenie's expensive powder, all over. Life was for living. The speed of her knitting was electric as she sat back in front of her fire; calm carried energy into her fingers which knitted with ineffective speed the sort of sweaters she realized she would hate to wear. The thought made her judder with laughter, but she still went on knitting. Still a fool, Margaret, after all these years. Tomorrow, Eenie and she would really talk, or perhaps they would. Everything took time. She would cope with Logo if he deigned to arrive, oh, for heaven's sake, she still loved them both and love conquered all provided you didn't look for reward. When he did knock at the door, she wasn't even surprised, let alone alarmed, and that was before the whisky.

'Oh, it's you, is it?' was all she said, opening the door and turning back to her chair. The one opposite, old and worn with a brash new cushion, welcomed him as if he had not been absent from her company for more days than had ever passed between them before for many a year. He looked terrible: the sight of him shocked her, but she wasn't going to remark on that, not yet anyway.

'Where've you been?' she said, in her familiar tone of scolding and grumbling. 'Thought you were dead.'

He looked at the whisky bottle and the two shining glasses all standing to attention on a lace cloth.

'Dead?' he queried. 'I may as well have been dead, for all you cared.'

'Now, now,' she said placatingly. 'Don't go on. You know you don't really want me banging at your door all hours of the day and night any more than I want you banging at mine when I've got company. But if you needed help, you only had to ask. Get us a drink of that, will you? Stop standing about looking like a lemon.'

He grinned. Like herself, she noticed, he had made a bit of an effort. The shirt was cleaner, the shoes had been rubbed up and down the back of his trousers where streaks of dust showed disarmingly. His face looked frightening, like a hand put through a mangle, but he still had eyes and he still had teeth. Living with the dying as she had done, Margaret had seen worse and she knew Logo's reaction to any kind of pity he had not personally solicited.

'Walk under a bus, did you?' she asked as they sat, facing the fire, each with a huge glass in hand.

'No, it was a train. What do you think?'

They both chuckled silently. 'Hope the other fella looks worse,' said Margaret nonchalantly.

'Oh, she does, *she* does,' said Logo, lingering on the 'she' with deliberate crudeness, then gulping, while Margaret failed to flinch. Instead, she took the proffered cigarette. She thought about lotion for bruises, wondered what she had and calculated at what point she would produce it. They were worrying, those bruises, but not fatal. She could tell the doctors about those bruises and then they might listen. She could tell them he beat his head against walls. They understood real injuries like that, nothing else.

'Has that horrible little girl been round again?'

'She's not horrible. She's just got parents who are trying to do too much. Anyway, you should feel sorry for her. Her granny came on a visit, but she was sick and she died. Awful for them, isn't it?'

'No, not really. People have to die. No work for the grave-diggers, else, is there?' He laughed uproariously. Margaret felt uncomfortable, continued with her knitting, sipped the whisky which he gulped. Half a bottle was not going to go far with him in this mood, but at least he was laughing.

'Guess who I saw today?' Logo's voice was oddly croaky, she noticed, but still loud. 'Just you guess who I saw!'

'God,' she said, knitting faster.

'Oh better than God, much better. More of a goddess. Maybe it was the devil. Sometimes it's difficult to tell. Sometimes the things which look innocent are the opposite, you know? Sometimes something very beautiful has to be wiped out for all the damage it can do. Killed, burned in the fire. Stoned outside the city walls, then burned.' He was murmuring, Margaret growing more and more uncomfortable, but keeping her veneer of placidity with admirable calm, gazing at her knitting for inspiration.

'What are you talking about? Who did you see?'

'Eenie.' He looked at her cunningly. 'You know, Eenie.'

This time she reached for her whisky tumbler and took a gulp as large as his. 'You never did,' she said.

'No,' he answered. 'I never really did. I just thought I did. I just felt her close to me, that's all. I don't suppose you've got anything to eat, have you?'

Margaret relaxed. 'You and your dreaming,' she said equably. 'There's some bread and cheese hanging around. Get it yourself. I'm knitting this sweater for you, you know. When you've got your snack, you can help me make this wool into a ball.'

A wave of noise hit the house, the roar of the football crowd she had seen foregathering as she came home. Not even an irritation any more, nothing to remark upon after all these years, less of an event than thunder and less frightening than a storm. Eenie used to complain, but then Eenie had been a difficult child. Margaret remembered Eenie holding a skein of wool between her hands while she wound it into a ball until the child was bored and then they swapped. She could have bought wool in neat, ready-wound packets now, but the cheaper wool on the market still came like this, pieces which had to be joined. Her bag was full of wool from decades ago, unpicked jumpers washed and saved: she remembered old economies. All those tasks were soothing, imposing continuity. Maybe the winding of wool would soothe Logo as well. She sighed, foraged in her deep bag for the next, comforting lump of royal blue, while Logo foraged quietly for cheese. There was a rattle of sound as he looked for a knife. Oh let him be: she was tired, so tired, she closed her eyes for a minute and let another roar from the crowd wash over them. If you listened, the fire made more sound than the rest of the world: it could speak to you, it was company. Maybe all she needed was a cat.

'I think I'll get one,' she said out loud.

'So,' he said, sitting in the chair opposite, picking up the new skein of wool which had fallen into her lap, holding it in one hand while the other held a lump of cheese, cut into a neat square.

'I think I'll get a cat.'

He looked at her with an expression of sad disgust, the look she might have given to a damaged city pigeon, some poor earthbound piece of vermin.

'Help me wind the wool, will you?'

'I can't. It'll stick to me, my wrists, they're all sore. Look.' He held them up.

'What's wrong with them? I can only see dirty tidemarks.'

With a lightning movement, he sprang towards her and stuffed the square of cheese into the mouth which was opening to speak. Two ounces of solid, sticky, soap-like cheddar lodged with violence between her gums. Margaret spluttered, tried to spit it out, but he held her hair and put his palm over her mouth. She tried to chew and swallow, thrashed with her arms, dug her nails into his wrist, her eyes bulging and her face changing colour, until he relented and stood back. Margaret coughed, disgorged the cheese, continued coughing, supporting herself on the arms of the chair,

144

staring wildly, trying to rise. Logo patted her on the back, firmly but kindly. Then he squatted at her feet, picked up the skein of wool he had dropped, fingered it.

'A pullover for me, Granny? Now whoever asked you to do that? I didn't. I wouldn't ask you for anything, not now. You knew where she was all the time, didn't you? All the time.'

'Who,' she whispered, massaging her throat, trying to sound calm, croaking as he croaked. 'Logo, stop messing about. Get out of here. I'm too old for horrible games, don't.' Her eyes travelled beyond him to the back of the kitchen and the knife drawer, standing open. Two pieces of paper were on the floor. The remainder of the cheese stood on top of the unit, the piece she had disgorged was on the floor at her feet. Oh dear God, why had she invited him to feed himself and look in the knife drawer? Letters for her eyes only and he had seen them. Logo stood up and ground the cheese into the carpet with his heel.

'You treacherous old cow. You knew when the pair of them were going, you probably helped them plan it, and you didn't tell me. How many letters has Eenie written you then? Keeping you up to date with the news, laughing behind my back, while all the time you pretend to sympathize . . . laughing at me.'

'One letter, Logo, I promise. Only one. One in four years, I promise.'

'You what? Promise! Don't make me laugh. You, knowing where she is, all this time. I bet it was her in here last Friday when you shouted at me to go away. Come on then, Granny, where does she live? Tell me, tell me, tell me,' he was wheedling, kneading her ankle in an attitude of comic begging. Margaret had a brief belief that she might get the situation back under control, then she knew she could not. Ah, the treachery of it: now she had betrayed them all, Logo, his wife, Eenie. She had kept secrets for none of them. The royal blue wool draped over her feet.

'I suppose I should have known. Ever since you got into the house with that child the other week. And went upstairs.' He spoke wistfully, still draping the wool round her puffy ankles.

'Why does it matter so much? Oh dear, stopit, stopit, you idiot, that black eye's gone to your head. Get us another drink, go on. Stop messing.'

It seemed best to treat him as a child, sound like the good-natured scold which had been her second nature, but somewhere in the depth of her fast-beating heart, Margaret knew it was too late. 'I've had one letter from Eenie, ever,' she said querulously. 'And why should it matter if I've been inside your house? Oh, I see.'

The vision of that suitcase at the top of the stairs floated back to her with a memory of her nervousness towards him ever since she had seen it, her lack of friendliness in these last days, all that to fuel their mutual suspicions. 'Tell me,' she said as evenly as she could, 'did she ever come back? Eenie's mum? Did she really just disappear off the face of the earth, just like that? It isn't right, is it?'

The wool was now wound round her ankles, fashioned into a clumsy knot. He had always been clever with pieces of string, clever with his hands, but lazy, preferring games to achievements, not like his daughter. She knew that if she got up now she would fall over and she felt weak at the very thought. Logo sighed.

'Oh yes, she came back. I brought her back, coupla days after, you were out, I know you were, but then she wouldn't tell me where Eenie had gone. I got angry, you see, very angry.'

'Why wouldn't she tell you where Eenie was?'

'To save me from her. Save me from that little temptress who'd eaten up all my goodness, made me lie with her. She gave me the apple and made me eat. She made me fuck her. She made me go to the devil, all on her own. Where does she live, Margaret?'

'No, no, poor child, poor child. Oh no, poor child.' Margaret was weeping, little corners of tears creeping round her bulging eyes.

'Where does she live?' he insisted.

'I don't know, I don't know,' she was shrinking from him.

'What does she look like? Black hair, all smoothed down, with a little plait at the back!'

Margaret screamed. 'What did you do with her, Logo? What did you do with her mother?'

He shook his head sadly. 'Only this. No blood at all. Only this.'

A great roar of victory from the football ground reverberated down the street. He could hear and feel the stamping of feet, the beginning of that swaying singing. It drowned the beginnings of her scream. His hands were round her throat, the thumbs gouging under her chin. Margaret was already weak and panting. She struggled again, vainly, one hand holding a knitting needle jabbing at him, catching him in the stomach, so that he yelped, but held. Her skin was purple, there were strange animal noises emerging from her throat as she went on and on struggling. It seemed endless, ebbing and diminishing. She acquired more vigour to resist after each successive wave of weakness. Then she slumped. He loosened his hands slowly, sensing a trick. Then dived quickly into her knitting bag, pulled out another hank of wool, put it round her neck almost reverently, twisted it in his fist behind and turned it. His hands slipped on the wool, felt hot and greasy: he realized he was trembling violently. Logo reached for the poker in the fireplace, inserted it into the wool and continued to turn it like a tourniquet. To stop the flow of blood, he thought irrelevantly. Finally there was no sound from her at all.

Logo stood up and drank some more of the whisky. Gradually the trembling ceased. He picked up the letters from the floor, read them again and threw them on the fire. He sized up the body of Margaret in his mind's eye, chuckled briefly and tapped his nose. When you were weak and ill with stitches in your stomach, it was so much harder, but he wouldn't make the same mistakes as last time, waiting until the limbs were stiff. He might have to wait to travel, surely the match was almost ended, half an hour to clear the ground, they were so good at it these days, then he could travel with his burden.

He pulled her from the chair by the ankles, then dragged her by the armpits to the kitchen door. She was the size of a bird, her blouse riding up to show smooth, white skin grazing on the floor. Outside was her chariot, lying on one side. First he took the blunt end of his axe and hit her elbows and knees scientifically: he had thought long and hard about this. Then he pushed her into the trolley, still warm, still malleable, but it was difficult. Finally, with a great heave, he managed to turn the trolley upright on the third attempt. All this took a while. In the meantime, crowds passed the bottom of the alleyway, whooping and yelling. He regarded that as encouragement.

Logo covered her head with a piece of black polythene, stuck a shovel down among her ribs. He trundled the trolley down into the street and out, past the little shops on the corner, on to the main road. It was not the route he normally took to work, but he had always found before that the more obvious he was, the less he was noticed. One whole hundred yards of the main road, before he detoured, left then right, into the graveyard, whistling. The ability to whistle always came back after a trauma long before the ability to sing.

Logo found the grave they were digging for the woman in Legard Street this morning. He took the shovel from the trolley, leaving Margaret as dead as she was, and leapt down into the trench. The gravediggers' footsteps were all over. He had brought a torch but did not need it: they were so close to the edge, the street lights would do, and anyway, he did not need to be particular. He had watched enough funerals to know the carelessness of city incarcerations on grey days like tomorrow; no one would notice the faintest signs of his presence tonight. They were buried here without a sense of place: Margaret would like it here. Inside the trench he dug like a demon. Soft, north-London clay, cold but free of frost, turning easily. No one looked at the sight or the sound in a graveyard late at night. Even the vagrants and the human residue from pubs, the teenage lovers went home at the merest signal of other life in here, drunk or drugged, they were easily spooked. Digging in a cemetery was only a sign of death, consistently ignored.

I do not want to die, Logo thought, but the thought was not unappealing after he had dug down a foot, neat but frantic, sweating in his black clothes. He smelt of powder, not earth, a sickly scent of talc clung to him like a mist; his lapels were white with the sheer moving of her. More powder billowed out of her in a thin mist to complement the fog as he hauled her, all lumpy and bumpy and huge, out of the trolley and into the hole, where she landed with a sound like thunder.

Then she moved: she moaned and moved and lay still. Logo had carried the whisky, took a swig, looked again. Margaret was so obliging. Freed from her polythene, she lay spread-eagled. He jumped on to her spine and with his hands, filled in the shallow covering of earth over her. She was still warm: not even the soil was cold; her presence rendered it tepid. So it was not without regret he covered her and tidied up. There was a certain economy in burying two at a time; they should try it more often. For himself there would be no family vault. They would all lie outside the city walls.

He packed up the trolley with his shovel and wheeled it towards the far gate. On his way, he saluted the same grave he had acknowledged earlier that day. After all, it was not the first time he had made this journey with a similar burden. First his wife, then Margaret, both treacherous. The wife had been heavier, he seemed to remember. Or maybe she was just stiffer and clumsier and he weaker with his stitches and fury. Logo touched his nose. He stank of talcum powder; he would never get it off; it was not fitting for a grave.

CHAPTER ELEVEN

There was something about a hospital ward. Perhaps it was the casualness, as if those who lay in bed had nothing to worry about at all. It reminded Rose of the foyer of the magistrates' court where people sat around as though nothing was going to happen and nothing ever would again. Hospital was all pervading: On Wednesday night Rose suddenly wished she belonged to this small community of souls who knew the manners of the place and revelled in its comparative security. Patients had to work for their visitors, please them in a way which would not have been mandatory at home, but Michael was delighted to see Rose. She looked at him anew, feeling a little jealous. He was like a man holding court in the kingdom of his safety, surrounded by gifts. These tributes to a man much loved by friends and family made her feel small and inconspicuous, a person who did not count.

'Mum and Dad,' he explained sheepishly. 'They keep sending things. I wish they wouldn't. I'm out of here tomorrow and I couldn't have eaten this lot in a month.'

'You'll have to leave them here, then. For the others.' Rose could hear her granny saying that.

She was holding his hand, loosely. With the other arm immobilized in a sling, she merely touched his fingers in a way which would leave him free should he want to scratch, gesture or simply abandon contact. They were both a little awkward; she was tense, full of her own anxiety, but determined not to undermine his optimistic mood. There was so much she wanted to tell him, but none of it was for the ears of a hospital case, the most handsome man in the ward, who looked so solidly secure that she wanted to crawl into his lap and stay with him there for ever, even though no one would believe that he was hers.

'How's the office, then? Still standing?' He was determined not to talk entirely about himself.

'Well, I've scarcely been in there. I expect so. You know what it's like. Another bit falls off every day. They've got notices up about IRA bombs.'

'Not again? I don't know why they bother with the notices. Any old tramp could get into your building.'

'Oh, I don't think so,' Rose said, shocked. She was defensive about the mausoleum she had always considered as solid as a rock. It was one of many reasons that she liked it, regarding it as the only impenetrable place she knew, because no one would ever try to get inside. Besides, Michael did not really want to talk about her work, let alone the place where she did it.

'Sergeant Jones came in today. And Smithy and that bastard Williams, getting in from the cold. I told him to fuck off.'

She didn't want to pursue this line either.

'They only come for the chocolates,' she said.

'Do you know, that's what I thought.' He shrugged it off, but she could tell he was flattered by the number of his visitors, slightly regretful that this period of being spoiled was coming to an end. Rose could see his point. His position in this bed made him quite invulnerable.

'What time tomorrow?'

'Oh, the morning, I think.' Now he was less comfortable, conscious of deserting her. 'Mum and Dad want me back for a day or two. It's probably as well. I won't be much use with the scrambled eggs just now. Gives Mum a chance to fuss.'

He was very proud of having loving parents, but also vaguely ashamed of them, with their chorus of soup-making and well-wishing relatives singing love from the sidelines. But Rose would have none of his guilt.

'Just what you need. Save me coming round to you with dishes of cold spaghetti bolognese so I can cut it into pieces for you.' They both giggled.

'Only for a day or so, and only in Catford. You could come and see me, meet them all. Saturday? I've written the address and phone number for you. Come on, Rose, say you will.' She shook her head, secretly delighted but terrified by the prospect.

'Yeah you will. And after that,' he was holding her hand very firmly with no sign of wanting to escape, gazing at her with eyes which felt capable of melting her bones, 'after that, you are coming round to my place. With your suitcase if you want. I love you, Rose. I want to bloody shout it.'

'Shhh,' she said. 'Shush, someone will hear you.'

'I bloody won't shush,' he said. 'I won't.'

On her way out via three sets of antiseptic, polythene doors, she was weak with a transient happiness, before the dark world beyond flapping exits intervened. Inside the ward next to him, she could see a future twinkling away, somewhere beyond the ever-persistent fog, but the trouble was how to survive the time before the future could begin. Somehow, inside that greenhouse warmth, Rose had managed to suppress the cough which now returned for revenge. With the sound of her hacking went the pleasure of illusion. Michael could not help. She would have to find a safe place all on her own. Logo was everywhere: no one could lock him up. Rose looked left and right before crossing the road. There was a taxi rank on the other side. Taxis were a luxury she could not afford, but there was no question of going home alone. Both girls would be in, Wednesday night was for complaining and hair washing. She would be fine until the morning, unless the doorbell rang.

Daddy looked round every corner. He had seen her.

Thursday dawned with a milky sweetness. The fog sank against Helen's basement windows as daylight pushed itself into her dreams. Nothing but the fog peered through the bars which covered the panes, and although she loathed the necessity for this iron security, she could not have slept alone without it. It was a slow January light, with the fog making her think of the sea and of being far away.

Thursday. For the untroubled it was a day of promise when the back of the week was broken, but Helen rarely came into that category. The morning's work would be easy enough, but all played to the tune of Wednesday's emotional hangover. Helen did not think of Logo as she dressed. Pondering cases in lieu of counting sheep was proving a distraction which no longer worked.

An obscure guilt was nibbling at her bones; guilt for things done badly or not at all; guilt for somehow missing the point and for not making sufficient progress with that girl, Rose, and for discussing her with Dinsdale the night before. Guilt for drinking white wine with Mr Handsome, as much as anything else, while knowing there was something wrong in this intimacy, however much she defended it by saying it was Wednesday and no phone call from Bailey this week, he deserved whatever he got.

Come now, there are no real, concrete commitments between Bailey and me. Oh yes there are, for all there is nothing on paper: the unspoken promises are the most important you have ever made.

'I don't know what ails that child,' Helen had been saying to Dinsdale about Rose, while they sat in a wine bar which was, by mutual consent, a long way from the office and prying eyes. Perhaps it was that which made her less comfortable, this definite movement towards the clandestine. 'One minute she's open, next, closed for the day. One minute an ordinary giggly girl, next sulky and unpredictable.'

'*Cherchez l'homme*,' said Dinsdale. 'Moaning hormones. How's the new man?'

'In hospital.'

'Not the best place for love to bloom, might have something to do with her moods.'

'I don't think so. Monday and Tuesday, she's brilliant, then this morning she didn't want to come to court at all, I practically had to force her. Then she kept her head down in her hands, did everything grudgingly, as if she was hiding . . . Don't know why.'

'Do you suppose,' Dinsdale ventured, 'there could be any truth in the Redwood theory? That Rose could be the one who's been sandbagging the system?'

'No. I'd literally stake my life on it. What a silly, dramatic thing to say.'

'Yes, it is. Anyway, you should know better than that.'

Helen watched his fingers round the stem of the goblet, holding it with the casual delicacy of a discriminating drinker. The bowl of his glass never became dirty, greasy or marked as hers did with fingerprints and lipstick long before the bottle was empty. She wondered how it was he managed to keep himself so clean, and also why it was she was struggling to keep the conversation on neutral, fixed to the main highways of law and objective gossip, away from anything to do with themselves. They had been playing with each other for several weeks, an element of teasing in all this chat. It amounted to nothing less than a prolonged flirtation, admittedly of an obscure kind, consisting as it did of two people listening to one another with the intentness only given to a potential lover. Now as the tenuous nature of the relationship began to slip, as it began to slide in the direction of an affair, and she knew he was teetering on the brink of either proposition or declaration, Helen, who had been as enthusiastic as Dinsdale for the flattery each gave and received, was thinking twice.

She had left the wine bar in full flight with an excuse which sounded as false as it was and now she felt furious with herself. She was a grown woman, she should have talked to him, she shouldn't have let things go so far. What she had wanted was the attention, she admitted bitterly. She had required fresh armaments in her war with Bailey, needed the uncritical, unreserved admiration which her younger colleague gave with such generosity along with Dinsdale's support while he laughed at her pathetic jokes. She had not really wanted to give anything back. Cock tease. And what is so wrong in that? She asked the mirror. Am I not supposed to *talk* to men and enjoy their company? You have every right, her conscience answered back; but you knew this was different. Did she really like Dinsdale, with his patrician manners, splendid articulacy and shining cleanliness? Yes, apart from the last. Yes, yes. So that was all right then. An honest cock tease.

The fog helped. It always helped but it would clear before noon. Helen West loved the cold anonymity of winter. It was as if the void left by the non-existent pregnancy had been filled with a strange kind of longing to be different, to acquit herself well by someone in the world, instead of failing everyone in a subtle fashion, all the time.

Sylvie's parents had debated long and hard the several issues raised by Granny's funeral. The first was, should Sylvie attend? Was this part of the necessary education of a child of such tender years, and would it make things easier to explain? Opinions had been canvassed, but they had come back in contradictory forms and it was pragmatism which won. An early morning call to Margaret Mellors had elicited no response; the child could have been shuffled off elsewhere, but there had been so much upheaval lately, it did not seem entirely right and there was no time to consider the alternatives. The second subject of debate was should they wear black, but there was no black garment in the house and no time to borrow. Mr and Mrs went to church in blue and grey and Sylvie, spoiling for a fight, in red.

It was the coffin itself which made Sylvie's mother weep, such a helpless weeping it had no self-consciousness and she clutched the child for comfort. Too late she remembered why children were left behind; not to spare them the sight of the coffin but the sight of the parent out of control. Letting go of the smaller hand, the mother clutched her solid husband instead. Sylvie forgot to fight in this alienating atmosphere. She picked up the hymn book her mother had abandoned and looked at it, before beginning to gnaw the cover with silent concentration.

'I am the resurrection and the life, saith the Lord; he that believeth in me, though he were dead, yet shall he live: and whosoever liveth and believeth in me shall never die . . .'

Sylvie twisted round with the book still in her mouth. She saw the last member of the congregation come in and sit at the back. Her jaw worked faster. It was the man with the fingers. Sylvie searched for her mother's sleeve, saw her huddled away against Daddy, both of them smaller, ignoring her.

'. . . We brought nothing into this world and it is certain we can carry nothing out. The Lord gave and the Lord hath taken away, blessed be the name of the Lord.'

It all went on too long. When the priest led his tiny flock from church to graveyard, the daylight hurt their eyes, but the movement was welcome, although as soon as the coffin shifted on the shoulders of the dull, professional pallbearers who had been outside for a cigarette during the ragged singing of a single hymn, the bereaved daughter wept afresh. The coffin was so tiny: she could not imagine it actually held the remnants of a life. She imagined her mother in there, sitting cramped like a small animal in hiding, squashed into that box the way she herself had once carried a pet mouse to school. There was a fine drizzle outside; the hair of the priest rose in a frizz, but he did not seem to mind. He enjoyed traditional funerals for the opportunity they gave him to raise his voice in prayer, the only chance in his current existence to remind the agnostics of the power of God and the futility of these little lives without Him. So he warned them in sonorous tones of our traditions of the graveside, warned them how the coffin must be lowered to the tune of his prayers and then they must each throw earth. Denied contact with her mother, Sylvie followed him closely, fascinated by the flowing surplice and the dash of colour in his sash. Boldly, she stepped up to the grave and peered down. The priest shielded her: this was no time for sharp words.

'In the midst of life we are in death: of whom may we seek succour, but of thee, O Lord?' He cast a meaningful glance at the twenty still gathered. Sylvie was gazing down into the trench, looking for worms, her eyes held by a bright skein of royal blue wool which seemed to shine artificially against the grey-brown of the crumbled earth. She knew without being able to say that there was a hand holding the wool. In the middle of the space left for the coffin, she could see a footprint and on the other side, half submerged, a shoe. No one else looked into the grave: all eyes turned elsewhere, even those indifferent to the deceased did not wish to examine the depth to which she would descend. Sylvie's gaze ranged the length and depth, looking for the other shoe, saw instead more threads of the same, blue wool, and then her whole, small, punchy little body arched itself into a piercing scream. Sylvie had no real idea of why she screamed as she was hoisted away, kicking as the prayer continued and the coffin descended effortfully, held by straps, everyone ignoring the extraneous sounds.

'. . . We therefore commit her body to the ground, earth to earth, ashes to ashes, dust to dust . . .'

'No!' Sylvie screamed. 'No! No! No!'

With a soul full of anguish and guilt and one hand stained with the dirt of the earth she had just thrown, Sylvie's mother turned back from the side of the grave and slapped her daughter on the face. The blow was automatic and the sound of it as loud as the silence which followed.

The current of the shrieking was abruptly stopped: the child's face was white with one dirty imprint to the left of her nose. Scooped into her father's arms, she did not turn the other cheek, but remained speechless for a minute more and silent until he had walked her back towards the entrance with his hand steadying her head against his shoulder. Then she muttered. 'No, Daddy, no, someone down there, Daddy. There is. Don't put the box on top, Daddy.' He cooed at her and patted her back, out of his depth and blushing for shame at the behaviour of his family in front of others. His anger embraced the whole world except his child, but it did not mean he listened to what she said. Out of the corner of his eye, he saw one mourner backing away from the edge of the crowd, a faintly familiar figure, looking towards him. He felt Sylvie stiffen in his arms and hold tighter.

'It's that man,' whined Sylvie. 'That one, the sing-songing man with the funny hands.'

'There, there,' he said. 'We'll all go home now, shall we? Nice cup of tea?'

In the early evening of Thursday, Rose sat in Debenhams' coffee shop, chewing her nails and letting her tea grow cold. She had raced down into the bowels of the Central Line to get here in time, and Margaret was late. Rose remembered the old lady teaching her how rude it was to waste all those particles of someone else's life, by being late. Then she thought, with a greater panic, how Margaret did practise what she preached, unfailingly, and this was nothing to do with tardiness, accidents or bombs. She simply wasn't coming. After that, Rose ceased to think in any consistent way at all. What she felt among the plastic ferns and wooden seats was merely a numbing hurt, followed by loneliness and finally fear. Margaret hated her, had decided she did not want to know her, had defected finally, did not care, had told her father about this meeting. On this thought, Rose was unable to move, even to pick up the cup. Shop tea, Margaret had said, not like I make in front of my oh so cosy little fire. Telling Daddy all about it. Oh no, surely she would never do that, could always, always keep a secret. And she isn't a bitch.

Daddy. In court yesterday with his malevolent, pale blue eyes and his tiny, destructive little self, his face like a coloured balloon, but still his face, passing her, reaching out to touch her, surrounding her with the smell of his dirt and his curses. That was fear incarnate, and yet she had pitied him too. As if she had not tried, tried to extract his papers and put them in the shredder, as she would the next time, so that their paths might never cross. But she could not do it, could not leave Helen West to face the music, had done her errands on Daddy's case like a good girl, and then hidden, wrenchingly sick, among the graffiti of the public loo, where the walls bore last week's legends. Level with her eyes as she sat staring, there had been a fading felt-pen scrawl which said, poignantly, 'Is there anybody out there?' and Rose knew there wasn't. Now that Margaret had failed to arrive, she knew it even better.

Rose looked round, surreptitiously, beset with a brand-new fear. Would Margaret have told her old friend Logo? Was he lurking round here now, waiting to follow her home to an address he'd already found from a postmark? Was that why Granny had not come, displacing one loyalty with another? It was dreadfully possible.

Rose felt safe in company, in shops and in large buildings. Dad used to take her with him office cleaning: it somehow dictated her present choice of destination. She picked up her bag with a degree of decorum she did not feel, catapulted down to the ground floor and bought a toothbrush and a shawl, waiting with bated breath to see if they were daft enough to take her overstretched credit card. Then she dived back on to the Central Line, still full of shoppers. At the other end she ran from the train, stopped at the hamburger shop on the corner and the off-licence next door just before it shut, spending her last pence. Then she bounded up the steps, past the comforting railings, to the office entrance where the night doorman sat blearily.

'I bought you something,' she said, handing him the bottle in blue paper. 'Oh, and I'm going to be working ever so late, don't mind me, will you?' He smiled, bemused. Rose tramped upstairs. There was something corrupt about earning a man's goodwill with a half-bottle of whisky, particularly a horrible, leery man like that, but it had worked between her mother and her father.

A chill began to descend on the place. Rose did not mind. The office was eccentric, but it was big and above all, it was safe.

Helen met Redwood in the corridor at about five. He was looking aimless and defeated and she found room to feel sorry for him. He did not see her until she was upon him and it was too late to turn back.

'What's new about the office thief?' she demanded. All of them had been ready to confer, then they got the message, Don't bother and don't ask why. It was her best-natured sharp tone, but he still shrank.

'Oh, nothing to report, I suppose, that's why,' he mumbled. 'No point in having you all sit down to tell you that. Besides, I'm busy, I've—'

'So you'll let the office saboteur ride his bike, will you?'

'What else can I do? No one else has complained. I can't disrupt the whole ship with an official inquiry, we're sinking as it is.'

But you were ready to blame Rose to make it look as if you'd done your duty, Helen thought furiously. Sack someone to make it look as if you've tried.

'Won't do,' was all she said, firmly. Redwood scowled. Challenges only frightened him initially; after that he remembered to become aggressive.

'What do you mean, it won't do? It's got to do. But security's being tightened up, dramatically overhauled, electric locks, that sort of thing.'

'When?' she asked solidly.

'When? Over the next month or so.' He was getting angrier the more defensive she made him feel. 'Look, if you don't like it, you don't have to work here. Or you can find out who or what is playing with the system. I give you my blessing. We've decided it might be some kind of computer virus—'

'Which also removes the paper? Clever little bug.'

'It fits the bill. But as I say, if you want to find out more, feel free.'

'All right, I shall. As long as you aren't busy blaming the clerks. I'll report back if I find the virus lurking in a cupboard, shall I?'

'Oh, very funny.'

They parted on almost friendly terms. Avoiding Dinsdale's room with a feeling of discomfort, Helen set off to find Rose. Their conversations in and out of court today had been all too brief, perfunctory almost, but Helen did at least know about darling Michael going to his parents' home that evening, and she had it in mind to grab Rose before she left, suggest a drink, a shop, or something to prevent their recently broken ice from forming all over again. Her own passionate curiosity for Rose was far from satisfied; it defied logic and had been there for a long time. It was Helen's unerring instinct for vulnerability in people who hid it by shouting. She stopped at the door of the clerks' room. Too late. The bird had flown, unaccustomedly early.

A note on the desk, defiant. 'Gone shopping.'

It didn't seem a bad idea at that. Helen was ludicrously calmed by crowds, warmed by lights, seduced by displays, could sit in a shop for hours. The tawdry splendours of Oxford Street beckoned and she moved towards them like a pilgrim.

She went down the escalator to the Central Line. It was late already, half six. The office was empty, her flat at home was empty, and she longed for that populated vacuum in between. It was an old escalator which protested at the weight of feet as she descended with a thinning stream of people at Holborn. Passing on the other side, ascending to the air and looking like a person distracted, was Rose, clutching a bag and staring straight ahead. Helen shouted and waved to no response. Other people looked, then kept their eyes fixed on the posters. 'Pregnant and happy? Fine', or other pictures describing the magic effects of alcohol, pizza, books and clothes, trundling by as they sniggered at Helen's gestures as if they were the sudden, funny aberration of a madwoman.

Helen lost her taste for the shops.

Geoffrey Bailey realized that he missed things like shopping in this structured existence where all was found, but he did not miss it to any great degree. Shops had become so alien that when he and Ryan sat in the local hostelry which had become their regular haunt, with the same two, attractive women, he did not immediately realize that the older one was wearing something so obviously brand spanking new he fancied he could almost smell the tissue paper and see the marks of the hanger. The woman, called Grace, had a house near by: they'd been there before, why not again now? Plenty of drink in. The invitation had been sidestepped for a while until, with an operation which was so smooth as to be painless, they had seemed to transfer themselves from the snug of the pub to the splendours of her living room via the mechanism of Ryan's scented car which had acted rather like a time capsule. It was only when they sat on a moquette sofa, which Bailey both noticed and hated without quite knowing why, perhaps because it was so deep it immobilized him completely, that he realized what it was all about. He craved beer and skittles. Or the prospect of Helen, guiltily and noisily home from the Thursday shops to sit with her nose in papers on a worn, chintz settee while he sat reading a book in her armchair with its springs straining against his behind, not minding the habits of her furniture. Helen had a cat, so did he, both of them the independent, alley-cat, beaten-up variety which could never have house room here. The impressions passed like quicksilver, leaving no visible mark on his face. Where he was now, there were three bedrooms upstairs, one each and one for their consciences, should any of these considerations apply. Bailey thought of the homework he should do before the rigours of tomorrow, remembered the opportunism of his relative youth and decided Grace wasn't such a bad alternative, conscience was soluble, she reeked of perfume and sympathy. He might not like her furniture, but she was from the same stable as himself with the same humour; she smelt of uncomplicated generosity.

At what point Ryan and his lady disappeared upstairs, Bailey did not quite gauge, midnight or thereabouts. 'I'm going to bed,' said Grace, with a yawn like a cat. 'I think you may have lost your lift back to school. You'd better stay. The bathroom's on the right at the top of the stairs. You can either come in with me or sleep on this thing.'

'Oh,' he said sheepishly. 'I'm sorry. I'm not . . .'

'Used to doing this?' She hesitated and he knew it was not feigned. 'Nor me. Which is why I'm wearing a new dress and being so brisk.'

He could not bear the risk of humiliating her and yes, he liked her. He liked a woman with an accent who spoke her mind and talked his own language.

'Yes, it's all right,' he said.

There was silence on the upstairs landing of this new house in a new estate full of picture windows mirroring closed lives. One of the rooms full of teddy bears gave witness to an absent child. The door to Mother's room was open, she was in there, taking off her new clothes. Bailey went into the bathroom. He was depressingly sober, depressingly helpless and he wanted to stay in there as long as possible.

The crash from downstairs hit him like a blow. His face, with all its multiple lines, stood solid as a map as he stared into the mirror with the fixity of a ghost. A door slammed. It took him several seconds to move and feel grateful he was still dressed. Out on the landing, Ryan's plump torso with the bottom half clad only in a fluffy towel, cannoned into his own thin and steely rib cage. It was bone meeting flesh; he knew Ryan's fist yearned to punch him for the stranger he was.

'Shit,' said Ryan. 'I think we got burglars.'

'Put some bloody clothes on,' said Bailey. 'For Christ's sake.'

The stage-whispers alone could have won them an Oscar. Grace appeared at her door, the stage-left entrance in négligé somewhat impaired by her white face.

'Stay put, I would,' said Bailey, mildly. It was years since he had seen a woman deliberately *déshabillé* to please, an uncommonly pretty sight. She did as she was bid and shut the door. Ryan re-emerged, with an unbuttoned shirt, a jacket on top, trousers zipped as he moved, shoes, no socks and, as Bailey rightly sensed, no underpants.

'Talk to me, Chief,' Ryan said in the same hoarse whisper. 'But make it loud.'

'What?'

'Make a noise. Sing or something.'

'We've got burglars.'

'Naa. This house might have burglars,' Ryan hissed, grabbing his arms. 'But we mustn't catch them. What do you want? A headline in the paper? Sing, will you? Give them time to get away.'

Bailey coughed, loudly. Coughing seemed to be infectious. Ryan coughed, but only as a preliminary to yelling, 'Is there anybody there?' in a voice so loudly artificial it made Bailey wince and then want to laugh. Then they went downstairs.

It was an awful room, Bailey thought sadly in the absence of its owner. A room which tried and failed to be all things at once, a comfort, a luxury, potted both inside and out. The glass doors led to a version of the tropics beyond. One of the palms had fallen through the window in nothing more than a fit of pique. Two huge plants lay embracing one another among broken glass.

'Thank Christ,' Ryan muttered fervently. 'It's only the wind. Time we were going. Sir.'

'In a minute,' said Bailey. 'In a minute.'

The women appeared as he was Sellotaping cardboard to the glass while Ryan swept up the broken fragments. They all did what they could whilst making the noises that go with the end of a party, laughing with a cup of coffee in one hand before, all desire spent, Ryan and Bailey left in a silent, cowardly posse.

'Sleep well,' said Bailey, something he said automatically to Helen if he should leave her late at night.

'I shall,' said the woman, smiling without a trace of bitterness. 'See you soon.'

Bailey blushed.

Sleep well, my sweet, be good tomorrow, awake refreshed, the aim of every man. Logo sat back on the cold kerb, gazing at the lights which still blazed in the windows of the building he surveyed. Didn't they ever turn off lights? Yes, they did. They turned off most lights on each floor, but forgot to extinguish them all. In the narrow street which flanked the back entrance to the vastness which he watched, Logo could see the silhouettes of clumsy furniture behind the net curtains of the huge ground-floor windows. There was a doorman dozing in there, but Logo knew how to get in; one or two sash-windows had already welcomed him, but he had doubted the point of the exercise. The offices of the Crown Prosecution Service whose address was so easy to elicit from the big-bottomed usher, or even from an old alibi notice, guarded itself against terrorists only. He was not one of those. Logo was only a man who wanted his daughter and had come to collect her from kidnappers. And, had he doubted her presence here, his doubts were soon destroyed. There were symmetrical windows in the basement below his eyes, all lined in a row, all dark save one, where the light flickered against dirty net curtains, and someone, against the back wall, was conducting a little concert.

She might have had head phones plugged into her ears: she was acting out a rhythm, but she knew about shadow play. There were long thin fingers in that room making an eagle against a yellow wall and Logo could see it, clearly.

He moved towards the railings, looking into the well of the basement, easy, with time, but a huge post office van rumbled by with radio blaring and stopped at the door. Logo retreated.

Tonight, tomorrow night, another night; rest up first, what did it matter when he was so close? He liked the expectation. The shadow play went on.

Now there was a rabbit: now, a church with a steeple.

She was still his own child.

CHAPTER TWELVE

The office building was the only place where Rose had never been afraid of the dark, but nothing could prevent her from missing the comfort of all her frills and teddy bears. Down in the bowels of the basement, she had been able to select from a number of rooms, each more private than the next. The cabin she chose out of this luxurious suite was the size of a cupboard with a smeared sash-window below the railings which flanked the front door of the building. The top of her head was well below the outside wall, the glass so dirty and the view of the street so restricted, the feeling of safety was complete. The yellow-painted walls were lumpy with layers; the stone floors had been painted with red tile paint, the whole brutal effect subdued by age. Outside and down the hall, the central-heating boiler for the whole vast palace hummed with harmonic fury behind a locked door, clicking disapproval from time to time. In the subterranean space, Rose felt she might have been in the bowels of a ship, with all the reassurance of noise and the vicarious life of the engine to chase away ghosts. Lighting in the cabin took the form of a single bulb hanging dolefully, augmented by the anglepoise lamp Rose had borrowed from Helen's room to illuminate her bed. Here, the mattress consisted of piles of old papers taken from store and formed into an oblong, covered with an abandoned curtain shaken free of spiders and on this makeshift arrangement Rose lay and aspired to sleep after playing games with shadows on the wall. Fully clothed except for shoes, covered with a winter coat and the shawl, she turned off the lamp into a darkness which was suddenly complete and then, before terror struck, her eyes adjusted to the oblong of light from the window and her ears to the roar of the boiler, and she was able to close her eyes.

But at 5 a.m., uncomfortable and cold, the stupidity of it all sank in. Sleeping in a dungeon on a mattress of paper with sweat gathering in her armpits and ice round her feet, Rose thought, So this is what I have become. A vagrant, a dosser, moving my shell each day with no good reason, always looking for a new corner because some little old man is chasing me. Down in the basement in the bleakest reaches of the night, Rose could not begin to congratulate herself for what she had done with her life to date, nor perceive even one of her extraordinary achievements. She was literate, presentable, employable; she was a mass of scars but she was not a cripple, and all she could see of herself was a snivelling thing, hiding in a cellar like a rat, the way she had hidden out with men. In the last analysis it was the terrible vision of what Michael would think if he saw her thus which drove her to groan. She thought of Helen waiting all week for her to talk without prompting. She thought of Dad in court and cringed.

She could sense the wind outside, smell the rain. From the well between the railings and the wall there came the steady sound of dripping water from the distant eaves above. The boiler burst into a new phase of life, then reduced its volume to a sinister muttering. Rose felt dirty. At six, she ascended the back stairs, feeling her way, dying for daylight, found the washroom on her floor where all the clerks ran to hide. Ever fastidious, she stripped, lingered over her ablutions with the powerful office soap and the harsh paper towelling. Upstairs, the silence was astounding apart from the minute sounds of her own effort, until she heard footsteps. Footsteps and a cough, which made her suppress her own. A pair of feet, walking along the corridor outside, unhurried but purposeful, receding shoes with steel caps sounding on the worn bits of carpet. Rose put her damp hand on the door of the washroom, opened it a crack, just in time to see a slim figure disappearing through a set of old swing-doors at the end. The doors were heavy: he was forced to pause long enough for her to recognize the set of his shoulders and the colour of his hair. Mr Dinsdale Cotton, carrying a couple of files, a sight which sent her mind snapping into sharp connections.

Rose knew in that moment the identity of the office thief. She was unable to move, looking out into the empty space with the door still juddering at the end, paralysed with anger. Of course Rose knew about someone purloining the files, fouling the system, getting cases deliberately lost, she was equally well aware that the inefficiency of her own team had been casually blamed, none of them told anything, all under suspicion, herself in particular. She did not need Helen West to hint by way of warning: she wasn't a fool; she had tried to tell Redwood about it long before, but had been told to make an appointment and she wasn't going to do that, let them rot if they wouldn't listen. So what had she done? Told Dinsdale, once, weeks before. She trusted Dinsdale, presumed he would act, tell his buddy Helen all about it at least, but even when she knew he had done no such thing, she had still trusted him.

What time was it? Half-past six, still the middle of the night and she had grit under her eyeballs. Rose carefully made up her face in the mirror, to offset the effect of her crumpled clothes. It wouldn't be the first time she turned up to work looking like this. She shivered as she thought of nights in the section house, surprised herself by thinking, You've come a long way, Rose, in a short time; don't go back, will you? Thinking of favours, she also reckoned she owed Helen West one: she'd better blow the gaff on her bloody boyfriend before anything went further between them. It was strange how one problem displaced another; in Rose's life that had been the history of her sanity.

Outside the loo, she coughed loudly to warn anyone else of her presence. She also whistled. The cough was still painfully real while the whistle was tuneless with nervous artificiality.

Even with this complication, it was still safer in here. Her gran had always wanted her to work in a place like this.

Three hours until Helen came in? Rose had the feeling that once she started to talk, she might not be able to stop.

It was a rain-soaked, blustery, purple-sky kind of day where the sun would never rise and the winter was interminable. The same kind of savage day in which Helen had encountered Mr Logo on the rooftop. She remembered him as she woke on Friday, for no reason except for the rain slapping against the window and her own, foul temper. No phone call from Bailey. All right, she'd unplugged the answerphone, but it was still his fault. She guessed by now he wasn't returning today, wondered if he ever would, didn't much mind; she wanted time to slouch, think and be a slut. Far fewer of us, Helen thought, swinging herself out of bed with the usual violence, need a constant man than any of them ever imagine. Three days a month would do nicely.

It was only when she crashed into the bathroom wall while reaching for a toothbrush that she realized that the symptoms of this depressive malaise were not merely mental. Her tonsils rose to close her throat like a portcullis; toothpaste tasted fiery; she felt as if her neck had been held to a flame and yet her face was unnaturally pale with deep red rings under the eyes. Rose's cough had been passed like a gift. Put make-up over that lot and she'd look like a corpse dolled up for a funeral. Take the day off *again*? Who cares? Who'll miss you? Point taken, they won't even notice, apart from Dinsdale, lovely dangerous man with the silly name. That fixed it. She wasn't going anywhere: she could make up the work before Monday. Helen sat instead in her basement living room with the dirty winter windows sluiced by the snarling rain, watching other workday feet go briskly by while she considered all her duties and personal obligations, finding them too numerous to contemplate without screaming. By reflex action, she phoned Rose on the number she'd noted down from the phone inside the girl's house (like the sneak she really was), simply to ask Rose to present her excuses at work (like the lazy coward she also really was). Only to find a girl who said hallo, nicely, but Rose hadn't been home last night and wasn't there now, and Helen found herself saying, 'Fine, it doesn't matter,' while feeling that little jolt of alarm which was akin to electric shock, then sitting back in the chair, to watch more feet.

Her cat came in from the great outdoors via the flap, wet and disgusted, sniffed at her feet in pure cupboard love and disdained to come closer. All right then, one phone call like a prisoner in custody allowed to say where he is, and then she would wait since she was in no position to do anything but fall over. Story of her life. Nobody loved her and she deserved nothing better.

'Then came the woman in the dawning of the day, and fell down at the door of the man's house, and her hands were upon the door of the threshold.

'And when he came into his house, he took a knife and laid hold on his concubine, and divided her together with her bones, into twelve pieces, and sent her into all the coasts of Israel.'

Logo was well acquainted with those biblical passages which smelt of blood, while he chose to ignore all those which favoured forgiveness over hideous retribution. His present serenity owed much to his loving contemplation of blood as well as to the lethargy of his limbs following all the dreadful exertions of the last thirty hours. Lifting heavy weights, lugging, lying, spying, mourning at a graveside, and suddenly some kind of end was in sight, only he was not sure what the end was. The reverie was broken by someone knocking at the door. He stood behind it and shouted, 'Who's there?'

'Mr Logo?' Assuming it was, the voice went on, young, brisk and efficient. 'Dr Smith, Mr Logo. Only your neighbour, Margaret Mellors, had an appointment to see me yesterday evening. I sent her a letter about the date for her hip operation, only she didn't turn up. She gave you as her next of kin; you wouldn't happen to know where she is, would you?'

'I am not my neighbour's keeper,' yelled Logo.

'I didn't expect you were. But do you know where she is? I don't want her to miss this chance—'

'Margaret who?'

The voice went away. He was suddenly afraid. People would come looking for Margaret, of course they would, a popular woman with friends, which in the case of someone over seventy, meant a visitor a day. He'd left the kitchen tidy, locked the door, thrown away the key. No, no, he would say, he hadn't seen her for a day or two, and it wouldn't be the shadow of a lie. And where did you see her last? Knitting, sir, only knitting. Oh yes, he could imagine the question and it made him put his fist to his face and giggle out loud.

Today he'd make amends to the old dear, put flowers on her grave if he could find something suitable left on another and no one was watching. Something to do on the way to work; he supposed he had better turn out, knowing as he did how far to push the line of absenteeism and today was a day for scoring points, what with the weather like this and everyone else playing truant. Then he'd rest, maybe take a long walk later . . . Logo rumbled the old trolley through the nine-o'clock streets, glaring straight ahead, his substitute for singing, frightening people another way. A man needed a tribe. To be disenfranchised by blood or sin was a terrible fate. Eenie had done that to him. She had made him the man who always walked alone, with others making their signs against the devil in a dozen different languages as they passed him. She had consigned him to hell. He paused by the graveyard gate. There was a man by the distant grave with a little girl, a smart-looking man with a suit, holding a bright show of daffodils in the one hand and the child's gloved paw in another. Then the man stooped and put his arm round the child's waist, intimately. See? Logo crooned to himself. Look at her flirting. Look at him! We all do it.

Daffodils, Rose thought, just daffodils. They were suddenly in tight-budded profusion on barrows near the office, bursting from buckets by the Underground, lining the street. They had all laughed today, must be the promise of spring, Rose their cheerleader, cracking jokes, mimicking the bosses, flying round, sharp and brittle as a thorn, hooting and yelling, hoovering work like a machine, flirting on the phone and making eyes at men. Everyone loved it. Rose on insolent form made the day go quicker, and as she led the gang out for sandwiches, the daffodils stood to attention along with the man on the stall, mesmerized by four noisy girls. Rose stopped and stared back.

'What you looking at?' she demanded.

'You, darling,' he answered.

'Cost you a free bunch of them.'

He gave them a flower apiece. Rose pretended to eat it. 'Lovely,' she said. They all snorted.

Anyone would think I was normal, she thought. Thinking, If I went round to Aunty West's flat with a bunch of daffs, would she let me in? Why's the silly cow off sick, when I need her? Promise me she won't mind. Can I please, please trust her? I'm not going back and I've got to tell her about that little fucker anyway. The bank machine ate her cashcard, a punishment for overspending. She winked at the girls and cashed a cheque at the counter without anyone being shot or yelling stop thief, and they huddled out like conspirators. In the middle of the afternoon, because of something else decided in the nether regions of the night, about how she couldn't face his parents, not as she was, she phoned Michael. Her heart thumped like a bass drum when she heard his voice, but she'd already made it into a public joke, about parents and everything, what a bore it would be, so she was brisk, said she couldn't do Saturday, she had to work. The lie was apparent; he was hurt and offended, but she was on a course of action she couldn't change, not even to avoid the corners. She threw a file across the room, let the papers spill out like confetti, teased her hair into spikes, chewed her pigtail, shouted some more. Put more files in the goods lift beyond the door, pressed the red button and shouted down, 'Egg and chips twice, please!' Dreading the ending of the working day, wanting it too, and it was still raining.

Enough stolen from the bank for the taxi fare and three bunches of daffs. Dark at five forty-five when she rang the bell to Helen's flat, and when there was no immediate reply and she was shivering on the doorstep, the old terror struck again. Until Helen appeared, looking like an alien without her make-up, letting her in, coughing like a car with a flat battery, but welcoming, oh yes. No fuss. Put your coat on the radiator and shove that cat off the chair, let's have a drink, excuse the way I look, all in one sentence. After that it was all right. It really was all right. More than all right, after all this time, to dump some of the shit on another pair of shoulders. She never could have done it if Helen hadn't told her about biting that bloke.

There was an interruption around seven when Bailey phoned. They'd covered quite a lot of ground by then, one bottle empty, a bit dry for Rose's taste, but not bad, and then it was Helen's turn to play the fool. Making faces at Rose while holding the phone. No, he wouldn't be coming home this weekend. As if I didn't know, Helen whispered with her hand over the mouthpiece. Neither mentioned the other's neglect. Bailey was always tense on the phone, sounding like someone in a call box with a queue outside.

'Other fish to fry?' Helen was asking lightly, while Rose took lessons. Truth to tell, Helen was feeling a whole lot better since Rose had arrived, deeply troubled but a damn sight more useful and therefore better. At least she and Rose coughed in unison.

'No,' he said, equally lightly. 'Work. They work us like slaves.'

'Can I ask you something?' He half hoped it would be something personal, but it wasn't.

'If a chap has paid someone to get his drink driving charge dropped, by say stealing the papers or bribing the copper, what do you reckon it would be worth?'

He thought for all of a second. 'Oh, two, three thousand, if his car was vital. It would depend on the alcohol reading, who he was and how greedy the person was he was paying. Helen, are you all right? Why are you asking?'

'Oh, a little academic problem.' More faces at Rose.

'Helen, if you go around asking questions, you get what I get, black eyes. What are you up to?'

'Nothing. See you when I do. Have fun.' The alarm in his voice was revenge enough.

Bailey remained as he was, furious. He was angry for her being nice about his absence when he wanted her to shout, I still need you, come home. For leaving him free when he needed chains. For not screaming at him, as if last weekend's sweetness and closeness had counted for nothing. He needed to be told, for God's sake, he needed that all the time. She acted as if reassurance was her sole prerogative. Ah well. Then he phoned Grace.

It was the room which soothed Rose as much as Helen's langorous stillness when she was listening, but then it hadn't been dramatic reactions she had wanted. A room with warm red walls lined with pictures, all differently framed, and books standing crooked, nothing new, no furniture without wear and tear, the gleam of mahogany, a worn carpet but densely coloured and comfortable, an ash-littered grate below guttering flames, litter and learning, something to look at all the time when you didn't want to meet eyes. What was it Helen was saying? Rose felt her lids twitching, watching the fire after talking for two hours.

'People care for you, you know,' Helen said, bowling coke at the grate and making a mess. 'An awful lot more than you think, so phone the flat-mates, will you, stop them getting alarmed.'

'OK.' Rose was enough at home to take orders.

'And it goes without saying you can stay here as long as you like, you'd be doing me a great favour,' Helen added in a cunning throwaway line. 'Only there's nothing to eat until I go out to the corner shop. There's never anything to eat here. It's you ribbing me about carting home all those potatoes. I've never been the same since.'

'I'll go,' Rose struggling to find energy, thinking of the dark.

'No you won't. I've got a cough, but it isn't terminal. Open this bottle will you, we don't have to get up in the morning. Back in a minute.'

She wanted time to digest some of Rose's revelations. She had taken them calmly. Rose didn't want outrage; she wanted belief. Abuse, betrayal, the deep, murky waters of systematic cruelty, all described, but no names, no pack drill, simply facts, no weeping please, no cries of horror. Rose needed empathy, she needed love, therapy, she couldn't do it all on her own, no one could. She wanted to be normal, so Helen acted normally, a lawyer listening with quiet credulity. Out in the street she wanted to scream with pity and rage.

The wind had lessened, so the trees now swayed elegantly rather than furiously, whispering not hissing without their leaves. It was a street of handsome houses where people walked day and night, confidently, and despite her history here, Helen had forged a sense of safe belonging. She wondered as she walked down her own road to her own parade of shops, what it was like for Rose to live without that blanket. Everyone needs a tribe.

Redwood had thought twice about staying late in the office on this particular Friday, since it did not do, in the current climate, to act in any way out of the ordinary. Whatever was going on here, he was sure he did not want to know, but his habits of insecurity could only die hard and he needed this sneaking about as much as he needed the evening drink when he got home. And there was something he had to do, could only do with the place empty, and that was somehow secrete or destroy all those case records which had got inside his desk as the result of expeditions like these. All he had achieved this week was procrastination, shuffling jobs around and the invention of another form which they would all accept in the end provided he never had a meeting to discuss it. In the meantime, he had this worthless cargo to unload which, if found, would brand him as a sneak or worse.

His idea of upstairs, downstairs was sound as far as people were concerned, but he was less good at geography. He aspired to the discovery of a sort of incinerator device such as he had in his garden, and might otherwise belong in the cellar of a place like this. The building had a basement, didn't it? Files came up and down from somewhere like prisoners being shown daylight from the hold of a ship. Somehow Redwood imagined the paper moving itself into the ancient goods lift on their floor without human guidance; he also imagined that everyone here hated the place equally and that none of them ever ventured to explore if they could avoid it. Armed with cunning and nervousness he kept on descending stairs and wondered if he would ever find his way back.

It was dark down here, oh yes, extremely, but there were also lights and it was warm. By the time he rounded the corner to where the boiler was locked away, humming loudly, he already felt he was about to meet a ferocious animal and was glad there was no incinerator to be found. This building has *too much heat*, he decided, lights left on everywhere, disgraceful, and too much hot water, with the noise that thing made, a fiver a breath; he could do something about that, surely. Now, where could he hide these notebooks since they were not for burning. If he took them home his wife would notice them.

Blundering about he found a small room, just off a large empty space, and stopped in surprise. He could have sworn he heard someone throwing something towards the window. There on the floor was an anglepoise lamp plugged into the single point, recognizable anywhere. Helen West's lamp, old but coveted, and what was it doing down here? Redwood took the lamp, meaning to return it. On his way to search for the stairs he found a suitably old and disused radiator behind which he stuffed Rose's notebooks. Nobody who counted came down here; it wasn't even very clean.

Puffing up the stairs, confused by the alien regions of the first floor and the constant choice of exit, he thought about the lamp. Wait a minute, he wouldn't put it back, a dead giveaway of Friday-night sneaking. Some might call it evidence. Redwood was confused. He left the lamp in his own room: somehow that seemed better and less incriminating, although he didn't know why.

The doorman was not at his post, but there was nothing unusual in that and the overhaul of security didn't begin for a week. Redwood let himself out of the front door, feeling like the keeper of a castle but not the king, never too keen on signing out and signing in anyway, especially on Fridays. Clutching to himself the important-looking briefcase containing very little, he strutted down the steps. Straight into a little man standing in the street, rubbing his wrists, appearing out of the dark, bowing.

'Excuse me, sir . . .'

'Oh, sorry,' said Redwood, sidestepping and striding on, momentarily afraid until he reflected that muggers weren't usually middle aged and knee high to grasshoppers, even he could work that out, it said so in the files; all of which occurred to him in the first two seconds of his flight down the street before he realized that the little man was following, running to keep up.

'Excuse me, sir, excuse me . . .' Redwood wished people never said that. It created an instant obligation.

'What?' he barked, turning, holding the briefcase in both arms like a shield. 'What do you want, man? I haven't any money and I've got a train to catch.' Both were true. The face, on a level with his briefcase looked harmless and smiling, but showed signs of having been in a fight. He relaxed a little.

'I don't want nothing, if you'll excuse me, sir, but I was waiting out here for my daughter. She works alongside you, sir, said she'd meet me here . . . I didn't like to ring the bell, she must be working late.'

'Name of?' Redwood barked.

'Enid . . .' the man hesitated, but Redwood was already barking back. He knew all the names off by heart, but could never quite connect them with the right faces.

'No one left in there at all. Even the doorman's asleep, at eight o'clock, I ask you,' he added for good measure. 'And no one named Enid at any time of day. Wrong building.'

He marched off. Logo watched. My, weren't they all such dreadful liars.

'Her granny called her Rose!' he shouted after the retreating figure. 'Rose!'

Redwood looked back at the little figure standing by the railings, but did not stop.

CHAPTER THIRTEEN

Margaret Mellors' doctor was in the area and tried to call on her patient for a second time late on Saturday morning. Monday was the deadline for the old dear to claim both her bed and her new life, otherwise she went back to the bottom of the queue. Looking through the kitchen window, the doctor could see a clean and tidy room, the fire not cleared and a knitting basket beside it. There was nothing in any of it to raise the slightest suspicion. Walking back out of the alley to her car, she met Sylvie and mother bound for the house she had just left, her attention drawn by the screaming child being tugged along like a reluctant bulldog, feet skidding, snarling between barks. It was a quiet sort of street, apart from that, the doctor reflected; a pity it was so close to the football stadium.

'Excuse me, do you happen to know Mrs Mellors?'

'Yes.' The reply was tired, but affirmative. The child stopped making a noise and began to pick her nose.

'Only I've been trying to get hold of her. Looks like she's gone away, perhaps.'

'She never goes away,' said the mother in a voice flat with disappointment. 'Never.'

'Any idea where she might be then?'

'Around here somewhere. She always is. Have you tried next door?'

They looked at one another meaningfully.

'She's dead,' the child piped up. 'Dead and buried.'

'That's enough from you, thank you very much.' The mother was apologetic, recognizing a doctor, and suddenly chatty. 'Sorry, she's very morbid. We took her to a funeral, a big mistake.'

'Oh, maybe not. Look, when did you see Mrs Mellors last?'

'Yesterday,' the child said. The mother turned to her.

'Are you sure?'

'No.' Sylvie giggled.

'I don't know,' said the mother despairingly, in reference to what the doctor was not entirely sure. 'Two days? Three days?' Her brow cleared. 'Before Mum's funeral, she was fine then.'

The doctor went back to her surgery after four more visits. Winter was a terrible time for death. From there she called the police.

When Logo came home at about two, they were all over him like a rash, doubling up, he supposed, on him and football duty. There was that lippy little bastard with the hammer fists and the weak mouth, another callow youth and a big darkie. My, my, Margaret would have loved it, always had liked men, liked everyone, come to that. She would have adored a whole houseful to make tea for and feed home-made biscuits, might even have offered them one of her everlasting, ever-shapeless sweaters. He told them as much.

PC Williams was twitching and eyeing him sideways, waiting for him to say something provocative and refer to the yellow tidemarks of his bruises, but the other two were as civil as the kind he usually encountered and Logo held his tongue. Acted as Mr Meek and Mild: no he didn't know where she was, he wasn't his neighbour's keeper (the phrase was becoming tired), but he'd like to know, of course, if they should find out. She was a good old soul and they often called on one another, but no, not in the last day or so, he had to confess.

'So your fingerprints would be in her kitchen, if we looked, would they?' said Williams, tauntingly. Logo looked at him, all wide-eyed innocence.

'Of course,' he said. 'I often brought in her coal.'

They'd have a job finding cause for a search warrant. Old ladies were allowed to go on walkabout, just like young ones. The boys were only there with their bristling radios and razzamatazz to make sure she hadn't fallen over in the bath. Once they'd heard how able-bodied she was, they didn't seem to have much else to do now they'd shouldered down her door. There was very little damage, a skill they had. Logo helped them refix the lock and showed them where Margaret kept her spare key, like the fool she was, hanging on a piece of string inside the letter box. It made them feel idiots for all that wasted effort and not thinking first. I thought you learned things in training school, he told them, only you don't know anything about the habits of the old. To compound his subtle insults, he waved them goodbye like passing royalty, hoping someone in the street would see he was on such friendly terms, like the actions of someone who really did help a neighbour with her knitting.

But they would be back; it was obvious they would be back. They'd come back last time, like some recurrent disease, saying, Sorry to bother you, acting as if they were too, but that time he'd been crying all over the place, weeping his cotton socks off, crazy with agitation for the loss of his wife and daughter, and they really had been sorry for him then. Now he reckoned he had two lines of defence to stop them coming into his house, the first being that they wouldn't like the smell of it (it was beginning to get that ammonia-tinged, fusty scent), any more than he liked theirs and the second was he could prevaricate as long as he wanted because there was nothing to hide. But he didn't want that PC Williams and he didn't want attention, and besides, he was really tired. The football crowd would imprison him indoors if he stayed with all their racket. The best thing to do would be to go away, just for the weekend. He knew where; like father, like daughter, he knew exactly where.

I brought her up to be cunning, he said to himself sorrowfully, standing in the back yard; made her sly and fond of the dark and good at getting into things, clever with her hands. He sniggered loudly at that, still revelling in his triumph with the officers. Only once before had he encountered so many and not even been arrested. *Oh Lord, forgive them for they know not what they do.*

Without the trolley, as he had discovered on recent perambulations, he was first without an alibi, second without ballast. He found himself swaying from side to side and not quite sure what to do with his hands. Today, he was restless after three steps, turned round, went back indoors and for some obscure reason, changed his clothes from one very dirty set to one less dirty. The black funeral jacket he had worn when he went to see Margaret last, a little grimy, not bad, but the lapels covered in white dust which seemed to have penetrated the lining with a sweet smell. Logo punched his chest and the powder billowed. He only tried that trick once. The trousers were cleanish jeans, the shirt he left as was, only worn three days in the last week, maybe it went with the jacket, he couldn't remember. He liked both for the wafts of scent they sent over his head. Walking down the road in his training shoes, he buried his nose in his armpit and kept it there, nice. As well as the smell he carried a scarf and one of Margaret's home-knit sweaters hung round his neck. The combined effect, along with his open donkey jacket, made him look and feel substantially fat, a man who ate well. That reminded him about bread being the staff of life, so he bought some and gnawed it out of a paper bag. Stopping at another shop for three bars of chocolate, he worked out that the lack of a good pie might explain why he was so twitchy. He'd given up going to the pubs since acquiring his bruises and even drink had lost its appeal.

When he got there, though, after the long walk, he wished he'd bought some booze. He looked up and down and decided he liked the railings in particular. Shining black, a row of spears, including the gate he had discovered before, stiff to the touch, but movable, with an impressive padlock holding a chain so loosely his thin self could sidle through the gap. The well of the moat was slimy with water. In the shallow pools created by three days' gusty rain, a pigeon bathed, cooing. 'Shoo,' he said, 'fuck off, or I'll sing to you,' and as it struggled into flight with the grace of a slow torpedo, Logo felt beset, as he had all day, by the endless desire to laugh. He paddled through puddles underneath the steps to what looked like a grand entrance for trade, down the side. A delivery door, secure as the crown jewels, a window into the basement which was not. He knew all about offices, from having cleaned them. Inside, it was warm as toast.

Rose was sorry in the morning, for having said so much. She woke up with a feeling of emotional indigestion, worse than any hangover she had ever known. A pint of wine hadn't done this to Rose; she had coped with a pint of spirit before now, and last night's ration had gone down like water, but it wasn't right to talk so much and eat another person's food. Not that she hadn't talked to people before about her life; to do so was another clue to sanity, she'd found. But it had always been in dribs and drabs and mainly to strangers, because that was like talking to a wall; they wished you luck and you knew you'd never see them again. Anyway she'd never opened her big mouth as wide as this. Helen and she slept late; Rose had got up in the middle of the night to find all the lights still on, which was comforting, and had gone back to bed in Helen's small and barred spare room, thinking, I could stay here for ever; it even beats the office for safety, but with daylight, it seemed less secure and her own position untenable. She might have gone before Helen was up if she had known how to unlock the door and her sense of shame had not frozen her will, and the boiler hadn't twinked into life and made the place even cosier, so she stayed put.

Helen had woken, coughing like a dead engine, wondering what Rose might think. She didn't know what it was like to be sexually abused, but she did know what it was like to feel violent and she certainly knew the deep dark shame of telling.

'Christ,' she said, slumping at the kitchen table in a dressing-gown which cheered Rose for its sheer age. Will you look at that thing, she was thinking; even her own was better, and she was up and dressed, far too wide awake for comfort, with that guarded look over her face like a visor. 'Christ,' Helen repeated, 'I do feel ashamed of myself. Will you promise me, Rose, you'll never repeat to anyone what I told you last night, all that stuff about fancying Dinsdale and my sex life before, during and after Bailey, and about being frightened of the dark? Promise? Blackmail me until the money runs out, could be soon, but don't tell.'

It was a bit of comic turn with exaggerated gestures; Rose saw through it but smiled, the guarded look retreating. She has an extraordinary face, thought Helen; a face which turns from hunted to haunted to hard and insolent and then into the softest and most vulnerable beauty you ever saw. I wish I had a daughter. Looking at what had happened in the life of this mother's child, she thought again, perhaps not. Helen had often felt maternal, but it was mostly applied towards adults.

'Instant coffee or the real knee-jerk variety? Got both, usually have the latter. We've got things to sort out.'

Rose liked the briskness. It made her meek all over again.

'We've got to go and get some clothes for you. I meant it about staying here, by the way, don't think I was just being polite, so you need stuff, though you're welcome to mine.'

Rose looked at the dressing-gown, like some sort of old carpet.

'No thanks.'

'And after that,' Helen went on, 'I thought we might go and see your adopted Gran—'

'No,' said Rose, panicking. 'He might be in. He'll see us.'

'So? I'm big and ugly. I bite people and—'

'You don't know how he hates me,' Rose said. 'You really don't.' She was aware now how ridiculous it seemed in the cold light of day to harbour such fantasies of persecution, for which she could produce so little evidence. It was ludicrous to expect anyone else to accept that one small man could loom so large and be everywhere at the same time.

'All right,' said Helen, 'We'll drive. Cruise by.' Nobody cruises by in your car, Rose thought, specially not the way you drive it. 'You can duck down and tell me what to look for.'

That was better. 'Do you think,' Helen continued, 'you could speak his name? I mean his surname? You haven't told me that.'

'Darvey,' Rose muttered.

'It isn't Darvey. I know Darvey isn't your real name. Don't ask me why I know, but I know. You just don't answer to Darvey easily enough. I bet you've got a really silly name, as silly as Dinsdale's. You just want to keep it secret.' She was making toast in that horrible dressing-gown, busying herself.

Oh why couldn't she guess? She'd had enough clues.

'My mother's name,' Rose snapped. 'She used to call me Rose and her name was Darvey.'

'Which brings us,' said Helen, pouring coffee, 'to the vital point. We want to find your mum. We want your father rendered harmless.'

Oh, help me, Rose thought. Could no one ever understand how her own father could never be rendered thus? And would Helen never see, without actually being told, how it was that the idea of her father being punished or imprisoned was not pleasant either? So what if the talk last night had all been about hatred and fear and hunting, it had still failed to include all the sneaking parts, the dreadful bond of blood which even while fearing him, did not want him tortured either and could not abide him covered in bruises. That was what she was afraid to admit.

'So,' Helen was continuing with the same briskness, 'I think that means we should go to the police and get the whole thing looked at again. To find out what went on, where your mum went. And report your father.'

'That means Michael would have to know.' Rose was faltering, looking for the excuse which Helen might find easiest to understand.

'Not necessarily, and besides, if you're going anywhere with Michael, he'll have to know.'

Rose took one of Helen's cigarettes. They coughed in concert. It didn't do to be too sensible. The nicotine made Rose dizzy, yet cleared her head. 'I think I want to wait a day or two for that,' she said in her firmest voice so far. 'Can we clear up the Dinsdale thing first? If I help sort that out, I'll feel I've done something. Feel better. Stronger.'

'Fine,' said Helen, thinking, Don't push the girl, let her do things her own way. 'I've been thinking about that too. Dinsdale. We could go to the office, pull every file he's had in the last year, cross index it to drunk drivers, see if we can find a pattern.' The Dinsdale side of things was sad, distressing and guilt creating: she wanted it over and done with. 'Only I can't work that bloody computer.'

'I can,' said Rose.

Nothing happened quickly. The car would not start without an hour's persuasion. Another hour was spent collecting two of Rose's teddy bears, a ton of cosmetic equipment and, as an afterthought, more clothes. Then Rose changed her mind, said she did want to drive by the house which had once been her home, feeling suddenly braver. They were silent as they covered the two miles in the unhealthy sounding car; Rose terrified it would stop and leave them marooned on Dad's territory, but she dared not say, nor even state to herself the reasons for sitting like a stiff wooden soldier. In case she saw Gran hobbling down the street, alive and well. Or saw Mum, as usual with a shopping basket. She wanted Helen to guess, from the address she must have noted half a dozen times, who her father was without her having to say it out loud, and so save Rose feeling so resentful that Helen hadn't worked it out already. But it was a Saturday afternoon, football season. The road was blocked off, the surrounding streets triple parked, nothing moving until the end of the game. Rose heaved a sigh of relief. Now they could go to the office, postpone the issue, and the office was safe.

Logo squatted down on his haunches in the basement, winded by the warmth, disorientated and aware of the discomfort of the knife which lay inside his torn trouser pocket against his thigh, hooked on to his belt. Margaret's best kitchen knife, useful for cheese.

There were footsteps upstairs. He scuttled to a window facing the railings, craned upwards to see if someone was leaving, but no door slammed. The footsteps were so muffled they were almost infinitesimal and as they stopped he thought he could hear the distant murmurings of a television. Football, he guessed: the bastard doorman hypnotized for a couple of hours. He thought of those big arc lights for the winter games, thought how gloomy it was down here with the feeble supply of daylight fading and the railings gleaming wetly above. Logo began to explore. Empty rooms and rooms full of paper, dull little alcoves and meaningless passageways, a distant humming; he liked it a lot. There was a fire-detecting device winking and whirring after twenty steps in one direction and after that he encountered the boiler-room door and wondered how the place seemed to be full of such strange, heavy-breathing animals, but apart from these, quieter than a graveyard. He found a set of narrow stairs and next to that, a lift in the wall for goods, with the shutter doors open. This piece of equipment delighted him in particular. There were a couple of dozen files on the floor of the thing: he threw these to one side and squeezed himself in. Cosy, like the size of his trolley, an excellent hiding place for a little man, if a little cramped. The thought of Margaret fluttered into his mind and then out. He uncurled himself and continued to wander round. Paper, miles of paper, it would make a good fire. He liked the idea of that, but on reflection, decided it was the wrong kind of paper, and he was an expert on rubbish, it wouldn't burn easily.

Now he was here, he realized he had nothing to do and although it was late afternoon, night-time was a long way off. He sat on the edge of the lift, surveyed the stairs to the upper floors, listened to the boiler, ate one bar of chocolate with loud smacking noises, finished it with a sigh and took off his coat. He wanted to sing for this sense of safety and completeness, tinged with excitement: my, my, so Eenie came to work here on Monday, sometimes stayed over, hadn't she done well. But the chocolate made him thirsty, he needed a source of water, some cover in case the present warmth did not persist, and he needed a place to pee. None of that was available on this level as far as he could see, just paper. The stairwell beckoned; the wooden banister felt warm to the touch. He ascended in his best training shoes, silent, still wanting to laugh. There was a game he had in mind. That woman, the one he'd scared on the court rooftop, the one who had let him off the other day, who had the nerve to pity him, she worked in here too, she said. He could find her room if he wanted, use that as a toilet, show her: wipe his bottom on her chair. The stairs went on up to the ground floor, led into a corridor which fanned from the foyer. Behind a closed door facing him, the sound of the television was louder. Full of impudence, Logo knocked, ready to run, although it had been a quiet tap; he felt like playing games, but there was no response. He danced a jig where he stood, remembered the desire to urinate, found a door marked 'Women' and inside there he rationed his own relief, saving it gleefully, and flushed the chain without thinking. Still no response from the TV room. Onwards and upwards, having crossed the foyer and found a grander sweep of stairs, he progressed, walking down each corridor on each floor in turn until finally he was lost. That distressed him, but only a little. Those that are lost shall be found, he told himself, and there, like a message from the New Testament, was another version of the same goods lift, staring at him in the face, like home. Logo realized he had gone full circle. He suddenly fancied a ride in that thing, not the big conventional lift which he had also seen, marked 'Out of order'; all he had to do, surely, was go straight back down, if he wanted, and he'd be back where he had started, and whatever his boldness, he knew he wanted a way out, as well as a warm and quiet place to sleep. He pressed the red button; the lift whined up to join him. Here it was even warmer.

Logo looked into a large room with a grand chair, big desk, very tidy, organized and controlled. Ah yes, looked like hers, the room of a bossy-boots with pretty clothes, full of severe authority and better carpet than outside in the corridor, but it smelt of man, and whatever else Mizz West was, she was certainly not male, better be sure. He giggled, coughed back the ever-present laughter, still wanted to sing. Until, like an echo of his own mild noise which he carried with him as he moved back into the corridor, he heard more laughter, more coughing, a chorus line of sound coming closer. In a moment of panic, he was incapable of discerning the direction of the sound; in one second he thought it came from behind him in the grand room, then from his right, then from his left, but it came towards him up the stairs and he had no notion of where these people might go. He looked wildly for the smallest space to hide, wanted to curl up rather than stay still, spied the goods lift with open jaws, thrust himself inside with his knees to his chin. He pressed the metal shutter half together with the palms of his hands. Neat.

★

'That doorman ought to be sacked, never mind anyone else,' Helen was raging on the way upstairs, coughing. 'You have to phone from a call box to get him to open the door, and even then, we might have been anyone. No wonder Dinsdale—'

'And me,' Rose cut in sharply. 'And me. He let me stay here on Thursday night, like I said, so don't knock him. Or shop him. I'll have a word if you want. He needs a job like everyone else.' She was somewhat sick of the diatribe which had lasted two flights. The lift was broken. Helen was being a nag. Sometimes she understood, other times she knew sweet nothing about anything and she looked sick. Keep reminding yourself you like her, Rose was thinking as they puffed to the door of the clerks' room, you do really.

The room was always a mess, less so when Rose ruled it, but discipline had slipped on Friday. Helen found herself resenting the way they were all cramped in here, while others, like Redwood, had rooms as big but all on their own. Rose went to where the computer sat, behind a screen on a kind of pedestal as befitted its status, pressed buttons and inserted disks with the ease of a pilot.

'How do you know how to do that?' Helen asked, feeling inept.

'I watched,' said Rose. 'I'm a quick learner.'

'Quicker than me. Give me something useful to do.'

'You can sit and knit. You aren't well, you know.' She was mimicking Helen's solicitude. They both laughed.

'I think we'll start,' said Rose thoughtfully, 'with the finished cases from last month, beginning with his, Dinsdale's, I mean. If he was deliberately losing papers, there'd be files he was given either to look at or take to court first time, that's how he'd know which ones he wanted to lose. He'd often get bloody cross if he was sent to a different court at the last minute. I reckon the ones you and John got, you got by mistake. He was supposed to go out there and lose gracefully. Right, let's have his list.' Helen watched the screen in amazement. 'It says the first twelve have gone to store,' said Rose, proud to act as interpreter. 'That means they're in the basement somewhere. We just shove 'em down there, and then file them every now and then, we're supposed to keep them for five years . . .'

'I wouldn't know where to start down there. Are there rats?'

'Course not,' said Rose scornfully. 'I wouldn't have slept down there otherwise, would I? All the rats are upstairs. I'll go down. You have a look in Redwood's room. He keeps the main diary in there, showing where everyone is. Make a list of the courts old D

183

goes to most regularly. There might be a clue in that.' Rose was showing off a little; Helen, humbled by her lack of knowledge of the office machinery, demurred slightly, but it seemed best to let Rose control.

'Why don't I come down to the basement with you? Aren't you a bit nervous going down there?'

'I'm never nervous here. It's the only place I'm not. Save your breath.'

Her footsteps pattered away down the stairs with light speed. Oh, for youth, Helen thought, wandering out into the corridor, down a few doors and into Redwood's room. Hot in here, close, with an odd smell, like old air freshener. She noticed her anglepoise lamp on the desk, you're welcome Mr R, I'm sure, turned it on, fished in her bag for a cigarette, enjoying the sensation of doing what was normally forbidden in the throne room, went across to the huge window behind Redwood's desk and flung it open. She looked out briefly into the street where a single mean lamp reflected a fine drizzle now descending into an area which was never light. They had been chilled and coughing on the way here; now she wanted cold air to clear her head, so she approached the other window, guilty for being a trespasser, thinking, I can quite see why Redwood likes sneaking around, fun really. Then stopped. Coming from behind, reflected in the old and wavy glass, a creature tiptoeing like a child sent out to hide and seek. Even before she turned, she could smell him. His was the scent of the room, artificially sweet, menacing, not immediately recognizable, and there he was, creeping towards her with a silly smile on his face. Helen spun round before he reached her. He was still five paces away over the dun–coloured carpet when she spoke, the voice not reflecting her panic as she measured the length between herself and the telephone.

'Hallo, Mr Logo,' she said neutrally. 'Who let you in? Perhaps you better tell me before I call the doorman for the police.'

He giggled, followed her eyes to the phone, shook his head. Helen got the message.

'I want my daughter,' he announced. 'I want Eenie. You've got her here. All of you, you keep her locked up, away from me.'

'Your daughter? There's no one called Eenie here. What's her real name?'

'That's what the man said, no one here called that, what a stinking load of liars you are, and you gave me these, people like you. You like my handcuff burns? Her granny used to call her Rose. Never liked calling her Enid.'

He was dancing in front of her, little swaying movements from foot to foot, pushing back the sleeves of his powder-stained jacket, releasing more of the same sickly smell and showing her his thin wrists, ringed with brown marks she'd seen before.

'See these?' he said. 'Gives me strong wrists. You give me handcuff burns. People like you.'

He stopped thoughtfully, inches away, Helen pressed against the glass of the window which seemed to creak against her weight. Truth was emerging with alarming confusion. Logo, the father of Rose, of course, of course, and in that split second she could at last understand the reason for the child's terror.

'Her mother used to call her Rosie Lee. After tea,' he added inconsequentially. Helen gazed at his wrists, hypnotized. Saw the knife hanging from his belt, thought, Oh, God no, I cannot be brave, I cannot bite back, not this time, not again, I have used it all up, whatever little courage I used to have.

'I don't think those are handcuff burns, Mr Logo,' she said contemptuously. 'I think it's just dirt. Show me.'

He stopped, open mouthed, distracted, held his hands, palm upwards. 'Come towards the light,' she ordered. He did as he was bid, never once taking his eyes off her face, shuffling to the desk, moving his hands to the light; he smiled suddenly, angled the lamp neatly, and began to twist his hands into shapes. Shadows sprang against the far wall, moving monsters, a pig with a snout and a tail, full of strange energy. Helen turned to look, her heart thundering in her ears, her eyes rounded, her left hand feeling for the telephone and her voice forming a scream.

'It isn't you I want,' he said suddenly. 'You're in the way. Where is she? I heard her.'

'I sent her home,' said Helen. 'There was nothing for her to do until Monday. She's gone. Come back and find her on Monday. She'll be here then. There's only me here now.'

The shadow play stopped abruptly. 'I don't believe you,' he said. 'And it isn't just dirt. There's no such thing as just dirt.' The anger was sudden and malevolent. The brown wrists were level with her eyes, his hands grabbing great chunkfuls of her tied back hair, shaking her head about like a rag doll, his spittle landing on her face to add spite to his words. Then he twisted her round, so one arm was across her throat, bending her neck back, the wrist of the other hand was in front of her eyes. 'Dirt,' he said. 'Dirt, is it? That's what she is, dirt, but you, you're the real filth.' The pressure grew stronger. Helen bent and jerked her elbows back into his abdomen, flung herself free and ran for the corridor. She ran blindly, glancing wildly into the darkened rooms as she passed, looking for salvation, somewhere with a lock on the door, a weapon, enough time to be with a telephone, open a window, scream, but her legs were leaden, her mind in the paralysis of futile fear, unable to stop running. There was a sense of *déjà vu* about personal attack; as she ran, she was in the throes of the last, remembering it, full of the images of her bedroom and Peter's brother, stinking with his own bitterness. She knew she would not bite this time and kept running. Too late, she realized, even as she sensed how his pounding footsteps behind her had faded, that she had run the full square of the floor and was back where she had begun, with him behind or in front, it made no odds, but the smell was with her, in her hair and her eyes. She paused, uncertain, by the goods lift where the scent was strongest. It was darker, someone had turned off the corridor light. Helen turned and shouted, 'Rose, Rose! Get out, get out!' hoping against hope the sound would travel. Silence and dark; for a moment she breathed easier.

He leapt from the lift, a black sprite with his kitchen knife, lunging. 'There!' he hissed. 'There! You were lying, you were lying . . .' Oh not my face, she remembered thinking, please not my face, let me die pretty, please. Putting up her arms to shield her eyes she kicked wildly, connected with thin knees, heard him grunt in pain, shift his balance. There was a thud as the knife dropped, whether because of the impatience of his violence, or clumsiness, she did not know, but his hands were in her hair again; she was pinned against the frame of the lift, nerveless, his braced legs prising her own apart as he banged the back of her head repeatedly against the metal surround, until she slid down, leaving him holding her half upright by the hair alone. Logo let her slump, bent over and hissed, 'Where is she? Where is she? I don't want you, no one would want you.' There was no response.

He let go of her hair. She rolled over on to the floor. 'Filth,' Logo muttered with a quick kick to her ribs. 'I don't need you.'

As if he could not have guessed if he used his wits. Rose would be hiding where she could play with shadows. He stood and waited to see if Mizz West would move. She didn't. That was all right then. He hoped she was dead.

★

Oh why had she not run downstairs, instead of in this hopeless circle? Helen wanted to be dead, wanted never to have to fight back against anything ever again. Her eyes were closed, but she knew she had rolled on to the knife, the wooden hasp of it digging into her waistline, the scenery inside her eyes a mass of purple, exploding clouds. Stay still: let him do what he wants, it doesn't matter, just finish it. She heard him giggle, then footsteps going away, unhurried, purposeful. She could sleep then, simply sleep, wait for someone to come, Monday would do, nothing mattered, she wanted to let go of everything. Rose, though: somewhere down there without the rats, was Rose. It was only Rose Logo wanted and the doorman was useless, wouldn't hear a bomb. Move, Helen, you've got to move, there's nobody else, there never is, but it was difficult. So she rolled, tried to sit up, half successful, but hurting. The light was still on in Redwood's room, insinuating itself into the darkness. The red light button for the goods lift shone in reflection, the only way of issuing a warning, give Rose a weapon. As she picked up the knife with a shaking hand, Helen could feel herself fading. There was blood on the knife. Oh please, not my face; it doesn't matter about your face, you should be ashamed, come on. She struggled to her knees, let the knife drop into the open mouth of the lift, pressed the red button, listened to it whirr away, and then sank back. In a minute I'll move, in a minute: not now. Find a telephone. Slowly she crawled in the direction of the light from Redwood's domain, wanting to keep her face near the floor, then raising herself half upright, began a different and shuffling progress on her knees. She debated briefly in the middle of the crawl: go forwards to the light, or back to the clerks' room? She made the decision to go forward, called by the light, thinking, I don't think this makes sense. Oh Rose, please run, I know what you mean, just run, out the way he came in, any way, but run. And halfway there, still gathering speed, she heard the sound of a phone. From the direction she had abandoned, the clerks' room, the logical place to go, but dark in there. Rose, phoning from the basement before Logo reached her? The doorman at the end of the football game, sensing drama? She crawled back, her knees rubbed raw against the harshness of the worn carpet, reached the door on the twelfth ring, managed to get to her feet on the leverage of the first desk and then it stopped as she reached and fell, down into another kind of darkness, lay quiet and winded, praying it would ring again.

Oh let me not be afraid of the dark.

★

Michael put the phone down in his parents' house, vaguely angry. So she'd said she could not come and see him today because of working, but he didn't think that was the way Civil Servants ever worked, even her kind, and if she was at work, why not answer the phone? So she wasn't at work, she was somewhere else, with someone else, doing God knows what, he didn't want to know. A girl like that wasn't for changing, he could hear it said, chanted by a thousand voices sounding as loud as the Red Army chorus or a first-division football crowd. Easily bored, was what she was, playing with someone else, off and away as soon as the new boyfriend was immobilized, that was what it was, it had to be something like that. Couldn't-wait Rose, that's what she was, and he had been taken for a sucker, played it all wrong.

'She doesn't answer, Mum,' he said savagely. A woman sat in the corner of a comfortable living room a few feet away from him, sewing. They had just turned off the football. She became a travesty of her normal, tranquil self when she watched her team, even though she still continued to sew, with big, stabbing movements.

'And I suppose that means that you think the very worst. You don't think of an innocent explanation, do you? She's been let off early, something's happened, she's out, that kind of thing. Even after she came to see you in hospital how many times? You men. You policemen.'

Michael sat back, absurdly comforted but irritated as well.

'I think about her all the time. I don't seem to be able to stop it.'

She put down her sewing, eyed the arm in a sling, sighed.

'Well, think nicely then. If you've got to go up west, your dad'll give you a lift. And back, if need be.'

'Thanks, Mum.'

She took up her sewing again. 'We were robbed,' she was muttering under her breath, 'robbed blind.'

It took him a while to realize she was talking about the football.

CHAPTER FOURTEEN

Rose was looking at the files thrown out to lie on the floor, when the lift thudded down beside her, level with her waist. Ha, ha, ha, Helen upstairs joking, asking what the hell she was doing all this time. Rose smiled, pushed up the shutter and thrust her head inside, grinning and muttering, 'Silly cow.' Her mouth, still creased open in a smile, was suddenly full of a familiar smell laced with an undertone of nausea. Someone's favourite powder, passed from body to body, sickening and cloying, mixed with dirt and sweat. That was her first impression, forming quickly, the second glance, from a distance, showed a kitchen knife, its blade swinging towards her like a wavering compass, faintly smeared, unmistakably a tool for cutting meat, suffering from use. Her whole body became rigid with shock; she put a hand towards the knife, withdrew quickly, extended again and forced her fingers to close round the handle which had the warmth of a reptile. Rose did not understand the message; it crossed her mind that Helen was playing with her. For a minute she thought the woman was mad, and stood winded by the cruelty of the joke, then some kind of logic prevailed. There was no sound but the ticking of the basement machinery as Rose stood gripping the knife, seeing its present purpose in a rush of images which came with the traces of scented powder and body-dirtied clothes, saw herself lying on a bed, and Daddy with his shadow play and his clothes not changed from work and herself stealing Gran's favourite powder as she would a talisman. Daddy in the kitchen as she sliced at him with another knife, warding him off, hurting by accident.

Rose did not think she would be able to do that again.

Flight was the course she had always adopted and that was what she was going to do now. She wasn't going to think of anyone else, she was going to run, leaving behind any loyalties and hopes in that headlong rush as she had before. Go home, don't bother saying why because there is no point, pack a bag, never come back, find another job, it was silly to have come so close; there was nowhere safe, not in the whole wide world, if it wasn't safe here. She had believed in this place. In one hand she had a sheaf of notebooks she had found behind the radiator. Rose dropped them on the floor, ran towards the back of the building, still holding the knife, but loosely, looking for the delivery doors. She took only a few steps, then turned back to stare at the open mouth of the service lift, big enough for a body. She ran left for the stairs, foolish and indecisive, feinting towards ideas like a fencer with a blade. Somewhere over her head, there were small sounds; the doorman, the enemy, both of them the same since the doorman must have let Daddy in; must have told him, pointed, go upstairs, that's where she went. It might even have been the doorman who provided Daddy with the knife. She held it to the light. Smears without colour, perhaps used to cut a sandwich, even Daddy had friends. Suddenly Rose stopped. He wasn't the only one with friends. Helen was upstairs.

Rose bent down and eased off her shoes. Instead of the wider, main stairs which led off from the right of the lift, she sprinted left down the stone corridors, turning off the lights as she went. Past the fire-detection unit, the noisy monitor of water supply, the ticking boiler, she sped up the narrow iron steps two at a time, pushing through a stiff swing-door at the top. If there was ever a fire here, no one would know how to get out. On the ground floor, there was a distant sound of a television, towards which she was drawn and then she pulled back, inexplicably disgusted by the excited sounds of sports commentary, flew round the corner and up the next narrow set of stairs. She had lost the desire to sit and sob: by the time she reached the second floor, breathless, aching to cough but afraid of the sound, she was consumed with a terrible, attacking rage, the rat in the corner which would die rather than not fight. It was a familiar sensation, she had felt it sometimes during her loveless sex, biting back the desire to snap and snarl which moved her now, something remembered from the time she had lashed out at Daddy, not knowing or caring who or what she hit, hating them all, anything within the sweep of her arm would do.

Someone had turned off the lights. Someone running in that wild way she herself had been running downstairs, she could feel the panic. In the corridor, the only light came from Redwood's room. With her mouth clamped shut against the desire to shout and cough, Rose tiptoed towards the door and went in. The anglepoise was turned at a drunken angle to illuminate the far wall, the desk was as rumpled as a newly abandoned bed, there were papers on the floor and one of the windows was open wide to the floor sending a fresh draught of air. She was drawn to it, leant out, coughing, then caught the sides of the window frame in the midst of a spasm, suddenly dizzy. Careful, Rose, she said; it would be high enough if you fell into the basement well, but that's no way out. The rain had begun again, spiky cold against her face, head clearing. The impulse to scream for help, on and on, into the silence of the side street, died in her chest, it was easily stifled; she might have been yelling into an Arctic waste for all the help it would bring, and she was still ashamed to scream. Helen: where is she? Where is the cow?

There was a sound, a mirror of her own, spasmodic cough. Rose leapt away from the draught, poised for more flight. Helen was in the doorway, leaning against it, slipping slightly, the pose at first looking nonchalant, like someone lounging at the entrance of a party, ready to make a scene, languorous in the pose of a model but playfully pissed. So contrived was it that Rose was furious all over again, yelled at her with all the pent-up fury, 'What's your game, then? What's your fucking game?' The words out of her mouth as the resting position of Helen's slender figure became less natural, sinister, the head supported on the arm, but lolling, the knees buckling, legs straightening in a sudden staggering lurch towards the desk, moving like an uncertain toddler aiming for the nearest knee, missing, ending up kneeling with a thump, her torso over a chair and her head bowed in contrition. There was a stickiness on the back of her neck, one sweater sleeve hung by a thread, and as she raised her head she stared fixedly at Rose, trying to summon the last powers of concentration.

'Did he cut my face?' she asked almost conversationally. 'Only I need to know. I can't tell.'

'No,' said Rose. 'He didn't.' She stuck her fist in her mouth. Blood was running down the fingers of Helen's left hand, which she stretched upwards with a strange elegance, focusing, bringing the fingers towards her face to rest gently on the bridge of her nose. Slight though it was, the movement cast a huge, brief shadow as the hand flickered down out of range of the light.

'Are you sure?' Rose wasn't.

'Yes, I'm sure.'

'Oh, good. Listen,' said Helen. 'Did you get the knife?'

'Yes.' A whisper.

'Good. I can't get the phones to work. They're switched through to the doorman on weekends, incoming only. He should be up on his rounds soon. Every hour, he does, Redwood says.'

'The security bloke doesn't do his rounds,' Rose said, tersely. 'He shirks. And he let my dad in, didn't he?'

'Oh,' said Helen. 'I didn't think of that. Have you seen him?'

'Who, the doorman?' Rose asked stupidly.

'No. I mean have you seen Logo? Your dad?'

'You mean you knew who it was all the time?'

Helen sighed without exasperation, as if everything she said was very, very difficult. It still looked as if she was playing a game of being drunk. Rose wanted to believe it.

Under the sigh, Helen's words came faster.

'No, I didn't know all the time, but I do now. He went downstairs, to find you. Did you see him?'

'No.'

'And now he's coming back up,' said Helen dreamily, shaking her head slowly from side to side. 'Like a plate of spaghetti. Go and jam the lift, quick.'

Rose was slow, traumatized, mesmerized by that fluttering, bloodied hand, watching for more shadows on the wall.

'Which lift?'

'No, don't: it's too late. Listen, will you?'

From below, came the grumbling of machinery.

'Run,' said Helen, her voice suddenly clear. 'Will you bloody well run? It isn't me he wants. Just run. Go on downstairs, I'll keep him happy for a while. I'll nag him.' The face found the means to grin. 'Keep moving till you find a way out, take the knife, threaten the doorman, but will you please run?'

The lift was whining now, groaning beyond the first floor, coming closer. 'Oh for God's sake,' Helen yelled, the languidness entirely gone. 'Will you just, for once, do as you're told?'

'No.'

But Rose ran, into the corridor. She was still holding the knife. The red light for the lift glowed. Rose dropped the knife, seized the steel handles of the pull-down doors, picked up the knife and shoved it down between them, jamming the wooden hasp flat. Got you. The silence was deafening: the lift seemed to have stopped without any of the usual bump, stuck somewhere, below her feet. There was a dampness on the frame of the lift against which she leant, listening. Rose lifted her hand away in disgust, wiped it down the side of her skirt, not wanting to look at what was on it. She backed away in sudden exhilaration. Stuck, that's what he was, let him rot. The smell of powder and body odour lingered. She shouted, barking like a dog at a safe distance, her voice full of gleeful venom.

'You just stay in there, Dad. You stink, Daddy, you know that. You stink.'

The use of her voice bought relief, then guilt. She stepped forward, less venomous. Was he all right? She tried not to care if he should smother, but did care a bit. Then she thought of Helen, bleeding all over Redwood's floor. He'd done that. Rose could feel the onset of sobbing, confusion, doubt, tried to retrieve that brilliant feeling of rage which was such comfort, stood irresolute. Should she go forward or back, down to the washroom for towels? What did one ever do with blood but stare, fascinated and helpless, smothering the same old instinct to run? Then, like Helen before, the decision was made by the phone. Pealing from the clerks' room. The response was automatic. Rose was in the room, banging the receiver against her ear in haste, wincing, no time to wonder why it was that the telephone's sound was always first imperative, anywhere, anytime, even if it promised nothing.

'Is Mr Cotton there?'

'No, listen—'

'He told me to ring him, this number, this time.' The man's voice was smooth, ragged at the edges with nervous irritation, not a man to be kept waiting. 'Give him a message from me. Tell him it didn't work. I've got a letter saying I've got to go again tomorrow, it didn't work. Tell him I don't like paying for something I haven't got, and why hasn't he done something. You tell him . . .' The voice grew angrier, words a little slurred, fear lurking behind.

'Shut up and listen,' said Rose, the fury beginning to return. 'Listen. I am locked in this building with a woman who's hurt, a maniac and a phone which won't dial out. Help me, please, phone the police. Now.'

'. . . to stop mucking about,' the voice went on. 'You tell him what I said—'

'Listen,' said Rose again. 'I'm stuck in this building with a maniac and someone hurt bad, will you please do something and call the police . . .' This time the man registered. After an incredulous pause, he burst into a splutter of outraged laughter.

'Call the police? What me? After what they've done? You must be joking.' The line went dead. Rose continued to hold the receiver, looked at it in disbelief, began to punch numbers, any numbers, 999 numbers, the number of her flat, listened to the buzz of uselessness. She could not bring herself to fetch the doorman, didn't know why, but she sensed the enemy, remembered him the other night, taking the whisky, leering a bit. Run, Helen had said, run. The doorman would let her out if she showed him the knife, though, wouldn't he? But then she couldn't take the knife out of the handles of the lift, could she, in case it decided to work again and . . . So she ran back to Redwood's room and closed the door, dragging another chair across it, useless, the desk so old and heavy, it was unshiftable, but any kind of barrier was better than none.

Helen was lying on the floor, her head against her wounded arm, the pose uncomfortable. Rose angled the lamp to see better, winced and looked away, then stripped off her jersey, took off the T-shirt underneath, looked around. A vase of flowers on a filing cabinet at the side, Christ there were enough silly chairs in here to seat an army, she thought impatiently, tossing the flowers to one side, sloshing water on the T-shirt. She dared not go out into the dark corridor again. The water from the flowers, early spring daffs, was none too clean, but it was cool. Rose cradled Helen's head on her own lap, folded the arm with the tattered sleeve over the chest, thinking inconsequentially what a nice sweater it was, classy, she'd admired it this morning, hadn't said so, of course. She dabbed at the clotted blood which had transferred itself to the cheeks, embarrassed somehow by the intimacy of this strange physical closeness.

'Will someone please come?' she said loudly. Then she looked down, adjusted the profile on her knees, more frightened of the sound of its breathing now than anything else, terrified it would stop. Hesitantly, she traced the line of the old scar with one finger.

'He didn't get your face, this time,' she murmured. 'Honest.'

There was no reply. They would have to wait.

It was quiet and warm, even with the window open wide. Rose began to feel unreasonably calm.

Dinsdale Cotton was more than an hour late. He had missed his meeting in the pub, caught in the football crowds, and now he had missed the phone call. He bumped his car on to the pavement round the corner from the office, with scant regard for its ridiculously inflated value and sharp, metallic paint, not a car he could ever trust to a magistrates' car park or want placed anywhere in sight of a colleague, even though he could pass it off as part of an inheritance. They would believe that, of course, in the same way his contemporaries at the Bar had believed his patrician background at first, the fabled public school (never quite specified, only suggested by the uniform, the speech, the tie, the well-worn-in quality clothes which looked as if they were part of an inheritance too), the patrician thinness, like a lean-boned racehorse. All of which belied the foundling survivor of endless scholarships obtained by cheating. There was nothing wrong with his intellect, but Dinsdale never could resist a short cut. Nor the materialistic ambition which did not equate with his instinctive imitation of a duke.

The Bar rumbled him after a year or three; it was the women who sniffed him downwind with their nose for a thoroughbred, but the Civil Service, blindly egalitarian, had been easier to fool. And then he'd met Helen. Just at the point when she had begun to change her mind about him, the way women always did in the end, he had begun to think how nice it could be not to act all the time. She wouldn't give a damn about his lineage. She had seemed to like him, might even forgive what he was with those big blue eyes, but really she didn't want him, and he didn't like the discovery of how much it mattered, just a game, but coinciding with everything beginning to go wrong.

The car door shut with a satisfying clunk. There was an old wreck next to it which he didn't recognize.

Dinsdale understood the world of the *nouveau riche*, had been adopted into it, pushed up like a piece of forced growth under the green-house roof, fatally flawed and prone to insect life. He knew how to choose from his own corruptible kind. Nothing wrong, surely? He wasn't taking bribes from murderers, merely those who wanted to keep their cars and he hadn't even been greedy. Only two more, the ones he had already approached, maybe do something to square the one which was going wrong, one more drunk driver with a small business and a large car. Then he would think again.

He rang the bell, a big, brass brute lacking polish; the kind of thing he would have liked on the front of his little house, with a butler to respond, instead of this shuffling, ever indolent but still suspicious slob of a night doorman whom it was best to confuse rather than persuade. The man took his time, the second ring reverberating into silence before he was on the other side saying 'Who's there?' but unlocking the door at the same time like a Shylock unlocking his own vault, grumbling. The doorman was flushed red, cross from afternoon sleep. Drunk, Dinsdale thought, amused for the first time in hours.

'You should have phoned,' the man said.

'Should I?' asked Dinsdale, drawling, eyebrows raised, flicking the fine mist of rain from his coat. 'I wonder why?'

'So you might. Them others did. Like Paddington Station, it is.'

Halfway across the foyer towards the lift, Dinsdale could feel his hackles rise.

'Oh yes? Which others?'

'Coupla gels.' The doorman was mimicking Dinsdale's accent, revenge for the provocation. 'They been sending that goods lift whizzing up and down like there was no tomorrow. Oh, by the way, don't bother waiting for the other one, I mean, it ain't working. Sir.' The 'sir' was loaded.

'Nothing changes in this hole,' said Dinsdale, making for the stairs with elegant speed, but stopping round the first turn. On the landing, he saw a belt curled like a snake lying on the carpet. There was a slight smell which could have been urine. Two girls, looking for a warm space on a Saturday evening? He doubted that, but not his sense of unease, sat where he was and lit a cigarette.

Everything was coming unstuck; he was never going to get what he wanted, whatever that was, though he thought that in some obscure way, it had included Helen West, if only on the periphery. He remembered them talking about evidence. She had never given him evidence of anything more than liking. Silence. He did not want to move. Sit here for a minute to make it look as if he'd come to collect something, then go home.

The swing-doors at the top of the stair well moved. Slightly. A light appeared through the glass panels. From his vantage point in the semi-darkness, Dinsdale saw a face passing, not looking down. It wasn't a girl.

Helen's breathing came quieter, even and peaceful.

'We aren't well, are we, Aunty?' Rose murmured, coughing. 'Neither of us. But at least we haven't got to cope with Daddy.'

She had moved the lamp on to the floor next to them, played with the shade, angled it against the wall so she could send out shadow signals to herself with her fingers. Beyond Redwood's desk an enormous V-sign appeared on the yellow paint, cheering her. Rose smiled, looked down at Helen with her head pillowed on Rose's sweater, twitching and frowning this last half-hour. With sweater and T-shirt deployed to Helen's use, Rose was beginning to get cold. She hadn't noticed at first.

'I know you've got the flu and all,' said Rose reasonably, 'but don't you think this has gone on long enough? If you don't bloody well wake up soon, I'll brain you.' Saying that made Rose laugh. She was talking out loud, better than crying and hiding the fact that she was beginning to feel kind of guilty for being passive for so long, even though she felt as if something was being resolved in her head without her having to do anything. Querulously, she started to sing, the tune and the words coming from nowhere.

'The day is done, its hours have run,
And thou hast taken count of all;
The scanty triumphs grace has won,
The broken vow, the frequent fall . . .'

Logo had found himself disorientated again. It came from being distracted, stumbling down all those stairs, knocking against something sharp, his belt snapping. All the way back down to the basement, slowly, all round it even more slowly, admiring those pipes in the ceiling which looked like links of giant white sausages, turning on the lights again and somehow knowing she wasn't there. Thinking that maybe the woman he'd hit had been right after all, maybe Eenie had been sent home, but then, why shout for her? Then he'd found a pair of shoes which hadn't been there before. They didn't look like Eenie's shoes, more like bovver boots, Eenie would never have worn those as a kid, but it was enough to make him set off again. His voice echoed round the stone passages, more confident now, loudly plaintive, then getting shaky. 'Come out, Eenie. Come on out, my lovely. I loves you, Eenie. I always loved you, that was all.'

He could not understand why he had begun to cry. Level with the goods lift again, he leant against the wall and sobbed. Couldn't she see that he only wanted to love her? He punched the wall, punched the red button in frustration, startled when the lift juddered and disappeared, jumped back, thinking something was going to leap out at him just as he had done upstairs. Then he peered at the thing shrewdly, getting angry again, wiping his nose on his sleeve. They were playing games with him, and where was his knife? He began the weary march back upstairs, this time going into every single room on the ground floor, except the doorman's where the telly was still on, making music now, above the sound of snoring. Up one more flight, beginning to move a little faster after he had stopped for a bite of chocolate. All those rooms, losing his sense of which side the street was on, looking out of windows into brick quadrangles, panicking a little until he found the goods lift on that floor and got his bearings. Up one more set of stairs, looking for it again, and there it was with doors jammed shut and his knife acting as the bolt. He stared in disbelief, working it out slowly.

That's what Eenie'd done, was it? Thought he was in there; tried to put him in a box and leave him there to rot, stab him with the knife again if he tried to get out. The anger rolled back like a clap of thunder, burst inside his head and descended to a low growling.

He prowled towards the clerks' room, hesitating to touch the knife, turning back towards the other direction as he heard the sound beyond the door of that posh room. His trousers were slipping without the belt. They felt as if they were held in place by the tightness of his stomach when he heard that sound, the sweet hesitant sound of someone singing for courage.

'. . . Through life's long day, and death's dark night,
Oh gentle Jesus, be our light.'

He turned the handle quietly, but it would not be quiet. Turned it once, tried again, pushing gently. The voice faltered into silence.

Helen stirred and moved with grumpy abruptness. Rose eased her into a sitting position, head between knees, patted her back, watching the door as she did so. She did not for a minute consider it might be the doorman; she knew exactly who it was, never really doubted that Daddy could play Houdini. Stood up now, holding the lamp, backed towards the window, stopped by the desk, not thinking much, simply reacting, put it down there with the hot shade facing the door, so the light shone on that useless barrier of the flimsy chair, waiting. If the unconscious desire to blind him was the motive, the effect was lost as he crashed through the door, a bent little man, carried far into the room by his own momentum. Rose stood, thin shoulders bare, nothing covering her bare torso but a skimpy bra, short skirt and thick tights below, no shoes, her legs apart, braced against the window frame, paralysed. The little plait lay sweetly against her neck. Logo looked at her in wonder.

'I only wanted to love you,' he said. 'I've never loved anyone else and you wouldn't understand, would you?'

She was stony faced. That look of mulish insolence which said, You stinking little worm, put it away and yourself with it. Her eyes flicked from his face to his waist. Disgust, pity.

'Come home, Eenie.'

Silence. His anger had not died. Logo went up to his silent daughter, took hold of both sides of her head and kissed her fully on the mouth. She stood as still as before, her lips sealed hard, each muscle of her body rigid.

'Open your eyes,' he commanded. Rose would not, could not. He tore at the lace of her bra, put one hand round a nipple as hard as a nut: she remained a resistant, sullen child. Then erupted into movement, her knee crunching into his groin like a hammer, making him stagger back, wild eyed.

'Like that?' he said. 'You liked that, did you?' He came back towards her, eyes full of tears and murder, hands stretched for her throat. Pressed himself against her so she could not kick. Her bravery was gone.

199

'Your mother's in the graveyard,' he said softly. 'Underneath someone else, the way she liked to be. So's Margaret. Buried with her neighbour. I'll take you too, if you like. Why can't you love your father? I only ever wanted to love you.' Then his hands began to tighten and she could not fight, not this time.

They formed a strange tableau when Dinsdale reached the door. He came through the band of light, blinded for a full second, until he saw someone on the floor, clutching at the leg of a man who was braced by the window, grunting. Helen was on her hands and knees, pulling at the ankle, looking as if she was about to bite. There was a sickening glimpse of white buttock where the man's trousers had slipped, a sound of choking, a rich, full smell, a mixture of vomit and parma violet; it made him want to retch until he saw a hand, clawing at the back of this double-headed beast, a helpless little hand. Dinsdale could not bear to see a woman abused. He simply measured the length between himself and that bent back like a football player eyeing the ball, ran forward and kicked with all his strength. Kicked again at the ankles, sensing Helen rolling out of the way, kicked again as Rose fell from the grasp of the hands at her neck and Logo twisted round. Again as the little man turned to catch the full force in the abdomen, roaring with pain. Logo seemed to trip over the trousers, scrabble for the window frame against which he fell as Dinsdale kicked him one last time, a vicious thud against the knee, he could hear the sound of bone. Logo howled this time, let go of the frame to clutch the area of pain, and then toppled backwards without a sound. For a moment, Dinsdale could not understand where he had gone, what he had done himself and why, until from far enough below, after what seemed an interval of minutes, not seconds, there rose through the rain a thin, watery scream.

Michael had tried to talk himself out of this. So had his father. You don't chase women, especially if you don't know where they are, you let them chase you. That's not what you did, Dad, grinning, feeling a bit silly. Is this the street where the office is? Do you want me to wait? Well yes, just until I see if she's there, if she isn't I'll buy you a beer. It's OK to park here, Saturdays, place is like a grave.

They turned into the side street, Michael looking up. He knew the window of the room where Rose worked because she'd leaned out and waved at him when he'd come to collect her one night last week, no, the week before, so nice and reassuring at the time he would always want to see it again, couldn't fail to look. Three weeks, was all, of coming here and it felt like he'd done it a million times. But all he saw was a sack of clothes hanging over the magnificent railings, probably blown there by the wind, he thought. Until, as the car stopped, he saw it flutter, jerking like a scarecrow on its back, moving all the time, the hands waving and the mouth on the upturned face open in what looked like a smile.

CHAPTER FIFTEEN

They were moving offices. That was today's news. Nothing to do with the incident two weekends before, but because the boiler had broken and, somewhere in the basement, there had been a small fire. No one knew if the two had been connected, but speculation was rife, hidden beneath a deluge of groaning. When were they moving? Soon. In Crown Prosecution terms, that could mean months. They worked to the indifferent heat of a hundred electric fires, mostly provided by themselves, cheerful in adversity. Redwood had a meeting, but not in his own room, conceding that the recent security survey had shown that proper precautions against the IRA would take seventeen guards, six Alsatians and a bank of electronics, none of which was in the budget and, besides, the lease was up.

His other news was that yes, rumour was true; a tramp had got in and for reasons best known to himself, jumped from a window, and yes, it was his room the intruder had chosen, yes it was fatal, no he was not going to give details, only that death was not immediate . . . Oh, yes, and just by the way before we finish, Helen West, Rose Darvey and Dinsdale Cotton were still suffering from a particularly virulent form of influenza and in these hard-pressed times, he would take it amiss if anyone else followed suit. Especially now, as they were expecting a surge of cases from the last big football match in North London, which seemed to have ended in a riot.

When they had all gone back to their desks, forgetting to ask questions because it was so cold, Redwood went across to the window and looked down at the railings. It was just as well Miss West was off sick, convenient really, since hers wasn't a bad room, and his own room was thick with tape, powder, dried blood, and locked. Dinsdale's seat was also vacant, but in view of the shock waves which would rock the office when the golden boy was charged, it didn't seem tasteful. They were still gathering evidence to build the wall round him.

The day was bright and dry. Helen's anglepoise lamp stood on her own desk. Redwood did not admire the railings as much as he had. He was full of resentment for the inconvenience, using that as a device to quell the nightmare. It was all down to Helen. She should never have provoked a defendant so much that he came in to their citadel to take revenge. And put Redwood's job on the line. What about me? he thought to himself. What about me? Everyone who matters thinks all this is my fault and I don't know the half of it yet. I'm having to take Counsel's opinion on the law on exhumation. He wondered if there was such a thing as a lawyer who knew every inch of the law. A bit like someone with every volume of the *Encyclopaedia Britannica* sticking out of his ears. Friday. He would never stay late again.

In the corridor, waiting for the lift, he could hear a chorus of goodbyes.

'What I can't understand,' said Geoffrey Bailey, corkscrew in hand, pretending to be calm, 'is why you never told me. You told me about missing files, the way you sometimes tell me about work. You had me harnessed to that damn computer because you were too scared to go into the basement, you tell me nothing—'

'That isn't quite fair. I might have told you all about Rose if I'd known, but I didn't, I didn't bang on about Logo, because you get sick of me talking about my cases and so do I. Not hearing about yours, talking about mine,' she added. 'I want to hear about yours much more than I want to talk about mine; what I can't stand is you thinking all the time that you're boring me. You leave out all the best bits, as if I was a real lawyer who only wanted to hear what you should have noticed instead of what you did. And anyway, I don't own you. You've made that patently clear. One weekend's whole-hearted devotion is supposed to go a long way with you—'

'You're sidetracking, Helen.'

He had got the cork out of the bottle, setting about it like an amateur, she noticed, crashing the bottle on the table. Good red wine, she also noticed. Good job she didn't much mind about the polished surface, easy come, easy go: things were meant to be used and surfaces scarred but it was a shame to waste the stuff by spilling it, even if there was plenty more. He'd arrived at the flat, at the end of his course, with a load of supermarket bags, most of them clanking with bottles, possibly the remnants of their end-of-term midnight feast, she thought maliciously. Not enough to allay her fears, but then all the crises of the last two weeks seemed to iron one another out, leaving her light headed.

'What did I do wrong?' Bailey shouted. 'Tell me what I did wrong!'

'Typical male, turns everything into a personal accusation. You didn't do anything wrong.'

'Well why were you so brisk with me when I phoned last Friday, before all this happened? Why not ask me to come home and help you with Rose Darvey et al, instead of just telling me afterwards about being hurt and then saying airily, "Doesn't matter, I'm managing fine . . ." How do you think that makes me feel?'

'I didn't ask you to come back because it was perfectly obvious you'd rather not. I wanted a volunteer or nothing, but you were all hooked up with your course and whatever you and Ryan were up to – don't tell me, I don't want to know. After the weekend before, when you got here half drunk, not exactly eager—'

'When you had us spending half Sunday in your office!'

'What's that got to do with it? After a week, I wanted you to be all over me, dying to see me and you weren't, that's all.'

He didn't venture to say he might have wanted the same, was silent, poured some wine with an unsteady hand. Helen had all the answers and his conscience was – how could he put it? – cloudy, like this wine.

'Anyway,' he said without a trace of bitterness, 'you seem to have recovered from everything very well.' Oh no, don't do that, she thought. Don't go back into your professional detachment. I know I haven't been fair, I'd want to shoot you if you did to me what I've done to you this last fortnight, but I had to see if I could cope alone, or I never shall, and please don't retreat like that, I want you to come out and fight.

'You know the worst thing that has happened to me since you went away?' she asked. 'The very worst thing? It's the reason why I'm so calm about everything else.'

'What?'

'Not being pregnant when I thought I was. Even though it scared the hell out of me, that was the worst. Puts all the rest of it in the shade. Even all the cowardice, the running scared round the office, the being absolutely useless, as well as blind, everything. I didn't care too much if I survived anyway. I thought it was far better if Rose did, because she can have lots of babies. And you didn't seem to see how much it mattered.'

He put down his glass.

'I know it mattered. But you never wanted a baby anyway. What about you comforting me for what might have been and wasn't? It didn't cross your mind. The more I sympathized, the more you'd think I was putting on pressure . . . Oh, what's the point?'

'Whatever it is, that isn't it.'

He was silent again, drinking rather quickly, a bit defensive, quiet, even by his own standards. He looked at his watch, needn't have bothered since he always seemed to know almost exactly what time it was. He was just filling the silence with a gesture. Typical male, she thought again, if they ever had any idea how closely they are observed, they'd resort to permanent blindfolds.

'You wanted me to remind you to phone someone before eight,' he said. 'In case you forgot, it's now seven forty-five. By the time you've done that, I might be halfway through some cooking.'

'We could go out, spare you the trouble.'

'No.'

'Why didn't you tell me?' Michael asked Rose. 'Why couldn't you tell me, when we first met, even after a week, what you told my mother and she told me?'

Rose and Michael's mother had been a case of love at first sight. Rose had been unnaturally calm like some creature caught in the headlights before death, poor little bird, you could feel her heart beating and her bones about to break when she was thrust into the bosom of the Michael family in the early hours of a Sunday morning with only enough warning to call a doctor and make a bed. Days of grieving and talking, poultices placed on wounds, ripped off again, replaced, an intermittent healing. Making statements from the living room to endless supplies of tea, with Michael holding her hand until by fits and starts the whole thing emerged with the ease of a Caesarean birth. Now they were in his flat. He wondered if it was too soon, he wondered what he'd got, but it was better, just by themselves. Like children playing house, she seemed to enjoy that. And she couldn't get over the fact that he was still there, not bossing her around or anything, but still there, knowing exactly when to shoo the people away and when to let them in, even his mother.

They were lying with their backs to his sofa. There was a fair bit of dust around, but he kept everything presentable. Helen West had sent over her two teddy bears, which was a nice thought, but she didn't want to think of Helen West. Chinese takeaway was a relief after relentless home cooking, but Mrs Michael wanted them back for Sunday lunch. Rose thought she could get used to it. She twisted her plait. Time to cut it off, it was beginning to annoy her.

'I couldn't tell you. You wouldn't have wanted to know. I didn't want to know either.'

'Look,' he said, 'I didn't think you were a virgin, did I? I couldn't have thought that. But I always knew you were still a kid at heart, innocent. Didn't make any odds, either way.'

She considered it, nodding. 'Nope. But it makes a difference, doesn't it? Going with blokes because you're frightened of the dark, and going with your dad—'

'Stop that,' he said, suddenly authoritative. 'Just stop that. You didn't go with your dad. Your dad got his dick out and hit you with it, that's what. And nobody is ever going to do that to you again.'

She was silent again.

'I think Dinsdale's all right,' she said suddenly. 'I hope they don't fix him.'

'Why "all right"?'

'He wouldn't let me look out of the window.'

Yes, that did make him all right, whatever else he'd done. Michael shuddered. Rose began to cry. 'Shh,' he said. 'Shh. It'll get better. I promise it'll get better.'

'I wish he wasn't dead. Not like that, not like that. I wish they weren't going to find Gran in that graveyard . . . I wish . . .'

'It's getting cold,' he said. 'Here, cuddle up.'

He moved closer, nuzzling her bird bones into the warmth of his chest, the clean smell of him, the comfort of beginning to believe him and oh, this terrible wanting which should not have been the birthchild of grief for Gran and Mum and everyone else, but was.

'You won't leave me, will you, Mikey?' she mumbled finally, her voice low and childish.

'No. Not until you're fed up with me, don't want me there.' He wondered how long, pulled her closer.

She extended her hand over the lamp next to them on the floor, let a huge shadow fall across the wall. Then snuggled back against him.

Steak, salad, ridiculously expensive new potatoes at the wrong time of year, followed by cheese. She could cope with this. Second bottle, nearly gone. Any invitations cancelled. Helen knew that what she had to say might have to bear the brunt of several repetitions. Bailey put down his knife suddenly, smiled at her, on the brink of laughter.

'You look as if you've just been exhumed,' he said with grim relish. 'Steristrips in your head, eight stitches in your arm and skin the colour of a lemon. You're an awkward, unreasonable woman and I still fancy you rotten. You're a walking nightmare, for me, do you know that? What am I going to do with you?'

She wondered. Had been wondering for a long time, but never as much as when she was helped out of the office into an ambulance last week, insisting she could walk and knowing she was going to have to fight for ever to quell her fear of the dark. Dinsdale being kind, but still a thief, Rose with her champion, everyone with someone, and she as she always was, alone, slugging it out with the whole universe.

'I thought we might get married,' she said. His knife clattered to the floor.

'I'm a pain in the neck, I know I am. It just struck me that the way to cure going backwards was to take a leap forwards.'

'Quite a leap.'

'You always said you would.'

207

He took a deep breath. 'Perhaps I meant at any time when you weren't speaking out of fear and a reaction to being attacked.'

She did not know whether to be disappointed, angry, humiliated or relieved. Dear Bailey had had his taste of freedom. Better to make light of it. She got up to clear the table, make the thick black coffee which he liked and which never kept either of them awake. It was nice to know a man's habits, even if they did irritate.

'I suppose that means you've gone off the whole idea? Marriage I mean.'

'Yes, for the time being. Doesn't mean I don't love you. Means it's my turn to be ambivalent.'

'That's all right then.'

She stood by the kitchen window with a tray full of dishes which would wait, looking into the dark winter garden, aching. There was a line from a hymn running through her head . . . Oh thou who changest not, abide with me.

Dear God, if you exist, don't let me be afraid of the dark.